GENTLEMAN
NINE

PENELOPE WARD

First Edition, February 2018
Copyright © 2018
By Penelope Ward
ISBN: 978-1-942215-75-2

Cover Model: Lucas Garcez, @lucasgarcez93
Cover Photographer: Sven Jacobsen,
svenjacobsen.com
Cover Design: Letitia Hasser, RBA Designs,
rbadesigns.com
Formatting: Elaine York, Allusion Graphics, LLC,
allusiongraphics.com

GENTLEMAN

NINE

CHAPTER ONE
AMBER

The ring of my phone startled me as I was mindlessly scrolling through photos online. The name on the caller ID made my pulse race.

Channing Lord.

Channing?

My heart began to beat faster.

Why would he be calling me?

Before I had time to ponder that question, I picked up, trying my best to sound chipper despite the fact that just moments earlier I was in tears while stalking my ex, Rory's, Facebook page.

I ran my hand through my hair as if it mattered what I looked like. "Channing!"

A deep, sexy chuckle vibrated against my ear, but somehow I felt it between my thighs. "How did you know it was me?"

My nipples stiffened at the sound of his voice. I didn't want to react this way, but for as long as I'd known him, I reluctantly and secretly crushed on Channing. For one reason or another, he was always off-limits.

1

When I first met him, he'd been my best friend's big brother. *Off-limits.*

Then, our relationship evolved into a friendship I valued. *Off-limits.*

Crossing the line with Channing wasn't a possibility, especially after I fell in love with his best friend, Rory, which made Channing once again...*off-limits.*

But the fact that I'd always considered Channing off-limits didn't mean I could ignore how attractive he was. The man was beautiful, and there was no denying that.

"Your name showed on the display. That's how I knew it was you," I said.

"Really?" He laughed. "Shit. This is my cell. I didn't know my name came up when I called people. I don't know if I like that."

"Well, it's because I have you programmed in. You must've called me from this number before—the last time we spoke. I think that was like six months ago."

"Oh, gotcha. Jeez. It's been a while, huh?"

"Yeah, it has. This is a surprise. What's up? How are you doing?"

Still hot as hell?

I couldn't help where my mind went with him.

Even though we'd talked on the phone occasionally, it had been a couple of years since we'd actually seen each other in person. From what I could tell on social media, he'd gotten even better looking with age. Channing was probably the most attractive human I'd ever personally known. Not only that, he had a larger-than-life personality and effortless charm. Women were always drawn to him, and that was precisely the problem for any chick who ended up dating him. Channing Lord loved women, and they loved him. That was the bottom line.

"I'm really well, actually," he said.

"Good to hear. I'm sorry that I haven't been in touch. It's been a rough couple of months."

A few seconds went by before he responded, "I heard about you and Rory. That was pretty shocking news. Are you okay?"

No.

The subject of Rory always turned me into a defensive, moody bitch. "Why do you ask? Did someone tell you I wasn't okay?"

"No. I haven't spoken to Rory or anything. Jordan told me." Jordan was one of my friends from back home who'd had a fling with Channing way back when.

"How nice of her to fill you in."

"You guys had been together forever. It doesn't take a genius to figure out that this must be rough for you."

"Well, I'm taking it one day at a time."

I didn't want Channing to know how badly the breakup had devastated me.

"That's all we can ever do, right? One day at a time. One foot in front of the other. That's a good attitude."

"So, to what do I owe this phone call, Lord?"

"Well, I sort of have a question for you—not sure if I'm overstepping my bounds in asking but..."

What was he getting at?

My heartbeat sped up a bit. "Okay..."

"I just got a temporary contract position with a bio-medical company in Boston. SeraMed. You ever hear of them?"

"Oh, yeah. In Cambridge."

"Exactly. The one in Cambridge. It's only for a few months, starts in early October. Jordan said you might have an extra room that you rent out to people? I figured it wouldn't hurt to ask if it's available. I'd need it starting on October first."

He wanted to stay here? With me? I didn't know how I felt about that. But I didn't want to lie to him.

"Yeah, actually. I do have a room. I rent it out typically through Airbnb, but I'm only booked through the end of August. After that, it's available." *What the hell.* "It's yours if you want it." I closed my eyes and cringed. I really should have thought it through a bit more before offering Channing a room. The last thing I needed at this point in my life was to have to listen to him doing God knows what with God knows whom across the hall.

He sounded surprised. "Are you serious?"

"Of course."

"You've rescued my ass. I owe you big time. I'll pay whatever you normally get—even more. I don't care. You just saved me the hassle of trying to find a place in the city. I was dreading it."

"Well, I'm glad. It will be nice to catch up, too." I meant that. Channing had a way about him that always made me happy when I was around him. Even though he and I were closer friends when we were younger than we were now, he was always fun to be around. We grew apart back when Rory and I started dating, but Channing was always someone I knew I could count on even if we weren't speaking regularly. He was truly like a big brother.

"Are you sure you're okay with this, Amber?"

"Completely."

"I promise I'll stay out of your hair. And by the end of December I'll be gone."

"We can touch base closer to October, but I'll hold it for you, won't book anyone for that time period."

"Fantastic." He paused. "Do you think Rory will be pissed?"

His question made me defensive. "I'm not even going to tell Rory. I don't owe him any explanations. I haven't been in touch with him in several weeks."

My ex lived about a half-hour away and had custody of our golden retriever. With a fenced-in yard, his house was a better fit for an animal. So, I only really contacted him to check in on Bruiser from time to time.

He was quiet, then said, "I'm sure you don't want to go into it right now, but I'm here if you ever need to talk about what happened between you and him."

"Thank you, but nope...no need to talk about Rory. Onward and upward," I said defensively.

No. I didn't need to talk about how my boyfriend of nine years, the guy I'd given my virginity to, up and decided that we needed a break because he hadn't sown his oats. He suggested we take some time to "explore other people." He'd completely blindsided me.

"If we're meant to be, we'll find our way back to one another, but I don't think either one of us is ready for marriage when we've never experienced being with anyone other than each other. Marriage is a vow you don't break, Amber."

Channing snapped me out of my recollection of Rory's words.

It sounded like a train was approaching in the distance. "Alright. Well, thanks again, Walnut."

Walnut. Now that was a nickname I hadn't heard in years. He used to call me that because of my last name: Walton. Channing used to tease me, saying that I was a bit of a nut—a walnut.

The train got louder. He continued, "I'll definitely have to eat you out when I get there."

What did he just say?

"I'm sorry. I can't hear you."

He shouted, "I said I'll have to take you out when I get there...as a thank you for letting me stay. Anyway...I'm just about to hop on the train. I'll talk to you soon."

Oh, mother of God.

"Okay. Sounds good."

"Take care, Amber."

"You, too."

⌒

The summer flew by faster than I was ready for. I couldn't believe that in less than a month, Channing would be arriving in Boston.

I decided that it was time to replace the ratty sheets on the bed in the spare room.

My friend, Annabelle, accompanied me to Bed Bath & Beyond one afternoon. Annabelle was a clinical supervisor at the human services agency where we both worked. During the day, I assisted in a special education classroom and worked with a special needs adult a few nights a week to supplement my income.

The store was filled with university students and their parents who were infiltrating the city for move-in weekend. A feeling of nostalgia hit me upon the sight of all the college kids standing in the checkout line with their shower caddies and reading pillows. Ah, to be that age again.

Annabelle lifted a set of shrimp-colored sheets that were encased in plastic. "What about these?"

I shook my head. "Not masculine enough."

She returned them to the shelf and picked up another. "What about these beige ones? Egyptian cotton?"

Taking a closer look, I said, "The thread count is too low."

"You seem very invested in this choice." She laughed. "Are you sure you're not planning on spending some time rolling around beneath these sheets yourself?"

Hells no.

My cheeks felt hot as I explained, "Channing is the last guy I'd be frolicking around with under any sheets, believe me."

She raised her brow. "Why is that? He's single, isn't he? And I really think you could benefit from a rebound."

"I can think of a million reasons why nothing will be happening with Channing."

"Like what?"

"Let's see. One: Channing has slept with half of my friends back home. Two: he was Rory's best friend for a while. Three: I look at him like a brother. Those are just a few of many reasons."

"I can't think of a better way to get back at Rory than to take up with his friend."

"As much as I'd love to stick it to my ex, it won't be via Channing Lord. There's way too much history there."

"Do you have a picture of this Channing?"

I proceeded to pull up his Facebook page on my phone, laughing to myself in anticipation of what she was going to say. Scrolling though some of his photos, I stopped at the one I knew would get the biggest reaction. Channing was wearing a gray beanie and a black, collared shirt. A little of his lustrous, brown hair was peeking out from under the hat. He was looking off to the side, showcasing his perfect profile. Just the right amount of chin scruff peppered his angular jaw. The photo was apparently taken during a brief modeling stint for some designer out in Chicago. Even though he wasn't a model, he was literally recruited off the street and into a photographer's loft for an impromptu shoot, according to the caption. That didn't surprise me. *Only Channing.* I was apparently transfixed on this shot, because Annabelle had to swipe the phone from me in order to look at the photo.

Her mouth was agape. "Holy crap. You look at *this guy* like your brother? How is that even possible? Jesus Hector Christ...he's super hot."

"Hector?"

"Well, they say Jesus H. Christ. I figured the H stands for something. Anyway...yeah...this guy is really good-looking."

"Oh, I know. Believe me."

"If I wasn't married, I'd probably be hanging out at your place all of the damn time. Still might be. Tell me again why you look at *him* like a brother?"

"We have a long history." I closed my eyes and took a deep breath. "Channing is my best friend, Lainey's, older brother. I first met him through her. She..." I hesitated. It was always hard to say it out loud. It didn't matter how many years had passed. "She died...in an accident...when she and I were fourteen. Channing was about sixteen at the time."

Annabelle looked like she regretted asking. "Oh, my God. I'm so sorry. That's devastating. I didn't know."

"It was a very hard time for all of us. He was never able to talk about her death. But even so, her passing sort of bonded us pretty fast. He and I really only became friends after that. That was how I met Rory, who was Channing's good friend at the time."

"You probably remind Channing of his sister, or at least what life was like before she passed away. He must have taken comfort in having you around."

"That might have been part of our connection, yes. He, Rory, and I hung out a lot after Lainey's accident. Being in Lainey's house with all of her things comforted me. They don't have a big family. It was just their mom and them. Now, it's just Mrs. Lord and Channing. Their dad was never in the picture."

"So, Channing was the man of the house."

"Yes, and he took Lainey's death very hard. So did I. She was like a sister to me. But no one took it harder than Channing."

"So, you said you met Rory through Channing..."

"Yes. We were like the Three Musketeers for a while."

"You and two guys? That sounds kind of interesting."

"I knew you were thinking along those lines, but no, it was platonic, even with Rory up until a certain point. When Channing went out of state to college for a year, that's when things changed. Rory and I got closer and eventually became a couple. I'd never really viewed Rory in that way—romantically. He'd always seemed kind of nerdy to me, actually. I'd always been much more physically attracted to Channing. But Rory grew on me. With Channing gone, we got closer. I eventually fell in love with Rory. I trusted him. And basically, that ended up biting me in the ass years later, as you know."

"How did Channing feel about you and Rory getting together?"

"I don't think it bothered him, although he did seem to distance himself from us after he came back from college to find that we were together. Channing had only been gone a year, then transferred back home to go to state school. We all ended up at the same college, at one point. I was a freshman when Rory and Channing were sophomores. Naturally, Channing quickly became a hot commodity on campus. He was with a different girl every week.

"So, he's a playboy, then…"

"Oh, yeah."

"Well, I can't say I blame him with looks like that, but eventually that's got to get tiring. How old is he?"

"Well, I'm twenty-five…" I closed my eyes for a moment to calculate. "So, that makes him twenty-seven, but I don't see Channing ever settling down, at least no time soon."

After I decided on a set of dark gray, 1000-thread count Ralph Lauren sheets, we passed the wedding gift registry area on our way to check out. My heart sank. It was in this very store at that very kiosk that my relationship with Rory started to crumble. We'd been shopping for a new coffee maker when I brought up the subject of starting to think about getting engaged. He'd gotten into a car accident a couple of months before but was on his way to making a full recovery. In the weeks that followed the accident, though, I began to notice changes in him, which all culminated in "the talk" at Bed Bath & Beyond. The accident apparently caused him to ponder his life and determine that he didn't see a future with me.

Annabelle disrupted my daydream. "Are you okay, Amber?"

Shaking my head to fend off thoughts of Rory, I lied. "Yeah."

CHAPTER TWO
AMBER

'd sent Channing the key to my place so that he could get situated while I was at work. His flight got in to Logan Airport at 10AM, which meant I wouldn't be home to greet him.

I'd made sure the new bedding was washed and placed on his bed and cracked open a window to air out the room. I also left him a welcome note with two mints, the same gesture I afforded my Airbnb tenants.

Since the school where I worked was only a short walk from home, I decided to head over to my condo during the lunch break to at least say hello.

It was a cool, crisp day in Boston, the quintessential autumn afternoon with falling leaves and blue skies. The historic neighborhood where I lived—Beacon Hill—was known for its brick sidewalks and Federal-style rowhouses. It was definitely one of the more sought-after neighborhoods in the city.

As I approached my door, the smell of something cooking immediately infiltrated my senses. Music was blasting. He hadn't wasted any time making himself right at home, apparently.

Channing didn't even notice me enter.

I swallowed. The sight of him taking over my kitchen really caught me off guard. It wasn't because he was frying something on the stove, but rather because he was doing it in nothing but his underwear.

His muscular legs were on full display forming a path up to his gray boxer briefs, which left little to the imagination, hugging his package and round ass. And he was shaking that ass around. There was no doubt in my mind that if Channing ever decided to do this very thing for a living, he'd make a killing. *Homeboy could dance.* He must have been listening to an old school R&B channel because *Do Me!* by Bell Biv DeVoe was playing. That could have been his anthem, I suppose.

This was all very Tom Cruise in *Risky Business*—well, if Tom Cruise had been shirtless and shredded. Taking a deep breath in, I just stared at him for several seconds. For as long as I'd known him, I'd never seen him *like this*.

Deciding it was time to make myself known, I called out over the loud music, "Channing!"

He turned around suddenly and began to laugh. "Oh, shit!" He immediately lowered the music.

"Meow."

It was then that I realized what looked like a kitten was sitting on his shoulder. I hadn't noticed it before because the right side of his body wasn't visible. Also, because I was mostly looking down.

What the heck?

"You brought a cat?"

"Meow."

"No." He shook his head and chuckled. "Well, sort of. It's kind of a crazy story. I'll tell it to you over lunch."

"Do you always cook half-naked?"

Was he blushing?

"Actually...yes. But I didn't think you'd be here until later. Otherwise, I would've put some damn pants on." He approached then kissed me on the cheek, the warmth of his lips and body sending shivers down my spine. A bit of his saliva lingered on my cheek.

Oh. Fuck. I'm in trouble.

Sneaking a fleeting look at his tanned, washboard stomach, I noticed a simple tribal tattoo that started on his lower abs and dipped into the abyss of his underwear line. That was intriguing and made me wonder where the ink ended.

I pried my eyes upward. "I know you weren't expecting me. I decided to come by and say hello, since I don't work too far from here."

"I'm really glad you did." He flashed his beautiful teeth. "It's so good to see you."

"Good to see you, too."

All of you.

Something on the stove started to burn, prompting him to rush back over to it. The kitten managed to stay glued to his shoulder despite the swift movement. I laughed because suddenly my house had transformed into a circus.

He glanced back at me. "You can stay and eat, right?"

"That depends on whether you put some pants on."

"No *junk* food for lunch. Got it. No problemo." He winked. "Yeah, of course, I'll get dressed."

Stretching my neck in an attempt to see what he was cooking, I asked, "Is there even enough food? You weren't expecting me."

"Yeah. I always make too much."

"Meow."

"Do you mind telling me now where this cat came from?"

"I don't know where she came from, actually. She found *me* somehow."

"What?"

He shrugged. "Yeah. I was walking here, and she followed me to your doorstep. She found me on State Street and just kept walking alongside me all the way to Beacon Hill. I didn't have the heart to leave her standing there on the curb while I came inside. She kept meowing at me. I figured she was hungry. I gave her a little of the turkey you had in the fridge. I'll replace it. I was gonna find a shelter and take her there later or maybe tomorrow after work."

"Leave it to you to be a pussy magnet, Channing." I chuckled.

"I guess, right?"

Our eyes locked, and he seemed to be observing me.

I cleared my throat. "Well, it definitely seems like you've had an active couple of first hours in Boston."

"It's all good. I really like this city so far. Stopped at a nice, little market in the North End on my way here, too." He nudged his head toward his shoulder where the tiny cat was perched. "Before I ran into this one over here."

Maybe now wasn't a good time to break the news that pets weren't allowed. I couldn't help but swoon a little over the fact that he'd taken in a stray cat, though.

"Boston is a beautiful city, especially this time of year when the leaves start changing. You're gonna love it here."

"Keep an eye on the stove for me? I'm gonna go put some clothes on."

The kitten stayed on Channing's shoulder as he sauntered over to his room to get dressed.

He came back out a minute later wearing jeans and a fitted, white shirt. He was holding the kitten now, cradling it like a baby in his strong arms.

"She finally climbed down off of you?"

"Well, no, I had to pry her away so that I could put my shirt on." ·

The cat was purring as Channing gently scratched its head. His masculine fingers raked through the soft, white fur. That made the hairs on the back of my neck stiffen.

"Is it okay if I put her down? Not sure if you want her on your furniture."

I waved my hand. "Sure. Yeah, it's fine. Although, I'm pretty sure she'd prefer to stay with you indefinitely."

"I don't know what it is about me that she likes so much." He gently placed the cat on the ground. She weaved in and out of his legs while purring. Channing then headed over to the sink to wash his hands. "Anyway, hope you're hungry."

"What did you make?"

He wriggled his brows. "Ah...the chef never tells."

"The chef never tells the ingredients, but you can tell me what it is."

"No. I'd rather you taste it without judgment first."

Crossing my arms, I shook my head in amusement.

Channing proceeded to open a bottle of white wine he had chilling in the fridge. With a loud pop, he freed the cork then poured two glasses.

Holding up my palms, I said, "Oh, no. I can't drink. I'm going back to work."

"You *think* you're going back to work, but you're really not."

I knew damn well that if I took even one sip of alcohol, I wasn't going to be heading back to the school.

"You're a bad influence."

He flashed a mischievous grin. "You have no idea."

I got chills. "Oh, yes, I do. And some things never change."

He winked, and it felt like someone had turned the temperature up in the kitchen.

Once we sat down to eat, my body cooled off a bit as I became more acclimated to having him here. He'd fried us...these things...wrapped in bacon. Whatever it was, it was delicious.

Channing filled me in on his new position as a quality engineer at SeraMed while the kitten was by his feet the entire time.

"So what exactly does a quality engineer do?"

"The company I work for out in Chicago owns SeraMed. They sent me here to oversee a new medical product they've created that SeraMed is manufacturing. My job is to make sure it meets quality standards and specifications and then suggest changes, if needed."

"Sounds complicated. But I always knew you were smart."

"It can be a lot of pressure to not screw up, particularly when you're dealing with medical products and people's lives. But you know, work hard, play harder. I don't take my work home with me."

Once I cleaned my plate, I asked him the question that had been nagging me. "Okay, can you please tell me what the hell that was I just ate? It was delicious, but I had *no* clue what I was consuming."

Channing was laughing at me. "What do you think you ate?"

"My best guess would be fried clams wrapped in bacon."

He wiped his mouth and smirked. "It was fried escargot wrapped in bacon, so you got the last part right—the bacon."

Oh, my God.

"Escargot? Isn't that snails?"

"Yup. I picked them up at that market I told you about."

"I just ate snails? They tasted like clams!"

"Escargot fuck yourself, Channing? Is what you want to say to me right now?" He was cracking up. "Tell me you would've eaten them if you knew, though."

"I *absolutely* wouldn't have."

"See...sometimes it's better not to know things. We can enjoy something as it was meant to be enjoyed without preconceived notions. Snails are a delicacy—and an aphrodisiac."

"I remember hearing that. Oysters, too. But I don't get it. How is that even possible? How does an oyster, for example, make you want to have sex? Does that make any sense to you?"

He licked his lips. "I actually know where that connection came from."

"You do?"

"Yeah. It has to do with the famous lover, Casanova. Rumor had it that he ate fifty oysters a day to build up his stamina. Somehow, they associated the oysters with sex for that very reason."

"Well, it takes a Casanova to know a Casanova, I suppose." I winked. "So, really, what you're saying is, it's more like folklore. There really isn't a scientific reason?"

"Well, have you ever looked closely at an oyster?" he asked.

"No, can't say that I have."

"It looks like a labia."

"A labia..."

"Yeah, you know, the—"

"I know what a labia is." I briefly fanned myself with a napkin.

"Eating an oyster is kind of like..." He hesitated. "Well, you know what I'm getting at."

Chills ran down my back as I stared at his lips. "Yeah, I think I do."

"So, maybe Casanova was...practicing his technique," he said.

"Interesting theory."

"Isn't it?" He smiled.

Desperately needing to move away from the sexual topics, I said, "Anyway, what I just ate—snails—are absolutely *not* meant to be eaten."

"Neither are cows or turkey and all the other things we consume every day."

Pondering that for a moment, I said, "I suppose that's true."

"Speaking of turkey...have you spoken to Rory?"

Ugh.

Why did he mention him?

"No, I haven't, actually. It's better that way. And you don't have to badmouth him to make me feel better. I'm a big girl."

"Well, technically, I feel bad for *him*."

"Why is that?"

He took another sip of wine before he said, "Because he got dumped."

Wait.

What?

Did he not know the truth about what happened between Rory and me? It felt like the entire world knew.

"I didn't dump him. Where did you hear that?"

"Jordan didn't use those exact words, per se. I just assumed the break up was your choice. Rory was always so whipped."

"Well, it wasn't...my choice."

He'd been drinking his wine but stopped mid-sip. "Wait a minute. Hold up. He broke up with you?"

I nodded.

He repeated, "*Rory*...broke up with...*you.*"

"Yes. You want me to have to say it?"

Channing's expression turned serious as he put his glass down. "I'm sorry...I'm just...I'm floored."

"Yeah, so was I."

He proceeded to pour me more of the chardonnay.

I held my palm out in an attempt to stop him. "What are you doing?"

"Call in sick for the rest of the afternoon. I want you to tell me what happened with that fucking fool, and I want you to have more wine and relax while you're doing it. Plus, it's my first day here and my only weekday off. That's reason enough to play hooky."

As a teaching assistant, I didn't exactly have the kind of job where you could just bail on work without a dozen things falling apart. But I couldn't remember the last time I took a sick day. I was enjoying Channing's company and really felt like unloading on him. I wanted him to tell me Rory was an idiot for leaving me. I wanted him to make me feel better, even if it didn't really change anything.

Channing tilted his head. "Come on."

"You're not going to let me say no, are you?"

"Fuck, no. I'll chain you to the chair if I have to."

I chose to ignore the muscles between my legs contracting at the thought of this man chaining me to a chair.

It didn't take much to convince me. I'd really made the decision to stay when I'd taken that first sip of wine. I knew we were fully staffed today at work, so in my mind I was able to justify calling out.

"Alright. I guess I can text my boss and make up an excuse."

"Perfect."

He got up to take our plates to the sink while I sent a message to work, making up a sudden illness as the reason why I couldn't return for the remainder of the afternoon.

He called over to me, "Stop feeling guilty, Amber."

How did he know that was exactly how I was feeling?

"Perceptive, aren't you?"

I noticed that the kitten had followed him over to the sink.

Channing loaded the plates into the dishwasher. "Up for dessert?"

"Considering what we ate for lunch, should I be concerned?"

"I promise, it's not anything weird. In fact, I'm a hundred percent sure you're gonna like what I got."

He grabbed a small paper bag off the counter and brought it over to the table before taking out two cake pops.

A big smile spread over my face.

He held them up. "You want the pink or the brown one?"

"What are we...five?" I laughed then answered, "Pink."

I took a bite and thought about the fact that white wine and cake pops really complemented each other well. *I should do this more often.* But the truth was, I wouldn't have even thought to do this, to take this time for myself in the middle of the day, if it weren't for Channing. My kitchen had never been filled with so much life.

Looking down at my half-eaten cake ball, I said, "These remind me of Hoffman's."

Hoffman's was the bakery in our old neighborhood just outside of Chicago. Growing up, Lainey and I used to get cake pops from there all of the time.

Lainey.

I wouldn't say her name. I didn't want to upset him. Channing always seemed to like to talk about things that reminded him of her without actually discussing *her*, so as not to have to remember what actually happened to his sister. That was how he handled the pain of her accident. So, I knew what these cake pops were really about. It was just one of the subtle ways he honored her memory.

"I know they're like the ones at Hoffman's. That's why I got them." He took a bite, catching a piece of the chocolate fondant that fell into his hand.

His eyes fell to my lips as I licked the last of the frosting off the stick. The tone of his voice softened as he leaned into his elbows. "Tell me what happened with Rory."

"I told you what happened."

"I want the long version."

I knew I wasn't going to get out of talking about it. So, I took a long sip of the wine and began to unload on him.

Over the next several minutes, Channing listened attentively as I recalled Rory's breaking up with me, from the days leading up to it, to the Bed Bath & Beyond incident, to the exact words Rory said to me when he suggested we explore other people.

It was the first time I'd really gone over what happened in such great detail. It felt like I was reliving it, and I ended up breaking down. There was something about telling Channing everything that made me emotional enough to cry. Maybe it was because I didn't have a big brother to tell things to, or maybe it was because Channing was one of the few people who knew Rory and me from the very beginning of our relationship—who knew how trustworthy Rory was. Technically, without Channing I would never have met Rory. I felt like Channing was truly on my side, though. He seemed like he wanted to kick Rory's ass for hurting me. And that gave me some comfort. Sometimes, you just need a strong male friend in your corner—a protector. Channing was that person for me. Even if years went by and we didn't speak, I knew he would be there for me if I ever needed him. In a sense, that was happening at the moment.

"I know it may not seem like it right now, but Rory did you a favor."

"By wasting nine years of my life?"

"I think he's crazy for letting you go, alright? He'll never find someone like you again. But, in a sense, he's right. You haven't experienced enough to know that he's the one. You've only been with one man—one man in your entire life. I don't think he can do better, but quite frankly, I think *you* can."

"That's not a very nice thing to say about your former best friend."

"Rory and I were never as close as you thought," he was quick to say. "And even if we were, I call it like I see it. You were always out of his league."

"On a superficial level, maybe. Although, you haven't seen him lately. He looks really good now."

"You're wrong...on *every* level."

His words gave me pause. I didn't even care if he was blowing smoke up my ass at this point. It made me feel good to hear him say that. I just needed to feel good tonight, after months of feeling like shit. I would take his words and run with them.

"I didn't want *better*, Channing. I wanted Rory, someone whom I trusted with my life. He's a good guy and knows me inside and out. It will take me years to build that kind of connection with someone again. If you live your life constantly thinking that the grass may be greener, you'll never settle down."

"No, but if you never venture out of your bubble of safety, you'll never realize it's not the color of the grass that matters but how fucking good it tastes to smoke it."

I pondered that for a moment. "That doesn't make sense to me."

"I know. I just made it up."

"You suck, Channing." I laughed.

"If you think about it long enough, though, it starts to make sense. And you're smiling. That's what matters." He chuckled. "Okay, in all seriousness...sometimes people have to learn lessons the hard way. He'll figure out his mistake and come back. It's just a matter of whether you'll be there when he does. The question is, if he came back today, would you *take* him back?"

"I honestly don't know. A part of me thinks yes, only because that part of me still loves him. You don't get over that so easily after nearly a decade together. But then another part of me doesn't feel like I could ever fully trust him not to leave again. Anyway, it doesn't matter. He's clearly not here asking me to take him back."

"No, but he will be."

"You seem so sure of that..."

He crossed his arms. "I am."

Channing was looking me straight in the eyes, and the intensity of that prompted me to change the subject.

I sighed. "Alright...let's talk about something other than Rory. Like literally anything."

He crumpled up a napkin and threw it at me playfully. "How about moldy cheese?"

"Sure."

"I'm serious. What the fuck did you have growing in your refrigerator? I cleaned all that shit out, by the way."

Mortified, I said, "Oh. I thought you were joking. You're actually talking about cheese. I'm sorry...I've neglected the fridge lately. It was the one thing I didn't get to tackle before you moved in. I couldn't tell you what was in there. I—"

"You don't owe me any explanations. It's your kitchen...your moldy cheese. Not my place to judge."

"You think I'm a pig, don't you?"

"Far from it."

"Well, I have no excuse for that."

"I beg to differ. How about...you work long hours, and your head isn't on straight lately because your heart is broken. Fuck the cheese. I'm sorry for even mentioning it. I was just messing with you. You said to change the subject, and for some reason that was the first thing that came to mind."

Attempting to change the subject yet again, I asked, "When do you start your new job again?"

"Bright and early tomorrow."

"Wow. Okay. You know how to get there from here?"

"I need to check the train route online."

"You'll take the Orange Line to the Red. I think the stop is Kendall Square."

"I'll figure it out." He smiled, pouring me the last drop of wine. "Tell me more about this school you work at. You like it there?"

Now, that was something I could never get enough of talking about.

"Yes. I love my job, actually. It's a school for kids with developmental challenges, like autism and Down's syndrome. I'm a TA in one of the classrooms. Then, a few nights a week, I work with a special needs adult, taking him out into the community."

"That's got to be a handful."

"It is. But it's very rewarding."

"Well, they're lucky to have you."

I didn't know what else to say. "Thank you." I'd never been great at accepting compliments.

We opened another bottle of wine and spent the next couple of hours reminiscing. I'd forgotten how easy Channing was to talk to, and with each passing hour, I was less intimidated by his physical presence. The last time we'd really talked at great length like this was before Rory and I got together. It reminded me of those early days after Lainey's death.

After our extended lunch, I felt a great deal better about him staying with me. Channing was still the same wildly charismatic guy I remembered, but he'd definitely matured. He seemed sensitive to my feelings, and I no longer feared that he'd disrespect my space in any way. In fact, the only thing I really feared after our afternoon together was that I might get used to him being around and not want him to leave.

CHAPTER THREE
CHANNING

God, she looked exactly the same as when she was sixteen. It made me feel like a perv, even though I knew she was in her twenties and only a couple of years younger than me.

How she hadn't aged was beyond me. The same petite body. The same straight, long, dark auburn hair with the exact same bangs cut straight across the forehead. The same brown doe eyes. They used to be full of wonder, but tonight they were mostly dark.

Fucking asshole took away the light in her eyes.

My mother always told me I shouldn't go to bed angry, that it would affect my dreams and that the negative energy would carry over into the next day. But as I lay in bed that night, I really couldn't help obsessing over the bomb that Amber dropped. Never in a million years would I have predicted that *he* was the one responsible for their break up.

She was so upset and wound up over Rory; I wished I could have just kissed the fuck out of her to make her forget—or even better, show her what it's like to be with a real man. That may have been an inappropriate thought, but nevertheless, I had it. A lot of inappropriate thoughts were moving in and out of my head. And that was pretty funny considering I couldn't ever act on them.

Years ago, I'd come to terms with the fact that Amber and Rory were together, because I assumed at the very least, he would do right by her and cherish her. It was the only reason I didn't beat the shit out of him when I came home from college and realized he'd broken our pact, pursued her, and had fucking taken her virginity.

Back when we were teenagers, I'd always known that Rory wanted Amber. What I never considered was that she could return his feelings. The three of us would hang out together, watching movies or just chilling down in my basement, and I'd catch him staring at her when she wasn't looking. He'd be fixated on her, and I would be fixated on his fixation with her. She was oblivious to his feelings and even more oblivious to mine, because I hid them really well. It was no exaggeration to say I'd probably hooked up with all of Amber's friends. So, yeah, I was really good at throwing her off. I'm certain she never suspected that I liked her as more than a friend. My actions certainly never demonstrated that.

None of the girls I'd hooked up with in high school or college meant anything to me. Amber was really the only girl I'd ever developed feelings for at the time. They never escalated to the point of love, but I cared about her, wanted to protect her.

Before Lainey died, Amber was merely my sister's friend. After Lainey passed away, Amber and I got closer. She was the only person keeping me sane during one of the most difficult periods of my life—those months after my sister's death.

But actually dating Amber back then was never something I considered a realistic option. I was too young and unpredictable. Not to mention, I was the spawn of an asshole, womanizing father. What if the apple didn't fall far from the tree? I was certain I'd end up hurting her. She was like a sister to me—a sister I secretly wanted to fuck but knew I never would. And I guess my attitude was that Rory should have felt the same way since the three of us were supposed to be friends. He and I should've wanted to protect her, not take advantage of her. But yet, what we should've felt didn't matter. We both wanted her.

So, when Rory came to me and confessed his feelings for Amber one night, I felt like I needed to tell him how I really felt about her, too. My jealousy was through the roof, even though I didn't think he was any kind of competition for me. That had been the one consolation—or so I thought. We agreed that since we couldn't both have her, that neither of us would tell her how we felt. We'd come to the understanding that it was better to keep our friendship intact—both with each other and with Amber.

I therefore didn't feel like I needed to watch my back when I went away to the University of Florida, leaving my friends behind. I trusted that he wouldn't move in on her and even more so, I figured that if he did, she wouldn't return his feelings. It was like double security in my mind.

Homesick, I decided to transfer back to a state school after my first year in Gainesville was up. When I came home that summer and found out that they were together, it felt like the ultimate betrayal. I alienated myself from both of them for a while. During that time, my manwhore ways were worse than ever once the school year started up again. It was a bad combination of acting out due to anger along with being the new, hot guy on campus at the local college I'd transferred to.

Over time, though, I began to accept things as they were. After all, even if Amber had been available, I knew I wasn't the right guy for her anyway. She deserved someone who wouldn't screw her over, someone like...Rory. He was safe. I grew to accept them together, and she and I were able to renew our friendship, although things were never exactly the same again between the three of us—especially between Rory and me. And he knew why.

Had seeing them together still hurt like a motherfucker? Yes. But I'd accepted that he was the better man for her. Sucking up my jealousy and pride, I ended up moving on.

So, finding out that he'd broken her heart all these years later was a tough pill to swallow. If he were in front of me right now, there was no guarantee I wouldn't injure him.

I flipped my pillow around and fluffed it while Kitty purred and curled up into the crook of my neck. A sneeze from behind the bedroom door was the first indication that Amber, too, wasn't getting any sleep.

I got up. She was leaning against the kitchen counter blowing her nose.

"Are you okay?"

She jumped a little. I'd startled her.

Amber sneezed again then said, "I think I might be allergic to your pussy."

"Well, that's a new one. Can't say I've ever heard *that* before," I joked. Then, it really hit me that she was serious. "Fuck. You're allergic to the cat..."

"I'm not sure, but it's a good possibility, seeing as though I'm suddenly sneezing incessantly."

Shit.

As much as it pained me to follow through with my original plan to take Kitty to the shelter, I knew that was going to be even more necessary now. I'd secretly hoped to be able to keep her around.

"I'll find a place for Kitty tomorrow, make some calls during my lunch break."

"Kitty?" She laughed. "Is that her name?"

"Yeah. I know...not very original, but that's what I started calling her and it stuck."

"I'm gonna start calling you Stud." She stuck her hand out in jest. "Nice to meet you. I'm Bitch."

I took her hand, which was so small it felt breakable. "My friends call me Dick." My smile faded into a frown when I said, "Kitty will be gone by tomorrow."

"No." She blew her nose. "Don't."

"What do you mean?"

"It's only a few months. I'll get on some medication or something. That cat loves you. She belongs with you. It would break my heart to see you have to take her to a shelter. I can't let you do it." Blowing her nose again, she said in a stuffed-up voice, "By the way, I know where she came from."

"You do?"

"Yes. I couldn't sleep, so I was watching a repeat of the late evening news. A pet store on Devonshire was supposed to get a delivery of cats. The truck was parked while the driver left it unattended. They think someone broke into it and set the cats free."

"No shit? She's stolen property? Maybe I'll take her back there, then?"

"No! You can't."

"Well, I can't let you just...be sick."

"It'll be fine. Seriously. Sneezing never killed anyone."

"That's pretty insane that you would want to keep her around."

"Yeah, well, I might just be a little insane."

"Actually, no, it's how you are. You've always had a kind heart."

"A lot of good it did me." She rolled her eyes.

I knew she was referring to Rory and once again wanted to kick his ass.

"God, you must think I'm such a fucking Debbie Downer," she said. "I haven't stopped talking about my breakup since you got here."

"Debbie Downer? Nah. More like Negative Nancy." I winked.

She sniffled. "Have I mentioned I'm really glad you're here? I think I've smiled more in the last twelve hours than I have in three months."

And that's exactly the reason you need to keep yourself in check, Channing.

You can't risk crossing a line and hurting her.

Your job is what it's always been, to be her friend, to make her smile.

You weren't supposed to mess with Amber before she got her heart broken. But after? Now it's even more important not to fuck up.

33

"I promise to make an effort to be a little more up-beat," she said as she looked over at the clock on the wall. "You should go back to bed. You start your job tomorrow. I'm sorry for waking you."

Feeling more wired than ever, I shook my head. "You didn't wake me. I got up because I heard you, but I hadn't fallen asleep yet."

"Why can't you sleep? Are you anxious about work?"

I couldn't exactly admit to her what was really keeping me up.

"Something like that."

⌒

After work the following day, I decided to roam Cambridge before hopping the train back to Amber's.

Crowded with college students and homeless people, Harvard Square was bustling. The faint sound of live music registered, although I wasn't sure exactly where it was coming from.

Passing an outdoor café where a bunch of people were sitting around playing chess, it hit me that sightseeing alone in a new city wasn't really very much fun, so I called Amber to see if she'd want to join me down here. As luck would have it, she had the night off.

We planned to meet at this small, used bookstore that I'd discovered on Brattle Street. It was tucked away, and you had to go down a few steps to access the door.

The place smelled like burnt coffee and old paper. Rich with eccentricities from corner to corner, it was seriously one of the coolest places I'd ever stumbled upon.

I checked the door every few minutes to see if she'd arrived.

When Amber finally entered the place, I noticed that she was making small talk with a hunched-over old man on her way in. She was the type of person who always noticed people, didn't just walk by them in a fog, but really *noticed* them. Amber was smiling and chatting up the man before she finally held the door open for him. That was probably the highlight of the old fucker's entire year.

I loved observing people when they didn't know I was watching them. Getting to see how someone conducted themselves in their natural state without knowing they were being watched was a true window into their soul. And Amber had a kind soul. That had always been apparent to me.

I waved at her from the corner table I'd snagged.

Amber unraveled her scarf and took a seat across from me. My eyes fell to her neckline and to her perky breasts that were stretching against her pink, fitted sweater. Her hair was staticky from the cold.

She looked around at the musty shelves. "This place is really cool."

It smelled like incense all of a sudden. It was coming from the opposite side of the room where a woman with dreadlocks stuffed into a knit cap was selling crystals next to the occult book section. A man played guitar in the other corner.

"It's like a coffeehouse slash used bookstore. I stumbled upon it and thought you might like it here. I remember you used to read a lot." I suddenly got up. "I'll be right back."

After I fetched us two coffees that were served in ceramic mugs, I returned to my place at the table.

Amber blew on the steaming liquid before she said, "I thought I was supposed to be showing *you* around, not vice versa. I never even knew this place existed. Really cool find. I could spend all evening in here getting amped up on caffeine and searching for obscure books. Do you think that's strange?"

"No, actually. That's why bookstores make good first dates for people. I've taken a few women to bookstores—granted not one as cool as this."

She scrunched her nose. "I wouldn't have thought that."

"Well, for one, there's never a lack of things to talk about. Each book is a conversation piece."

The corners of her eyes crinkled. "Yeah, but you're really not getting to know the person if you're talking about books and not each other."

"I beg to differ. You can tell a hell of a lot about someone by what they read."

"Or what they *don't* read...if they've never picked up a book."

"Exactly. Now you're getting my point."

"I can imagine you've dated some women like that... who didn't read? At least from what I remember..."

"Plenty. And the truth always comes out. Not that I have anything against someone who doesn't habitually read, but sometimes it can mean there's an overall lack of interest in things outside of themselves."

A smile spread across her face. "I'm impressed, Lord. But given some of the girls you used to date, I didn't think such things mattered to you."

"Sounds like you're judging a book by its cover, Amber." I winked. "See what I did there?"

"I do." She laughed.

The sound of her laughter brought me back in time to our youth for a moment. There were very few remnants of that time, but her laughter was one of them. Her laughter used to be my medicine.

"I'm not exactly the same guy I was in high school and college."

"You mean, you don't..." She coughed intentionally. "Get around anymore?"

"Get around? You mean sleep around...fuck around... right? Just say what you really mean..."

"I was trying to be bookstore friendly."

"Look around. I'm pretty sure you can say and do anything you want in this place." I grinned and inhaled a curious scent that smelled an awful lot like marijuana. "By the way, do you smell pot?"

She sniffed the air. "I do."

I took a sip of my coffee and addressed her previous question. "I still appreciate a pretty face and a hot body, but it takes a lot more than that to thrill me now. A man can only take so much ass before he needs something more. My brain needs to be stimulated just as much as my dick."

Amber looked a bit flushed. "I see."

Needing to redirect my mind from focusing on how adorable her blushing was, I said, "You know what else is great about first dates in bookstores?"

"What?"

"If it ends up being a dud, you still get to take something new home to cuddle up with in bed." I wriggled by brows.

"I like the way you think, Lord."

My eyes landed on a situation happening in one of the aisles. "Even observing people in bookstores can be fun." I pointed to this dude I'd been watching before she arrived. "Take that guy, for example. Look how he's not even opening up the book he's holding. He's been watching that woman who's browsing next to him the entire time. He's pretending to be interested in *The Nightingale*, but really, he's totally getting ready to make his move. And that choice of book was no accident, either. It's a popular book. The likelihood that she's read it and liked it is high. So, he's counting on it as a potential conversation starter."

"That theory makes sense, but how can you be so sure of what's about to happen?" She drew her own conclusion. "Ah...you've picked women up in bookstores before, too."

Shrugging, I admitted, "I might have done the casual aisle thing once."

"Did it work?"

I simply smirked.

Amber rolled her eyes. "I didn't even need to ask. I'm sure everything works for you."

It amused me that she assumed things were so easy for me. "Why do you think that?"

"Because women have always been unable to resist you. It doesn't matter whether it's the bookstore aisle or the pet aisle at the supermarket, the story is the same in the end. You get the girl. You can have any woman you want."

"I'll have you know that's not always the case, Amber Walton."

"Someone rejected you?"

She was still clueless as to how I used to feel about her, never imagining that she was the first person who came to mind when she asked me that question. Even though it wasn't a blatant rejection, she had no idea how it felt for me when she got together with Rory. Besides Amber, there was only one other woman in my life whom I'd wanted but couldn't have. I don't think I'd ever spoken about the situation with Emily to another person. If anyone could understand, though, it was Amber.

"Yes, actually. Someone did reject me once."

"Really?" She leaned in. "Do tell, Channing."

"There's not much to tell. Her name is Emily. About a year ago, we met at the wedding of a buddy of mine. It was a three-day event in the Bahamas. We had this weird, instant connection. She was probably the first woman I can honestly say I could've seen myself in a relationship with or at least trying for it." I paused as I thought back to that weekend. "Anyway, we had an amazing time together. We were inseparable. I hadn't felt that way about someone in a long while. When the weekend came to an end, I went back to Chicago. And she went home to Massachusetts. We stayed in touch long-distance."

"Wait...she lives here in Mass?"

"Yeah...somewhere outside Boston, ironically."

"So, you'd gotten closer to her over the phone and then what?"

"Yeah. We were talking a lot—lots of Skype sex. And I found myself thinking about her a lot when we weren't communicating. I was supposed to come out to visit her, but she ended up getting back together with her ex-boy-friend out of the blue. I'd known about him all along, but she never gave me any indication that she was still into him. Anyway, she explained that she felt terrible for leading me on and all of that but that she had to follow her heart. There's really not much more to tell. It's nothing compared to what you're going through with Rory, but I'm not unfamiliar with disappointment."

She seemed truly shocked. Amber had definitely witnessed some of my biggest moments of vulnerability in those months after Lainey died. But over the years, I'd put up such a good front around people, that I made it easy for her to forget that I'd ever had a sensitive side. She probably thought I'd hardened a lot more than I actually had.

"Wow. Thank you for sharing that with me. I guess it was dumb of me to assume that you were immune to getting hurt."

"I wasn't looking for anything serious. But Emily just came out of the blue."

"That's how it happens sometimes, I would imagine."

I was done talking about Emily. I'd pretty much gotten over that whole thing, but rehashing it made me feel like shit. This was a taste of how Amber must have felt the other night when I made her talk about what happened with Rory.

Glancing over at the man macking in the aisle, I said, "See? What did I say about him?"

The dude was now holding the book behind his back as he chatted with his female prey.

"Holy crap. You were right." Amber was cracking up. "Oh, my God. She's leaving with him now!"

"See. That was slick. Slow and steady wins the race."

"Apparently."

I took her empty coffee mug and returned it to the counter.

Back at the table, I asked, "You want to look around?"

"Sure. Now that the fiction aisle A through L is done being used for *Love Connection*."

As we browsed, I brushed my index finger along the books on the shelves while Amber followed close behind me.

"Now, I want you to really think about this question, Amber."

"Okay..."

"If there's one book here that you've read, that you'd want me to read, what would it be? It should be something that I would probably otherwise never think to pick up on my own."

She continued to follow me in silence until she finally said, "Probably *The Law of Attraction*." She pointed to the non-fiction section. "I saw it over there. I'm actually studying it right now and would love another person's take on what it teaches."

"Alright. I'm gonna buy it and read it. But you have to read whatever I pick for you. Deal?"

"Yes."

I picked up *The Alchemist* by Paulo Coelho. "Have you ever read this?"

"No."

"Okay, this is my choice for you. We'll give each other a month to read. Then, we'll discuss."

"This is shaping up to be an exciting few months for you, Lord. Cats...staying home and reading. What's next? Should I be looking for a Bingo hall?"

"Get on that. Also, don't forget living with Negative Nancy...that's another one."

"Yup. That, too."

I hoped she truly knew I was joking. "I'm really enjoying being here so far. More than I anticipated, actually."

"It must have been the moldy cheese that did it."

"Definitely the moldy cheese." I grinned.

We were standing in line waiting to check out when I asked, "Hey, you hungry for dinner?"

"Yeah, I'm starving."

I knew exactly where I wanted to take her. "I saw this Jamaican place down the street on the way here."

"I've never had Jamaican food."

"You don't know what you're missing, then."

"What's your favorite dish?"

Without having to think, I answered, "Curry goat."

"Did you just say goat?"

"Yup."

"Snails...goat...do you eat *anything* normal?"

CHAPTER FOUR
AMBER

I'd been deep in thought when Annabelle took a seat next to me in the teacher's lounge.

"How's Channing?" she asked as she opened her lunch bag.

I couldn't actually tell her the truth.

Well, Annabelle, I've masturbated to thoughts of him every night since his arrival. It's a problem.

"He's great, actually. I'm really enjoying his company."

Well, that was the truth, too.

She bobbed her head to the side as she looked at me. "You seem like you have something on your mind."

I have a lot of things on my mind, and most of them are not safe for work.

"Well...it's nothing...it's just..."

"What?"

I thought up an analogy to explain what I was feeling.

"You know how when you're on a diet...as long as you don't bring bad stuff into the house, you're fine, but as soon as someone brings over that box of cupcakes, all of your willpower is gone? That's sort of what having an attractive man around does to the celibate woman. Being around Channing is making me realize how badly I need to get laid."

Annabelle was laughing at me. "The solution seems simple to me."

She just couldn't seem to get it into her thick head that I refused to go there with Channing. Just because two people are single doesn't mean they're a good fit.

"I don't know how many times I can explain it to you. I could never be with him in that way."

She examined my face then said, "I worry that the real reason you're afraid to consider that is because of Rory."

The R word immediately triggered my defenses. "What about Rory?"

"A part of you thinks that Rory and you are going to get back together, and you know that sleeping with Channing would ruin that because Rory would never be able to accept it. Am I right?"

God. Maybe. Maybe, that was at the back of my mind.

"I don't know. Maybe, subconsciously. There is no doubt that Rory would never get over it if something happened with Channing and me. That's for sure. But first of all, even if I didn't care about the repercussions of sleeping with Channing, I don't think he looks at me in a sexual way. He never did. He sees me like a sister."

"How can you be so sure of that?"

"I can't entirely...but he could have almost any woman he wants. Well, everyone but some chick named Emily. So, it's a safe assumption."

"Emily?"

"Some girl he was telling me about that led him on then went back to her old boyfriend. I bet she's out of this world gorgeous."

He'd surprised me with that story. Emily must have really been something for Channing to want to consider settling down. That whole thing made me a little sad for him. I was jealous of Emily and kind of wanted to kick her ass for hurting my friend at the same time.

Her mouth was full when she said, "Have you looked in the mirror lately?"

"Yes, and I need to get my eyebrows threaded. Badly."

"You're selling yourself short. I'd kill for your body. Don't let it go to waste. You're only young once. We got to get you back in the game."

Annabelle would often compliment me. With her frizzy, black hair, prominent nose, and stalky body, we were opposites physically.

"My problem is...I'm not ready for a relationship. But at the same time, I don't want to just hook up with someone, either. There's really no in-between. You know what I wish?" I looked around to make sure we were still alone. "I wish I had like a superpower where I could have sex with a man and erase the whole experience after, so that there was no aftermath or guilt. I would never run into him again. In fact, he would stop existing after that. But that's just a fantasy."

"Uh...no, it's not. That's called a one-night stand."

"Well, you'd have to actually go out or online date to have a one-night stand. That sounds really daunting to me right now. I'm not ready for either one of those things."

"You just want to get laid by the magically disappearing cock."

I couldn't help but laugh when I said, "You need to lower your voice."

Annabelle squinted her eyes. She was giving me a weird look, making me think she was cooking up something in her brain.

"What do you have up your sleeve?" I asked.

"Who says you can't have what you want?"

"What do you mean?"

"When you just told me about your little superpower fantasy, you reminded me of something."

"What?"

"Okay, you know my cousin Shae, the single attorney who lives in Wellesley?"

"Yeah. You've mentioned her."

"Well...the last time I saw her was at my sister's wedding. She had a little too much to drink and began to open up to me at the reception." Annabelle lowered her voice. "She told me that she went to see a male escort."

Looking behind my shoulder, I whispered, "You mean a prostitute..."

"Technically, yes. But she said this guy was *amazing* both physically and personality-wise. She said it was one of the most enjoyable nights she's ever had."

"She only saw him once?"

"Well, it's very expensive—like a thousand dollars for one night. Shae said it was worth every penny. Apparently, it was just what she needed to feel confident and sexy again. A little while after that, she started to put herself out there and began dating the man she's now engaged to. But she attributes this escort with getting her out of the funk she'd been in. Not to mention, she said it was the best sex of her life."

"Really...well, I could never do something like that."

"Suppose you had the money, though...why would you say that you would never do it?"

She couldn't be serious.

"Because he probably has some disease, for one."

"Actually, I brought that up with her, and she said that they discussed it before they had any physical contact. He told her he gets tested frequently and is very rigid about practicing safe sex. He was very open about everything. They spoke quite a bit online before they met."

"Wow. Well, that definitely doesn't sound like what I envision a male prostitute to be like."

"It wasn't. I guess this company caters to the professional woman. They know that smart women want more than just a night of sex. They want to be with someone who is both sexy and intelligent. Honestly, if I were single and had the money, I would totally do it."

I wasn't sure I believed her. "Really? You would?"

"Why not? I agree with you that dating can be brutal. Sometimes, a girl just needs a good lay and nothing more." She whipped out her phone.

"What are you doing?"

"I'm texting Shae for the information on the escort service."

"Why?"

"Just in case you want to look into it." She winked. "You can start saving now. Skip the gel nails and the lattes for a few months."

"You're crazy. Don't bother."

She ignored me and kept typing. "Like I said, can't hurt to have the information."

We'd been so wrapped up in this conversation, I hadn't even heated up my lunch. I popped my bowl into the microwave, waited, and just as it dinged, so did Annabelle's phone.

"Oh, she responded!"

I blew on the escarole soup. "What did she say?"

"Let me read it verbatim." She paused. "It's called Newbury Gentleman's Club. They have a generic website. They obviously don't advertise the fact that they offer more than just escort services. The woman who owns it has a direct email. Most of their business is through word of mouth, since they can't be too blatant in their advertising. You contact this woman initially, and she gives you a password to a secure portal where you can choose the person based on physical attributes and a brief description of personality traits of the man you want to meet. For example, you can indicate whether you want to be with someone who's rough in bed or someone who is more gentle. You can indicate preferences like blond or dark-haired, bulky or lean. They don't show photos to protect the man's privacy, but they guarantee that on a scale of one to ten on the looks ratio, all of their men fall in the ten range." She turned to me. "God, this is better than being a kid in a candy store! Anyway, she just pasted the email address of the woman in charge but also gave me a password that she said might still work to bypass having to contact the woman in order to get into the secure site. I'm forwarding you all the information."

That made me nervous for some reason. "Why?"

"Because I want to live vicariously through you. I think you should look into it."

Annabelle had seriously lost her mind.

"And where exactly am I going to get this money?" I asked even though I wasn't really entertaining this.

"Where there's a will, there's a way."

I neglected to mention that I had quite a bit of savings, and that technically, money wasn't the issue. I could easily afford the thousand-dollar price tag without denting my bank account because I'd always been smart with my money and saved a lot. That wasn't the deterrent for me so much as my fear of disease and my pride.

⸻

A few days later, it was Sunday night, and my emotions were all over the place.

I'd just logged into Facebook to find Rory had been tagged in a photo posted by someone named Jennifer Barney. They were walking along the Charles River, both wearing athletic clothing. I assumed he must have been dating her. It was the first time I'd had to see him with anyone else, and it was absolutely devastating.

After thoroughly stalking her photos, I realized that Jennifer's features were similar to mine, which made it all even worse somehow. He'd broken up with me to spend time with someone who looked like she could be my sister. And that burned.

I did something I considered doing a long time ago but never followed through with: I unfriended him to avoid having to see his posts. It was time. I didn't want a front row seat to his moving on.

The condo was eerily quiet as I sat alone with my misery. Well, I wasn't completely alone. Kitty was sulking on the other end of the couch. It was the first time Channing had left her alone with me.

He'd flown back to Chicago for the weekend. I was grateful for the reprieve, not because I didn't enjoy his company, but because I was starting to enjoy it a little too much—his smell, his laugh, everything about him. It was also nice to not have to worry about what I looked like as I lounged around in my sweats.

But now I sort of wished he were here. He'd likely say something to make me feel better.

Desperately needing a distraction, I scrolled through my phone and came across the text message Annabelle had sent me containing the information for Newbury Gentleman's Club. My curiosity got the best of me. Pulling up the website, I must have stared at the screen for over fifteen minutes.

The truth was, I hadn't been able to stop thinking about the male escort thing since Annabelle's and my conversation in the lunchroom.

My heart was pounding. *Was I really doing this?*

I told myself that I was just innocently checking it out, that I wasn't really serious about it. An unsettled feeling in the pit of my stomach, however, seemed to contradict that. And an inner voice that felt new and untrustworthy was telling me that I deserved this, to put my carnal needs first, that no one needed to know.

A box prompting the user to enter a password popped up onto the screen. If the code that Annabelle's cousin had given me worked, then I would be convinced that was a sign. If it didn't work, then I would walk away. After I punched the code in, I was diverted to another site.

I was in.

The page was black with gold accents and sleek fonts. A slow and seductive piano tune played. The site featured a detailed description of the club's services. You could choose from a minimum half-day experience, full-day, or even an entire weekend, which seemed to be the maximum duration offered. The full-day rate was two-thousand dollars with the cheapest option being the half-day rate at a cool grand.

I clicked on a link titled *Meet Our Gentlemen.* It was essentially a menu of men, each numbered Gentleman One through Gentleman Twenty. A disclaimer noted that for the privacy of the men, photos would not be provided.

I began clicking through each profile, reading the descriptions.

Gentleman One is an actor by trade. He loves older women, gentle lovemaking, and intelligent conversation. With blond hair, blue eyes, and a tall, lean body, Gentleman One is an all-American dream. Celebrity Doppelgänger: Alexander Skarsgård.

Gentleman Four was born and raised in the Dominican Republic. Known as our gentle giant, with his massive frame and strong, muscular body, he's often mistaken for a pro-wrestler. Celebrity Doppelgänger: Dwayne "The Rock" Johnson.

I read through them all, eventually returning to the one who had stood out the most: Gentleman Nine.

Gentleman Nine is a Southern gentleman, raised right. He believes chivalry isn't dead, and his goal is to make you feel as comfortable as you will feel sexy. Celebrity Doppelgänger: Matt Bomer.

He had me at Matt Bomer.

Underneath the description was a button that said *Contact Gentleman Nine*. I entered my email address where it asked for it to activate the chat feature and began typing.

Hi,

My name is Amber, and I can't even believe I am writing to you right now. I don't even know what you look like or whether you're a psychopath. Well, given the fact that my writing to you is essentially synonymous with trolling for sex, I guess the shady one in this equation is me. I'm really not...shady. I'm not unattractive or desperate, either. I'm sure you see your share of those types, but I felt the need to let you know that I'm not...gross. I'm twenty-five, svelte, and have been told that I'm attractive, although I don't feel that I am the proper judge of that. I just want to be clear that I'm not contacting you because men aren't interested in me. I could definitely find a man to sleep with if I wanted to deal with all of the other things that go along with that. I am not looking for a relationship. This past year, I got my heart broken by the man I thought was the love of my life. And, well, since then, I haven't felt ready or able to open my heart to anyone. Not sure if I ever will. Some days, I miss him and that makes me even angrier...because you shouldn't feel that way about someone who dumped you.

I don't want to go off on a tangent here. I'm sure you're very busy...very busy getting busy. I'm sorry. I know. I'm not very good at this. Anyway, the reason I'm writing you right now is because I'm starting to really miss sex. I'm wondering if one night with someone who really knows what they're doing and who won't judge me or expect anything more from me might be what I need right now. I don't feel comfortable just showing up to a hotel room without knowing a little bit about who you are. And I'd also want confirmation that you don't have a disease. Not sure how that will work. Anyway, I'd love to chat. If we can come to some sort of an agreement, then I would take the next step to meet you for a half-day session.

Best,

Amber W.

CHAPTER FIVE
CHANNING

The Chicago trip was way more stressful than I thought it would be. I needed to check in on my mother and handle some other business, but the entire time, I couldn't wait to get back to Amber's place in Boston, back to Kitty and the calm.

I still couldn't believe Amber had insisted on keeping the cat around. But the sneezing had stopped, so that was good. I didn't think I could really keep Kitty if she was continuing to make Amber sick.

The sound of running water could be heard when I let myself in. Amber was taking a shower as she normally did in the evenings. I hadn't told her exactly when I'd be returning, so I hoped I didn't scare her when she came out of the bathroom.

Kitty started meowing right away as she purred along my legs.

Lifting her up, I kissed her softly on the head. "How's my girl? You take good care of Amber?"

A throw blanket was strewn messily atop the couch, and Amber's laptop was open on the coffee table. I was looking forward to catching up with my roomie, hearing about what she'd been up to this weekend. Even though we both worked a lot, it was always nice to chat with her at night before retreating to my room.

We would sometimes watch TV together or just talk about our days. Before this, it had been years since I'd had a roommate—not since college. I'd forgotten that living with someone could actually be enjoyable. Not to mention, Amber's condo was a pretty damn sweet place to live. It was spacious with high ceilings and white crown moldings, details that only an older, historic property would have. It was the nicest place I'd ever lived and nothing like I'd expected.

I couldn't wait to take a shower myself tonight. Since I had to wait for the bathroom, I decided to relax for a bit and surf the net. Plopping my ass down on the couch, I let out a deep sigh. Breathing in, I could smell the pumpkin-scented Yankee Candle that Amber had burning on the mantle. Damn, it was good to be back here.

Since Amber had left her laptop open, I figured I would use it instead of grabbing mine. Readying to log into my Facebook account, I noticed a website that was minimized. I probably shouldn't have clicked on it to see what it was, but we won't remind Kitty that curiosity killed the cat.

The website that met my eyes was definitely not something I was prepared to see. She'd left a chat window open. It was a message to someone.

With my heart pounding, I read it at least three times. *What. The. Fuck.*

My mind was racing. In what world does Amber need to go to a male escort? Does she have any clue how dangerous that could be? She didn't. Amber had always been a little too naïve and trusting.

Frozen, I couldn't get past the shock of this enough to figure out how to deal with it.

Was I supposed to just forget I saw this? Pretend like nothing happened when she came out of the bathroom?

The sound of the shower turning off started an internal timer in my head. There wasn't much time to think about how to react. There was no way I could allow her to do something so reckless as to sleep with some guy who'd probably been with thousands of women. Coming from me, I know that thought was like the pot calling the kettle black, but I couldn't guarantee that this person took the necessary precautions to avoid disease, not to mention her safety in a situation like this. She couldn't trust what he said no matter what bullshit he was going to feed her.

Needing to buy myself more time, I made an impulsive decision. Deep down, I knew it was out of line, but that didn't matter at the moment. Fuck that. All that mattered was looking out for her.

I hit the contact button. It required you to enter your email address to start a new message. Referring to my phone, I looked up Amber's email, hoping it was the same one she'd just used. I entered it, pretending to be her and typed:

Sorry. I had too much to drink tonight. Disregard that last email, please. I'm no longer interested.

I saw that you could delete sent messages from within the chat box.

Good. This is good. I can work with this.

I deleted my message from the "Sent" tab so that she wouldn't see it. I really hoped that tactic worked, preventing this guy from responding to her initial message. Then again, if she didn't hear back, she might contact him again or contact another "gentleman."

Shit. Think.

I had an idea of how to handle that but knew that I needed to get out of here to implement it. There was no way I could face her right now anyway. Making sure I left her computer open in the same spot in which I'd found it, I got up.

Taking my travel bag with me, I exited the condo and headed to the café down the street. She would never know I'd even come home in the first place.

Once at the café and seated at a table with my laptop, I decided to create a new email address under the guise of Gentleman Nine. Without overthinking it, I sent her a message.

Dear Amber,

Thank you for reaching out to me. I felt that your message warranted emailing you from this address so that you don't have to log into the site to contact me moving forward. It's

easier to correspond back and forth this way.
I can completely understand your wanting to
get to know me first, and I think that's wise.
I'm here for you if you want to talk or anything
else. Just let me know what questions you
have.

—Gentleman Nine

What the fuck had I gotten myself into? I should have
just had him tell her he couldn't help her out, that he was
too busy, but then what if she moved on, seeking the services of someone else? I couldn't monitor the situation
unless I controlled every step. It needed to be handled like
this. Also, to be honest, a part of me really wanted to know
what she was thinking. *Jesus*. I was going to hell.

Not ready to go home and face her, I ordered a hot tea
and decided to sit for a while before venturing back home.

A notification chimed, signaling that I'd received
a new email. It was a response from Amber. I probably
shouldn't have been surprised that she'd responded to my
message so quickly.

Hi Gentleman Nine,

Thank you for answering so fast and for pro-
viding me with this email address. You're right.
It's much easier to communicate with you outside of the portal.

I'm sorry if I sounded like a rambling mess in
my first message. As you can see, I am new
at this. My biggest concern is to ensure that

you don't have any kind of sexually transmitted disease. How do you protect yourself if you're with so many women? Do you have anything current from a doctor that you can show me verifying that you're clean? (I know you probably can't divulge personal information.) Beyond those issues, I guess I just want to know who you are. How old are you? Do you really look like Matt Bomer? LOL. How did you end up doing this? And what would a night (or half-day) with you be like? Sorry for all the questions.

—Amber

Shit. Deeper down the rabbit hole.

Bouncing my legs frantically, I raked my fingers through my hair while I pondered my response. Determined to lie as little as possible, I tried my best to address her questions in a way that the answers could technically be applied to the real me. That made me feel a little less guilty. I began to type.

Hi Amber,

Don't worry about asking too many questions. There is no such thing. I can provide you with whatever verification you need that I'm clean. I can assure you that I'm STD-free, but as a precaution, I always use condoms with no exceptions. Your safety is my number one priority.

How did I end up doing this? Well, how much time do you have? LOL. That's a long story I should probably tell you in person, but the bottom line is, I fell into this situation, and it's hard to leave now.

In answer to your age question, I'm twenty-seven. I don't exactly look like Matt Bomer, but you might like me even better.

A night with me consists of whatever you're comfortable with and whatever you desire. We could talk for a while or not talk at all. Basically, your wish would be my command. I can guarantee that for at least the time we are together, you won't be thinking about that fool who left you.

What brought you to me tonight of all nights?

—G9

That was really what I wanted to know.

This was so unlike Amber or at least the Amber I thought I knew. What prompted her to do this tonight? Something must have happened while I was away.

I took a long sip of my tea, nearly burning my mouth and waited. I knew if she hadn't gone to bed, she wouldn't take long to respond. I'd give it twenty minutes before giving up and going home.

Five minutes later, a new message popped up in my fake inbox.

G9,

Is that what your friends call you? I like that. Thanks for the answers.

That's an interesting question—why tonight of all nights? Well, I saw my ex tagged on Facebook with another woman, and that put me over the edge. But it's more than that. Lately, I've developed a strong attraction to a good friend of mine, and that's sort of screwing with me a bit. He's actually temporarily living in my condo, but he's someone I've known for years. I've always thought he was extremely handsome, but it's complicated. He and I would not be a good match romantically. He's not the monogamous type, or at least, he never used to be. We're better off as friends. He was also the best friend of my ex years back, so there's that. Having him around, though, has made me more sensitized to my sexual desires. Little things like the waft of his scent, the way he touches the small of my back when he passes by me in the kitchen...it's like my body is on this constant state of alert. So, I was thinking if I could just—for lack of a better word—get laid, maybe I could get this feeling out of my system.

—Amber

My jaw was open as I just sat there staring at the screen.

Holy fucking shit.

I read it again.

And again.

And again.

I honestly didn't think that Amber felt that way about me. She would always make jokes about me being good-looking, but her attraction to Rory proved that her taste wasn't exactly conventional. Now, I really felt like shit for invading her privacy, because there was no way she would've been okay with confessing that to me. I never imagined any of this had to do with *me*. I'd assumed it was solely about Rory.

She wanted to use another man to fuck *me* out of her system?

That revelation left me shocked and confused—not to mention hard as fuck thinking about the fact that Amber wanted me.

Knowing what I now knew, the right thing to do would have been to just abandon the entire exchange at this point. But then how would that have left her feeling if *he* never wrote back? I'd completely made a mess of this situation, although I still wouldn't have changed a thing if it meant preventing her from giving her body to some male whore who merely wanted her money.

This predicament kept getting more difficult for me to navigate. The café was about to close. Needing to get home and not wanting her to think she'd lost me, I sent her one final message.

> **Amber,**
> I can definitely relate to wanting someone you can't have. I think you should think about what you want to do a bit more. I'm here if you need to talk, but I have to log off for the night.
> Have a good evening.
> —G9

I closed my laptop and got up to exit the café.

My breathing was ragged as I sucked in the cold night air. Making my way down the cobblestone street, I pondered whether I should avoid Amber tonight altogether. My fear was that she would be able to tell that something was up just by looking at me.

Something was definitely up, and I couldn't have her noticing that, either.

Pretending to be arriving home for the first time, I opened the door and greeted Kitty as if we hadn't already reunited tonight. True to form, her meowing was just as enthusiastic as ever. It didn't matter whether we hadn't seen each other for hours or minutes, she was always purring and excitedly meowing her ass off.

Amber was sitting on the couch. She abruptly closed her computer and straightened up as if I'd caught her with her pants down.

"Channing! I wasn't sure when you'd be getting back."

Dropping my bag on the floor, I said, "Yeah. Late flight. I'm exhausted."

Silence filled the air as we stood facing each other. I sensed that she was still thinking about Gentleman Nine and probably feeling a little ashamed. Maybe my presence had snapped her back to reality a little. At least, I hoped so.

I'd known Amber since I was a kid...but somehow this moment felt like I was meeting her for the first time—seeing a new side of her, one that involved her wanting me and one that involved the understanding that she was no longer the innocent girl I once knew. She had needs—very adult needs. I didn't blame her for that. Hell...the fact that she was exploring her sexuality was hot as fuck. I just wanted to make sure she was safe; that was all.

"Anything exciting happen while I was gone?" I took two steps toward her and immediately noticed her body stiffen as she stepped back a bit. She was reacting to me. Had it always been like this? Maybe I just never noticed. I was now picking up on the body language that had probably been there all along.

"No. It was really quiet with you not here. Without the distraction, I ended up stalking Rory's Facebook page, which was a total mistake. He was tagged by some girl while they were out. I shouldn't have done that."

I had to act surprised because of course I already knew about that from our email exchange. "I'm sorry you had to see that."

"I unfriended him, so I don't have to see his posts anymore. It's for the best."

"Good." I scratched my chin. "That was a good idea."

She looked up at me, her eyes reflecting so many different things: sadness, desire, desperation, confusion. That jackass had left her feeling so lost, doubting herself. But the answer to her problems had nothing to do with him. She needed to get out, find herself, separate her own self-worth from the breakup.

There was no question that I was attracted to her. I was *very* attracted to Amber—always had been. That didn't mean I was the right person for her. She was too vulnerable to mess with. Not to mention, the mature side of me really didn't want to ruin a good thing—I valued her friendship more than anything, and this time in Boston with her was like a second chance to renew it. There weren't exactly a lot of people in my life whom I could depend on. Not to mention, Lainey would have been proud of me for looking after her best friend and not fucking things up.

Amber was generally smart. But her contacting that service proved she could be misguided. Paying for sex wasn't the answer to her problem. She needed help finding someone without having to resort to that. Even though the thought of pawning her off to some dude in a bar admittedly made me jealous, I sucked it up because the alternative of how she was handling herself was definitely the bigger evil.

"You need to put yourself out there, Amber. As hard as that might be."

"I tried online dating. It's not for me."

"What happened?"

"Well, as an example, one guy told me how much he wanted to give me a pearl necklace. I thought he had some kind of jewelry fetish. Annabelle had to break the news to me about what it was. That was pretty much the end of it for me."

Oh shit.

"Yeah, he wanted to bejewel you with his cum. Sick fuck. Also beware of someone who wants to shower you in gold."

"Yeah, I know that now."

"Maybe try a different route. You need to force yourself to go out more. You can gauge people better in person. We should go out Friday night. I can be your wingman."

"You're gonna what...pimp me out?"

The irony in her choice of words was not lost on me.

"No. But I'm very good at judging people on a first impression, so I can help you determine if a guy is worth talking to, help make a smooth introduction to avoid any awkwardness."

"I'm not really ready for that kind of thing."

"I know that. But you probably never will *feel* ready. Sometimes, you just have to push yourself to get out of the house. That's half the battle. Then, you just sit back and watch life happen. Nothing great can happen to you if you stay home all of the time."

She cracked a slight smile that I knew was masking a plethora of self-doubt as she tried to convince herself of all the reasons not to take me up on my offer.

"Amber...just drinks. Okay?"

She let out a breath and softly said, "Okay."

CHAPTER SIX
AMBER

Happenstance was a bar a few blocks from home. A co-worker had recommended it, saying the atmosphere was relaxed, and the beer was reasonably priced. So, I suggested it to Channing for our night out.

A jukebox sat unused in the corner. Maybe I'd get up and play something later.

The bar was channeling an old *Coyote Ugly* vibe. Hundreds of bras hung over rods along the ceiling, an indication that there had certainly been some wild nights at this joint. Unfortunately, tonight wasn't one of them.

"So, what do you have up your sleeve tonight, Lord?"

"Absolutely nothing. This is just a night out between friends. But if anyone happens to catch your eye, just let me know. I'm your man."

"And what exactly are you going to do if I decide I want to talk to someone?"

"I'll catch him at the bar, start a casual conversation with him. I need to vet the guy first to make sure he's not a tool. If it seems like he's worth talking to, I'll give you a signal. We'll have to come up with something. Like maybe I'll look over at you and scratch my chin."

My eyes were transfixed on Channing's masculine fingers rubbing against his scruff as he demonstrated.

"That'll signal that it's safe to come over," he said.

"Then, what?"

"I'll introduce you as my friend. I can casually slip away if it turns out you're getting along with him. If not, you can excuse yourself."

"Is this what you do for your guy friends?"

"I've done it a few times in the past."

"Does it work?"

"Sometimes, yes. Sometimes, no."

"Why?" I asked before the answer hit me. "Oh, let me guess...because the chick ends up disappointed that you weren't the one interested in her. She wants you instead."

He laughed guiltily. "That might have happened once or twice."

"Oh, my God, Channing, I would never let you be my wingman if I were a guy. That would be counterproductive."

"Well, it's a good thing you're not a guy, then, isn't it?"

Channing looked and smelled amazing. He wore a dark gray beanie that reminded me of the one in the photo on Facebook. His shiny hair was sticking out at the top. The wooly, fitted sweater he was wearing made me want to scratch it like a cat.

He looked around. "I don't see any viable options."

"I'd have to agree with you. It's pretty empty here tonight."

Channing took a bite of his fry and dipped it in my ketchup. "Some things to keep in mind if you're ever out and about without me..."

I straightened in my seat. "Okay...what?"

"Be wary of men who are by themselves in bars. They're lurkers." He pointed to a man in the corner of the room. "Like that guy over there. A dude is much safer if he's with a friend or a group. Much less likely to be a psychopath."

"Makes sense. And, well, you do seem able to read people. I was impressed by your observation of that couple in the bookstore."

"Look around, tell me what you want to know about someone here. I'll tell you their story."

Taking him up on his challenge, I pointed to a girl sitting at the bar. "What about her?"

The girl looked tense, like she was waiting for someone.

"See how she's looking around frantically? She's waiting for her Tinder date, and I think it might be the first time she's ever done this. She's already decided she's going to have sex tonight. She's not sure if she should, but she's going to do it anyway."

Interesting. That reminded me of something.

I pointed to the man in the corner. "What about him... the guy you said was a lurker. What's his deal, really?"

"He's probably here looking for you, but I'm with you, so thankfully that was intercepted. He's creepy."

"Totally." I looked toward the opposite corner of the room where a man and woman were together but completely ignoring each other. "What about that couple over there?"

"God, look at them. They're both on their phones, not even paying attention to each other. They've been together for a while probably and just don't give a shit anymore. That's kind of sad."

"Yeah, but we all do that from time to time, right?" I said.

His eyes widened. "You and Rory went out and spent half the night looking down at your phones?"

"Well, yeah, actually we did sometimes. You've never done that?"

"I can't even recall one time I pulled out my phone on a date. Well, not for the purpose of making a phone call or checking the Internet."

"What other purposes are there?"

Channing smirked, and that made me very curious.

"Maybe I don't want to know. But tell me anyway."

"A woman once asked me to go to the bathroom and text her a picture of how hard I was for her. So, I made an exception and pulled out my phone in that instance."

"That's not all you pulled out, apparently." I laughed.

"Touché."

Normally, the idea of Channing sending a photo of his cock to some woman would make me cringe. Maybe it was the alcohol, but right now, the thought of him sneaking off into a bathroom and doing something like that was turning me on. Then again, everything was turning me on lately. I really needed to figure out where the *off* button was.

I cleared my throat. "Okay, so you make exceptions for dick pics..."

"Only dick pics." He winked. "Otherwise, it's disrespectful and shows the person that I'm more interested in other things. If I'm with someone, I'm going to be mentally present, otherwise what's the point of being together?"

"Yeah, but after you've been with someone for a while, it's a little different. You've never gotten to that point with anyone. In a long-term relationship, gone are the butter-flies and the dick pics."

"Well, that's just a shame. Maybe that's part of the problem. If being online is more interesting than the person sitting in front of you, then what does that say?" He looked back over at the couple. "Those two haven't looked at each other once. If that's what a relationship is like, then I'm happy I'm not in one."

It was hard to argue with that.

My attention turned to two men who were looking in our direction. "What about those guys?"

"They're gay," Channing said without hesitation.

"Ah, you have gaydar, too?"

"Well, if they're looking at me and not you, then yes, that makes it pretty easy to figure out. You don't even really need gaydar, in that case."

"I guess you're right." I sighed and surveyed the room some more. "What do you think someone turning the tables on us right now would think? What impression would we give?"

"They would think we were either old friends or on a good date because we're actually comfortable with each other and engaged in conversation. And they would think I was entertaining because you're smiling and laughing."

"They wouldn't know what a miserable person I am normally."

His expression turned serious. "I don't see you that way at all, Amber."

"How *do* you see me? What's your honest impression of me since arriving in Boston?"

"You want the truth?"

"Yes."

"You're still sixteen to me." He laughed.

"Shut up, really? You think so? Well, you definitely look a lot older to me, but not in a bad way."

"You honestly look almost the same. But I'm not just talking about your appearance. When I look at you, I see my sister's friend, the girl who hung out in my basement and who used to kick my ass in air hockey. That's who I see, even though I know you're really not her anymore. Maybe I just *want* you to be her. I'm choosing to see that version of you for selfish reasons."

"You prefer her over the person I am now..."

He was quick to correct. "That's not what I meant... at all. You have every reason to be in a funk right now. And, of course, you've grown up a lot. I was more referring to the nostalgia of thinking about the connection we had back then. We lost touch when I went away to UF. And after that, it was never really the same between you and me. That's what happens when you're young. We evolve. But the mark of true friendship is that you can still come full circle, even if life circumstances change."

"I always knew you'd be there for me if I ever needed you, but I never would've imagined that I'd be sitting in a bar in Boston with you and certainly wouldn't have dreamt that we'd be living together."

"It's fate. The timing was right. The job brought me here, but the universe knew you really needed someone to give you a good kick in the ass."

"Have you started reading *The Law of Attraction*? You mentioned the universe..."

He winked. "I might have."

"I hope you don't think I'm a whack job after you get done with it."

"I'm surprised at how much I'm liking it, actually. And I think that what the book teaches about manifesting your own destiny can help you get over the R word if you apply it correctly."

"You can say his name. I won't freak out. I'm done crying over it."

Channing tapped my foot with his under the table. "Good."

"I just need to hit a reset button on my life."

He smacked the table. "There it is, the new R word. Reset."

"Love that." I sighed. "You know, my problem is...I've never dated. I never had to because I was always with Rory. I feel like I don't really know how to handle myself in that situation. I'm like a fish out of water."

"So, let's practice."

"How?"

"We'll pretend to be two people who are just meeting here. I can stay in character if you can. It'll be like improv."

"Oh, boy." I laughed. This sounded crazy but kind of fun at the same time. "I guess I should take advantage of the opportunity to practice with a true expert." When he suddenly got up, I asked, "Where are you going?"

"I need to enter the bar, pretend like I'm just meeting you." He winked. "Just wing it, alright?"

"Alright." I took a long sip of my drink.

Channing exited the building then reentered.

He was apparently not fooling around. He actually went to the bar and ordered a beer before his head slowly turned toward me. When his gaze met mine, his mouth curled into a sly smile. I covered my mouth in laughter before he gave me a scolding look with his eyes. He was silently reprimanding me for not taking this seriously. It was in that moment that I vowed to get my shit together and actually play along.

The only problem was, I couldn't stop laughing and worse: I got the hiccups. Whenever I laughed really hard, I would always get the worst case of them. Channing was cracking up now, too, because he remembered my hiccup issue. It used to happen to me all of the time when we were younger.

When the laughter died down, the sexy smirk returned to Channing's face as he once again moved into character, playing the role of my mysterious suitor.

Flirtatiously twirling my hair with my index finger, I returned his smile.

When he began to walk toward me, I actually got goosebumps. My physical reaction was no different than if this was actually happening.

"Are you alone?" he asked.

My heartbeat sped up. "Yes."

"Mind if I join you?"

"Not at all."

He pulled out a chair and sat down. "I'm Channing." He held out his hand, and when I took it, his touch felt electric. My nipples hardened. Maybe this wasn't such a great idea.

"My name is Amber." *Hiccup.*

"Well, excuse you. You okay there?"

"Yeah, I just get the hiccups when I laugh too hard. You made me laugh earlier."

"Is that so?" His tone was so flirtatious.

"Yeah."

"You know, I used to have a friend who hiccuped whenever she laughed too hard. You know what I would do to her?"

"What?"

"I would scare the living daylights out of her when she least expected it. That's supposed to make them go away."

"Please don't do that to me," I said seriously. It used to annoy me when he'd startle me.

"Well, what's a beautiful, hiccuping girl like yourself doing alone in a bar anyway?"

"Just relaxing, having a drink."

Over the course of the next thirty minutes, Channing stayed in character, asking me question after question about my job and personal interests—as if we were meeting each other for the very first time. Honestly, it was freaky how real it felt. I found myself getting lost in the experience, almost forgetting who we were and the purpose of the skit. He was so engaging and easy to talk to. Something told me that this wasn't exactly how it would be with most guys I'd pick up in a bar. I wasn't going to admit this to him, but if this were real, I'd be totally sold on him right now.

My hiccups still hadn't waned, though. At one point mid-conversation, Channing grabbed my glass of water and drank a sip before suddenly splashing it in my face. The surprise impact of the water hitting my skin caused a rush of adrenaline.

Drenched, I yelled, "What was that for?"

"For your hiccups!"

Wiping my face with a napkin, I said, "I told you not to scare me."

"I bet they go away now, though."

"Sure...now that I look like a drowned rat."

"No, you don't. You look beautiful."

After that comment, it was necessary to remind myself that he was still in character.

Sure enough, the hiccups never returned as we continued our little roleplay game. Channing gradually pushed his chair nearer to me. His face was close to mine whenever he spoke. I could smell the beer on his tongue mixed with his cologne. There was likely no sexier scent on Earth than the combination of those two things. I was trying to ignore the fact that my panties were wet just from the closeness of his body and from the feel of his breath on my face. That made me realize how hard-up I was.

God.

After several minutes of talking, he leaned in and spoke directly in my ear, "I'm not far from the bar at all. How about we get out of here. Go back to my place." His lips actually touched my skin, and his breath felt like it travelled through my ear canal and down to my vagina. It nearly did me in. This game was starting to play serious tricks on me. The urge to lean in, grab him by his hat, and bring him to my lips was enormous.

My heart started to pound. What would have happened if I said yes? Would I really go to his apartment— well, actually, my place?

Would the game continue beyond the bar?

Would we roleplay our way all the way into his bedroom?

Wishful thinking, maybe.

Finally, I answered him, "I would love to."

Channing just kept staring at me. He was stuck. I'd totally stumped him.

He suddenly fell out of character and flashed me a look of warning. "You wouldn't actually respond that way, would you?"

If we weren't us, and you were you? I probably would.

Feeling stupid, I shook my head. "No. I was just playing along."

"Good. Because you should never go home with someone you just met. Ever. I don't care how good his game is," he scolded. He was even hotter when he was angry.

Channing was staring off and looked seriously worried. Guilt washed over me, thinking about Gentleman Nine.

If he only knew about that. He'd kill me.

Channing never resumed character, and much to my chagrin, it seemed the game was over.

"Thank you for the practice run," I said.

He simply nodded.

Surveying the room, I sighed. "It doesn't look like you're actually going to get to test your wingman skills out on me tonight, Lord."

He chuckled. "We apparently picked the lamest bar in Boston."

"It's okay. I had no expectations. In my experience, nothing ever happens when you're looking for it. You either have to make something happen for yourself, or it just falls into your lap when you stop searching. But when you're sitting around passively waiting for something, typically it doesn't happen. Sometimes, if you really need something, you have to take it into your own hands."

His eyes looked like daggers. "What do you mean by that?"

I knew what I was referring to, but I wasn't about to tell him.

When I hesitated, he said, "You know, I'm as wild as they come. But over time, I've learned to think before I act. When people are feeling vulnerable, they're more likely to do something stupid. You might believe that you want certain things that you may not *really* want. You might be more likely to act on impulse without thinking something through. Spontaneity in life can be both good and bad, but many of the mistakes we regret for the rest of our lives were born from a moment of impulsivity. Sometimes, when you know you're in a vulnerable state, it can be good to take a step back and check yourself."

His words were random and oddly cryptic given what I'd been up to lately. It felt like God was speaking through him. I took those words in, but unfortunately, the longer we stayed in this bar and the more drinks I consumed, the more uninhibited and impulsive I felt.

"I think I need another drink," I said. "How about you?"

"You want another Cosmo?"

"I would love one."

When I took out my wallet, he placed his hand on mine. "I got it." The feeling of his hand made my body react again.

As Channing walked over to the bar, I admired the curvature of his ass in the dark jeans he was wearing. He was charming the pants off the older, female bartender. I felt really fortunate to have this handsome man buying me a drink and to have his full attention tonight, even if we weren't together romantically.

I got the sudden urge to shock him a little. Reaching behind my back, I undid my bra and slipped it out of the bottom of my shirt.

"Hey, Channing! Catch!" I said before slinging the bra toward him.

What I didn't anticipate was my bra landing on his head. A wide smile spread over his face. Clearly, he was used to women throwing lingerie at him since he seemed amused but unfazed that my bra was currently hanging off his face.

He climbed up on a chair and hooked it over the bar where it joined the bras of over a thousand other women who'd lost their minds here before me.

CHAPTER SEVEN
CHANNING

Amber taking off her bra was definitely...interesting. It made me realize what shaky ground I was on because it was a full-on struggle not to make my gawking obvious for the rest of the night. She was so goddamn sexy without even trying to be. I'd always thought so, but I'd never really gotten to see that wild side of her until tonight. Of course, knowing what she'd told Gentleman Nine about me—knowing she wanted me—made my inner conflict worse.

I'd taken it too far with that "let's pretend" game, too. It felt too real. I was playing off of our attraction to each other and experiencing actual chemistry with her. My strong reaction to her saying she'd come home with me was a little much. It's not like I hadn't picked up countless women in that exact same manner. But I couldn't help feeling protective because her gullible response reminded me about the whole Gentleman Nine situation and how vulnerable she was.

It truly was my intention to try to hook her up with someone decent if the opportunity presented itself at the bar tonight. But the more time we spent there talking, drinking, and reminiscing, the more I hoped no prospects came along. I was enjoying having her to myself. But that was wrong, because I really did want what was best for her. And that didn't include me. And Gentleman Nine most definitely wasn't what was best for her.

I'd been relieved that she hadn't contacted "him" again all week. That made me hopeful that she decided to nix the idea of seeing him and.had come to the correct conclusion that it wasn't the right move.

As I sat up in bed unable to sleep, I decided to check the account I'd created just in case there was anything new.

My stomach dropped when I noticed a new message from Amber that came in about fifteen minutes ago. She must have just sent it from her room.

I braced myself and opened it.

Dear G9,

It's been a few days, and to be honest, I wasn't sure if I was going to ever contact you again. I was leaning toward no. But as much as I've tried to distract myself, I can't seem to let the idea of this go, even though it's literally the craziest thing I've ever done. So, I'm thinking I'd like to move forward with a meetup. What's the next step?

—Amber

My pulse raced.

Shit.

I needed to either not respond ever again or come up with something that would get my ass out of this situation. There was also the burning need to know the reason behind her sudden push to move forward. If anything, I'd hoped that my words of warning about impulsivity tonight would have helped steer her away from the idea of paying some man to fuck her. Clearly, that wasn't the case.

Angry and perplexed, it took me several minutes to figure out what to say, and I ultimately came up with something short and sweet that would put the ball back in her court.

Hey Amber,

I didn't think I was going to hear back from you. What changed your mind?

—G9

Hoping she didn't decide to fall asleep, I waited for the next message to come in.

Hi G9,

Thank you for the quick response. I just came in from a night out with my friend—the one I told you about. He was hoping to serve as my wingman tonight. But no one worthy of his efforts ever showed. We still had a really great time. Well, I already told you about my attraction to him. We'd done this roleplay thing

where he pretended to be picking me up in the bar so that I could practice my dating skills. We were flirting or pretending to, and his body was close. Anyway, I came home feeling very aroused. Also, I might be a little drunk. I don't want to wait months or years to satisfy the sexual need I'm feeling. So, I'm taking matters into my own hands. Or maybe into yours. (That was bad.)

Let me know what's next.

—Amber

Blood was pumping through my veins and rushing down to my cock. I just started writing the first thing that came to mind. This time the words were coming from a different place within me.

Amber,

It may not be my place to ask, but this man you live with...how do you know he doesn't want you in the same way you want him? How do you know that he's not the man for the job to satisfy you? Have you ever told him how you felt?

—G9

I knew one thing. I may not have been the best man to solve Amber's little problem, but I was sure as fuck a better option than this dude she thought she was talking to.

A few minutes later, she responded.

> **G9,**
>
> No, I've never told him anything and I don't plan to. I really care for him as a friend and wouldn't ever want to ruin that. I think I mentioned to you before that he was my ex's best friend for several years. We were all friends and have a long history. Yes, I'm very attracted to him, but I'm not looking to make my life more complicated right now. That's why I came to you. I just need to satisfy this physical need I have. I've only been with one person my entire life, and it's been a while since I've had sex.
>
> I know the site said that photos are not provided, but do you have a picture of yourself you can send me?
>
> —Amber

Fuck!
Fuck. Fuck. Fuck.

I needed to end this, set a date to meet her, then figure it out and be done with this charade.

> **Amber,**
>
> I'm not able to send you a photo, but we can plan to meet a week from Saturday, early evening if you'd like. Say 4PM? I can book us a room at The Peabody Hotel. We can meet in the lounge first. If you're having doubts at that time, you can walk away. I'll completely under-

stand. **No fees charged.**

—G9

How was I going to get out of this? Did I even want to? Should I come clean? Show up and confront her? Let her think he stood her up? I had no idea.

A new message popped up.

> **G9,**
>
> **Thank you for agreeing to meet me at a public place. I really appreciate that. The truth is, I won't know how I'll feel until I get there, until I see you. I'm sorry if that sounds really superficial. Please bring the medical paperwork you promised.**
>
> **That time sounds good. I can plan to be there.**
>
> **—Amber**

I had a week to figure this out. I typed.

> **Amber,**
>
> **I completely understand. Let's say 4PM at the lounge. I'll be wearing a black polo shirt and will probably be seated in the corner. Otherwise, at the bar.**
>
> **If you need to cancel, simply message me at this email address by 3PM. If I don't hear from you, I'll assume we're still on.**
>
> **—G9**

A final response came through.

G9,

Thank you. I will see you then.

—Amber

I shut my laptop and let out a deep breath.

Amber...why?

A part of me really wished I could storm down the hall to her room and ask her what the fuck she was thinking in agreeing to meet him. The other part of me was fighting my body's reaction to the idea that she was turned on tonight because of me. It wasn't fair to take enjoyment out of that thought given that I'd basically stolen that information. It was never meant for me to know.

Then, an unsettling thought hit me. If I tell her the truth, what if she doesn't understand that I was just trying to protect her? I could lose her friendship over this.

The clock ticking in my head was practically deafening.

My mouth was parched, so I decided to get up for a glass of water. I stopped short because I wasn't expecting to see Amber in the kitchen. Clearly, she wasn't expecting to see me either, because she was wearing nothing but boy short underwear and a thin tank top.

Fuck me.

"So much for sneaking a quick drink of water," Amber said.

She covered her chest with her arms, but it was too late. I'd already seen her breasts in their entirety through the thin white fabric, with their piercing nipples and tear drop shape.

I wished I hadn't.

For the first time that I could remember in my life, I'd lost my words in front of a woman. Pointing my thumb behind me, I stammered, "I can...uh...I can come back."

Returning to my room with my one-eyed trouser snake, I wiped the sweat off my forehead. She'd been messaging me—G9—half-naked. My rigid cock was sticking straight up in the air. I was a lost cause.

Then, a funny thought hit me. For some reason, this night reminded me of something from the animated movie, *The Secret Life of Pets*.

I'm Tiberius.

Holy shit. I'm Tiberius!

I started laughing to myself.

A date had dragged me to see that movie once. In the film, there was this sweet, little white Pomeranian named Gidget who entrusted the help of a red-tailed hawk—Tiberius—to help her find her friend, the Jack Russell Terrier who'd gone missing. The entire time, the hawk struggled with whether to help her—or eat her.

Yup. I was Tiberius and Amber was Gidget.

The next evening after work, I came home to a rude awakening.

Upon entering, the sight of a man sitting in the living room took me by surprise. My heart sank because my first thought was that I'd interrupted some kind of hook-up.

He didn't see me come in, didn't even flinch when I opened the door. His eyes were fixated on the television instead.

Kitty was weaving in and out of my legs as I stood frozen, observing this man who was making himself at home in the living room.

Was I about to interrupt something?

Amber brought a man back here?

My stomach churned, thinking that maybe she was freshening up, readying herself for something sordid with this guy.

Since he hadn't noticed me yet, I continued to stand there, sizing him up. He looked about mid-twenties, pretty good-looking, although he couldn't dress for shit. He was wearing a vintage *Fat Albert* t-shirt. What the fuck? Where the hell did she find this dude? And where was Amber?

Swallowing my pride, I took a few steps forward before I threw my keys down on the table. "Where's Amber?"

Turning his attention away from the television, he finally looked at me. But he didn't say anything, didn't answer me.

What kind of game was this guy trying to play?

I spoke louder, "Excuse me. Who are you?"

Nothing. Not a fucking word. Cracking my knuckles, I prepared to knock him out if necessary.

"Dude. Is there a reason you're not answering my question?"

The asshole not only continued to give me the silent treatment, but he then turned his attention away from me again and back to the television.

My mouth hung open. And what was he watching? *The Wiggles?*

What the fuck!

Approaching him, I leaned my face into his, "Who are you?"

The next thing I knew, his two hands landed on my head, pushing me into his face so fast that I had no time to react. His nose was buried in my hair as he pulled on it. It was like he was...sniffing me for dear life. *He was. He was sniffing my hair.*

Barely unable to break free of what felt like a super human grasp, I managed to pull myself away just as Amber entered the room.

"I see you've met Milo," she casually said.

"Who the hell is he?"

She was laughing, and at that same moment, realization struck.

Oh.

Ohhh.

Now, I felt like an idiot. A massive fucking dumbass. This wasn't her date. It was her client, the special needs adult she takes care of at night. She'd never brought him here, so I never suspected it was him. Everything made total sense now.

Rather than answer my question, Amber seemed to understand that I had figured it out. She looked utterly amused as she took a seat on the couch then wrapped her arm around him.

"Milo, this is Channing. He has nice hair, doesn't he? Did it smell good?"

He smiled and grunted.

"Yeah, I bet." She laughed then looked at me. "Milo loves to smell hair. It's his favorite thing to do. And if you're fresh meat like yourself, you're gonna get extra special attention."

I nodded then addressed him, "Sorry, man, for over-reacting. I didn't know." I looked at Amber. "Can he understand me?"

She got up and nudged her head for me to follow her before leading me over to the kitchen.

Whispering, she said, "Sorry, I just didn't want to talk about him in front of him."

"Yeah, of course."

"I'm not sure the extent to which he can understand something like an apology, actually. He can typically understand concrete things. He can request very simply but can't converse or talk about feelings, stuff like that. But just because it doesn't come out verbally, that doesn't mean he doesn't understand. There's still a lot even I don't comprehend."

"So, what does he...have?"

"He has autism. He lives in a group home with other adults who have varying needs. But as you know, I take him out a few nights a week. I normally don't bring him back here, but I ended up having to use the bathroom while we were out. Since we weren't too far away, I figured I'd just come home. He loves *The Wiggles*, so I knew if I put that on, it would buy me some time to get a few things done around the house. Now, I don't think he'll ever want to leave."

"God, I thought I was interrupting something, thought you'd brought a man back here. He looks so...I don't want to say normal, but...what's the right word...typical?"

"Typical would be what I would say, yes. That's the thing about autism. You can't necessarily tell by looking at someone that there are any developmental issues. It's only when you try to interact with them that you realize it. In Milo's case, he's child-like, even though he's close to our age."

"Wow. That's perplexing and fascinating at the same time."

When we returned to the living room, Milo was no longer paying attention to the television. In fact, he had turned it off altogether. Instead, he was playing around on an iPad.

"What's he watching?" I asked.

"He likes to watch YouTube."

I sat down next to him on the couch and leaned in. He was looking at clips from the show *Archer*. It was some kind of montage.

"That's a cool show," I said.

Apparently, my giving him that little bit of attention served as his cue to wrap his arm around me, once again pulling my head into his face. His nose felt like a vacuum atop my head. Closing my eyes, I let him do it, as uncomfortable as it was allowing a grown man my age to cradle my head and sniff me.

Amber chuckled. "He's definitely motivation to keep my hair smelling fresh and clean, but I feel like I'm not competition for you at this very moment."

When he finally let me go, I noticed that he was looking at the iPad screen then back at me. He kept doing this over and over.

"What's up?" I asked him.

Amber chimed in, "I think he thinks you're *Archer*. He's done this to me and other people."

"That's why he's watching it? He thinks I'm the character?"

"It's possible. I've seen him do that before."

"Who does he think you are?"

"Daria from that old MTV show."

That cracked me up. "It must be the bangs."

"Anyway, we were about to head back out to get some dinner," she said. "Would you want to join us?"

Watching Amber with Milo was actually really fascinating. It was an entirely different side of her life that I'd never gotten to see. So, I took her up on her offer.

Amber held onto his hand as the three of us walked down the street.

"Do you always hold his hand like that?"

"I don't have to, but it gives me a feeling of security. He's been known to suddenly run if he gets excited about something. It's not worth the risk. And he doesn't mind holding my hand."

People must have thought I was the third wheel as we strolled through Quincy Market, one of Boston's biggest tourist attractions. Milo was twice the size of Amber. No one would have ever guessed by looking at them that her number one job was to keep *him* safe.

After we stopped for Greek food—Milo's favorite—we browsed through some of the vendor carts surrounding Faneuil Hall. Milo pulled Amber toward a woman who was selling hats and sunglasses.

She was trying to get him to go in another direction. "Milo, no. We can't go here."

"Why not?" I asked.

"He likes to snap sunglasses in half. That's why I can only wear dollar store ones around him."

When he had his mind set on something, it was apparently hard to distract him toward anything else. Amber couldn't pull him away from the cart. Honestly, I didn't know how she took him out by herself because she didn't have the strength to control him on her own.

I intervened, holding onto his shoulders. "What do you want, Milo?"

He then grabbed a pair of the sunglasses, placing them on my face before taking one of the large, pink hats and putting it on my head. He then let out one of his big, grunty laughs.

"I'm sorry," Amber said to the saleswoman.

"No problem. He reminds me of my nephew," she said.

We were all laughing at that point.

Apparently, Milo had gotten his fill after emasculating me. He began to just walk away. Amber chased after him as I placed the items back on the cart.

When I caught up to them, she looked frazzled then said, "I normally wouldn't take him some place like this with a lot of knick knacks without a second set of hands. I'm glad you were here."

"I don't know how you do it."

"You mean...take him out?"

"Yeah, by yourself."

"Well, he has to learn. He has to learn to live in this world. If that means some embarrassing moments and what sometimes looks like male-female wrestling to the outside observer, then so be it. But if people don't like it, that's their problem, not mine."

I really admired her for that attitude and honestly, Milo was one damn lucky fucker.

We ended up getting ice cream from Ben & Jerry's. Milo got a massive cone of the strawberry flavor while Amber and I each got small cups of mint chocolate chip. We sat down on a couple of benches in the marketplace. It was now evening, and the sun had gone down over the popular city attraction.

Amber and Milo were across from me on their own bench when almost his entire dollop of ice cream fell off his sugar cone and onto Amber's chest. Before she could even react, he faceplanted into her cleavage, licking up the entire dollop back into his mouth in one swoop. It had all happened so fast that Amber just sat there looking stunned. Ice cream was dripping down into her shirt.

And no, I didn't offer to finish off the job.

I was too busy busting out into laughter, and then she followed suit.

"That was a good one, Milo," I shouted from across the way. "I think I'm gonna use that move someday."

When he also started laughing, I couldn't help wondering if maybe Mr. Milo was smoother than we'd given him credit for.

⌒

That night, after we dropped Milo back at his house, Amber and I were hanging out in the living room. She was keeping a good few feet away from me on the opposite end of the couch.

"I can't believe you do that several nights a week. You've talked about it, but I had no idea it was so much work."

"I can handle it."

"I'm really proud of you. Not that many people can do what you do. It takes a certain personality and a shitload of patience."

She blushed a little from the compliment. It was fucking adorable.

"Well, it makes me feel good that I can help him have as normal a life as possible. He won't have independence like you and me. He won't drive or be able to live on his own, but it's all about helping him get to his personal best, whether that's just knowing how to cross the street or getting him to practice waiting in a store line."

"Shit, woman. No wonder you're exhausted when you come home."

"It's true. Before you moved in, I used to sometimes just crash and go right to sleep."

"Ah...so, I've been disrupting your rest."

"Yes. But I wouldn't have it any other way."

Tonight had been a really great distraction from not having to worry about the dilemma of this upcoming Saturday. I still didn't know what I was going to do. I decided to test the waters to see if by some chance, she'd give me a clue of what was going on in her mind.

"I was thinking of going to see that new movie about shark-infested waters at the IMAX theater Saturday night, like an early evening show. I don't really feel like going alone. You think you'd want to join?"

As expected, she looked flustered. "Um...I can't Saturday."

I swallowed. "You have plans?"

"Yes. I'm...meeting a friend for drinks."

"Alright. Maybe another time, then."

"Yeah."

God, my stomach hurt. Her cheeks were turning red. I knew she didn't like having to lie to me. I was a prick for putting her into this situation. But I wasn't ready to confront her about it now. It had been a long night, and I really needed to think about how I was going to handle it.

We were silent for a while as we each pretended to be paying attention to Jimmy Fallon. She looked guilty, and I hated that I knew exactly why.

"I'm gonna turn in," she finally said as she stood up. "Thanks again for hanging out with us tonight."

"My pleasure. I'd love to do it again. If you ever want to take him somewhere that warrants an extra set of hands, I'm your man."

"Thanks. I'll try to plan something like that before you leave."

Before I leave. Fuck, that's right. I'd be gone by Christmas. For some reason, it felt like I was supposed to be here longer.

"Sweet dreams, Amber."

Back in my room, once again sleep was evading me.

Kitty was kneading on my abs, her little claws digging into me. Under my t-shirt, it looked like I was into kinky sex with scratches all over my skin. The wrong kind of pussy had done a number on me—the kind that left white hairs all over my bed, too.

I spoke to her in a low, soothing voice, "Kitty, what am I gonna do with you? You gonna come back to Chicago with me? Then, what? Huh? I'm stuck with you? Like for twenty years? You know, we really should've discussed this before you got attached. I don't do commitment."

"Meow."

"You're telling me I don't have a choice, huh? Okay, you convinced me. I think I'll keep you."

This was the nightly ritual. She'd listen to me speak to her ever so quietly, and I'd watch her eyes slowly close as she fell asleep to the sound of my voice. Thank God no one was witnessing this, or I definitely would have had to hand over my man card.

I was just about to turn the sound on my phone off when I noticed a new text had come in.

At first, I thought my eyes were playing tricks on me. But no.

It was her.

Emily: Saw on your Instagram that you were at Quincy Market today, and I haven't been able to concentrate on anything else. I can't believe you're in Boston. Are you here on business? I've been meaning to contact you for a while now. I just haven't had the guts and I've felt ashamed. I'm no longer with Tim. Long story short, I haven't stopped

thinking about you and realized soon after I went back to him that I'd made a big mistake. Do you think you could meet me at the Common tomorrow? There's a lot I need to say to you. I completely understand if you'd rather not. I figured it was worth a shot to ask. I really miss you and don't want to miss any opportunity to see you while you're here.

CHAPTER EIGHT
AMBER

Annabelle was helping me look through the clearance table at Victoria's Secret.

"So, I'm looking for size extra large, right?"

"Right," I said as I mindlessly sifted through the pile of lace undies.

"You're not even listening. You're not extra large. You're barely a small. Your head is somewhere else." She picked up a tiny piece of fabric. "What about this thong?"

"I don't wear thongs. I don't like the string. It feels funny in my ass."

"Get used to saying that," she joked.

"Are you kidding me right now?"

"Yes, of course, I am—sort of. Seriously, though, are you nervous?"

Throwing a pair of zebra print panties across the pile, I said, "Yes. I am. I've considered cancelling, but then I remind myself that I don't have to go through with it if I'm not feeling it when I meet him."

"That's a good plan. And make sure you have condoms. Several."

"I'm sure he has those."

"Yeah, but you never know. Buy the best kind and insist on using yours. You don't know where his have been stored. Make sure you buy lubricated."

"For someone who was pushing me into this, you seem more worried than me. And that's freaking me out." I threw some beige underpants at her. "Stop it."

"I kind of *am* worried. To be honest, I never thought you'd actually go through with it. You really surprised me. I talk a good game, but I think what you're doing takes balls. And I'm proud of you for taking control of your sexual needs."

"Lower your voice," I whispered.

"Everything is going to be fine, Amber."

God, I sure hoped I was doing the right thing for myself.

After racking up a two-hundred dollar bill, I left the store with a large, pink-striped bag filled with a multitude of thongs and other lingerie.

Annabelle and I parted ways out front as she headed toward the train station.

I opted to walk home since my house wasn't that far from the Downtown Crossing shopping area. A long, brisk walk sounded like just what the doctor ordered. Dried-up autumn leaves crunched under my Ugg boots as I strolled.

Cutting through the Boston Common, I glanced over at the swan boats, trying to forget about thoughts of riding on them with Rory.

Then, I nearly lost my breath when I saw him.

Channing?

It was.

He was sitting on a bench, talking to a tall, gorgeous brunette. She looked like the kind of girl who women loved to hate and a perfect match for Channing looks-wise. Her hair was long, the strands blowing toward him in the wind as they engaged in what looked liked an intense conversation. Her chestnut hair contrasted her fair skin, which accentuated her plump, red lips. Wearing dark, tapered jeans that looked like they were painted onto her legs and high-heeled boots, she basically looked like a supermodel.

They were seated very close to one another, their bodies turned inward, and their legs touching. I could feel the heat in my body rise. This shouldn't have upset me. I knew Channing probably picked up women in public all of the time. But this was the first time I'd ever witnessed it. And my reaction was really telling.

Really, Amber? You have a sack full of lingerie so you can have sordid sex with a male prostitute on Saturday, and you're considering hiding from Channing because you're upset he's talking to a girl? Grow up.

Giving myself a mental kick in the ass, I marched over to where they were seated but then stopped just short of where he could see me.

Channing wasn't acting like his normal smiling, flirtatious self. The tone of their exchange seemed serious.

He suddenly glanced over and saw me before I could opt to slip away unnoticed.

Channing instinctively moved his body away from the woman when he said, "Amber..."

Taking a few steps forward, I put on my best, fake smile. "Hey."

"What are you up to?" he asked.

Shrugging, I said, "Just did a little shopping. Now, I'm headed back home."

His eyes were glued to my shopping bag. He was probably wondering why I'd gone to Victoria's Secret when my vagina was more dried-up than a desert.

"Looks like more than a little shopping."

"Yeah, well, gotta have underwear, right?"

"Right." He turned to his lady friend." Uh...Amber, this is Emily. Emily, this is my friend Amber, the one I'm living with."

Emily?

THE Emily?

I looked between them, wondering if I'd heard correctly. "Emily?"

His eyes were telling me not to mention that he'd spoken of her to me. So, yeah, it was definitely *that* Emily.

"Yes," he said.

Emily smiled. Of course, her teeth were just as perfect as everything else. "Nice to meet you, Amber."

"What brought you two to the Common?" I asked.

"We're just catching up."

Wow, I had so many questions, but they were going to have to wait.

"Great. Well, I'll leave you two to...catch up, then."

"I'll see you at home later," he said.

"Yep. See you later." I turned to her. "Really nice to meet you, Emily."

Not.

"Same." She smiled.

I started to walk away. So flustered, I wasn't paying attention when a man walking his dog knocked into me. The leash ended up wrapped around my leg as the dog yelped like crazy. The animal then began tearing into my shopping bag with his teeth.

Channing and Emily were still looking over at me when all of my lingerie fell out of the now entirely ripped bag. The thongs and other pieces were strewn about the grass.

This was mortifying.

The owner apologized, but the damage had been done.

They had seen the entire thing unfold. Channing got up off the bench and promptly began to help me pick up my underwear off the ground.

I couldn't even look at him as he handed them to me. "I can just put them in my purse. Thank you."

When all of the panties were safely in my leather satchel, my eyes finally met his.

He looked concerned. "Are you okay?"

"I'm fine. That was really weird." I glanced over at Emily and whispered, "This is interesting? What brought her back into the picture?"

"Yeah. She texted me out of the blue and asked me to meet here."

"Wow. Is she still with that guy?"

"No. They broke up."

Why was my stomach churning?

"I see. Well, I don't want to keep you. Enjoy the rest of the afternoon."

He looked like he wanted to say something else but instead just answered with, "You, too."

Once home, I found it very difficult to concentrate. All I could think about was what Channing and Emily were doing.

Tonight was my night off from working with Milo, but I almost wished that weren't the case. I could have used a distraction from the thoughts floating around in my head.

Between my upcoming rendezvous on Saturday, to my irrational feelings of jealousy, my mind was all over the place.

A couple of hours later, I was just about to head to bed when Channing walked in.

I straightened up on the couch. "Hey."

"Hi." He plopped down next to me, smelling like cold air and cologne. He turned to me, and we just looked at each other for a bit, silently acknowledging the awkward run-in from earlier.

Examining him closely, I tried to figure out whether he looked different—namely whether he looked like he'd had sex. His hair was rustled. That could have been from the wind, or it could have been from her hands running through it. His lips were red. That could have been from the cold, or it could have been from her kiss. Images of him hovering over the sexy brunette flashed through my mind. Even the idea of him having sex with her turned me on, and that was a little disturbing.

I told myself I wasn't going to pry—unless he wanted to offer the information. But a part of me needed to know how the Emily thing came about, what he was thinking—whether he had fucked her. Everything. I needed to know everything.

Well, maybe I could pry a little.

My heart sped up as I initiated the conversation. "How was your date?"

"It wasn't really a date. It was just a meetup."

"So, what happened? I thought she was out of the picture."

"You and me both." He chuckled, then let out a deep sigh before rubbing his eyes. Then, he looked at me. "After you and I came home from taking Milo out the other night, I realized I'd missed a text from her. She messaged me because she saw I was in Boston from my Instagram. I rarely post anything, but I'd posted a shot from Quincy Market. She said she'd been thinking about me for a while and wanted me to know that she ended things with her boyfriend. She asked if we could meet."

"So, she broke up with *him*? The guy she went back to while she was seeing you?"

"Yup. Apparently, she says it's for good this time."

"What else did she say to you?"

"She said the feelings she had for me scared her at the time and that her running back to him was like a safety net. She said she didn't fully trust that I was ready for a relationship because I hadn't had any serious girlfriends. But she claims she couldn't stop thinking about me and that she regretted ending things and not taking a chance. She never planned to contact me, because she figured I wouldn't want to see her. She took my being in Boston as a sign that she should get in touch with me."

The jealousy meter was definitely off the charts at this point. I didn't know what to say. "Wow."

"Yeah. I honestly didn't expect to hear from her ever again."

"How do you feel about all of this?"

He blew out a breath. "I don't know. The whole thing is sort of complicated. I still have feelings for her and I'm very attracted to her, but at the same time, I'm going back to Chicago, too, you know? Then, there's the issue of not being able to really forget how she abruptly ended things. That left a bitter taste. I'm trying not to overthink it. I guess I'll just have to see how things go while I'm here."

A small part of me was happy that Channing had a second chance with the one girl he'd truly connected with. It felt like fate, him ending up in Boston and getting to rekindle things with her. But I'd be lying if I said I wasn't extremely jealous. I'd probably always be envious of any woman who could be with Channing in that way.

My stomach was unsettled, but I did my best to offer sound advice despite my biased discomfort. "I don't blame you for being cautious. Just take one day at a time." I needed water. I got up and walked toward the kitchen while still talking to him. "Where did you go after the Common?"

He followed me. "You mean after we stopped talking about my awkward friend with the mutilated bag of underwear?"

Taking out a glass and filling it, I laughed. "Did I embarrass you?"

He leaned into the counter. "I'm just messing with you. We did laugh about it after you left, though. I told her a little about our friendship and history. Then, we left the Common and grabbed a bite to eat at Fuddruckers. After dinner, I walked her to the train. She hopped on the commuter rail. She lives in Waltham."

"Did you kiss her?" I spit out.

"Once. Before she got on the train."

My face felt flush at the thought of that, and I wondered if my jealousy was transparent. I hoped not. I just kept staring at him for a bit. "I see."

That prompted him to ask, "Something else you want to ask?"

"When are you seeing her again?"

"I'm supposed to see her tomorrow night. But to be honest, I don't know if that's a good idea."

"You don't completely trust her?"

"I'm not sure. But honestly, I don't know if I want anything serious with anyone—even her. My frame of mind isn't exactly the same as it was when I met her. Stuff has happened since then. I don't know what I want anymore."

I wondered what stuff he was referring to.

"Well, she's really beautiful. I can see why you're drawn to her."

"She is." He smiled, unable to deny that. "Any other questions?"

"No. That'll be all for tonight."

He leaned his back against the counter and crossed his arms. "So...any particular reason why you were stocking up on panties, Walnut?"

"Can't let a good sale go to waste."

He lifted his brow. "That's it?"

My face felt hot. "Yeah."

He was searching my eyes. "Okay..."

I swallowed, feeling very uncomfortable. I didn't like lying to him, but telling him why I'd really purchased the underwear was not an option.

"Oh, check this out," he said, taking out his phone. "We ran into Steven Tyler from Aerosmith downtown. He was just standing around talking to people, so we snapped a few photos."

"That's so cool!"

"I'm gonna go change," he suddenly said before leaving me with his phone to peruse the photos.

In one of the shots, Emily and Channing were on each side of Steven Tyler. I couldn't tell which one of them had the more gorgeous smile.

I sighed.

As I tried to zoom in, I accidentally hit something that brought me to an index of photo albums categorized by year. Randomly, I clicked on 2015.

Big mistake.

I came upon something I never should have seen: a series of dick pics.

OhmygodOhmygodOhmygod.

There in all of its glory was Channing's beautiful cock, just as thick and magnificent as I might have, on occasion, imagined it to be. The crown was perfectly rounded and in perfect proportion to the shaft, his golden skin slightly veined yet smooth. And it was long. Really long and thick.

In the three photos, you could see the base of his tatted, carved V along with the thin line of hair forming a path down to his crotch.

Footsteps!

I freaked out as I heard him approach and accidentally dropped the phone onto the ground. He landed right in front of it, picking it up, and putting it in his pocket. "Whoa, be careful, butterfingers."

Oh, no.

I froze because I didn't know if it was going to open right up to the photo of his cock the next time he checked it. Had I somehow exited out? I didn't think so.

"How about a late dinner?" he asked.

"Didn't you already have something while you were out?"

"I'm still hungry. If I make something, will you eat?"

"Sure."

He examined my face, seeming to notice that something was off. "You alright?"

"Yes," I lied.

Unable to look at him for the time being, I went to the couch in the living room and prayed that I'd dodged a bullet while Channing cooked us something. I didn't want to be in the kitchen if he happened to look down at his phone.

Several minutes later, he called out from the kitchen, "Food's ready!"

When I took a seat at the table, I immediately noticed that his phone was now out and on the counter. That meant he'd likely checked it if he'd taken it out of his pocket. So, the damage was either done or had been averted.

He was acting totally normal, so I breathed a little sigh of relief as we dug into our food.

This was fine.

Maybe he didn't notice.

Maybe I had closed out of it.

109

Just eat and forget about it.

Yeah, right.

I looked down at the meal in front of me. "This is... interesting."

"It's something I've wanted to make for a while. It's melted chocolate cheese pizza."

"Kill two birds with one stone. Dinner and dessert," I said as I tried to remain calm.

It actually turned out to be really good. The tangy cheese and sweet chocolate atop the crispy crust made for an unexpectedly tasty contrast. Leave it to Channing to figure out the culinary potential in that unusual combination.

He was looking at me intently when he asked, "How did you like it?"

"It was delicious. Thank you."

He leaned in and crossed his arms. His voice was low. "I was referring to my dick."

The food caught in my throat. "Excuse me?"

"You were looking at a picture of my dick earlier, weren't you? It was open on my phone."

The pizza felt like it was coming up on me. "Uh...I can explain..."

His brow lifted. "Yeah?"

"I wasn't looking for those pictures...I swear. I was looking at Steven Tyler then hit a button and the next thing I knew, it was 2015 and cockapalooza."

He started to crack up as he rubbed his eyes. "Cockapalooza..."

"I'm mortified."

When his laughter died down, he said, "I'm the one who should be embarrassed, not you."

"Trust me, you have nothing to be embarrassed about."

Those words exited my mouth before I could think better of saying them.

Great. I'd basically just complimented him on his cock.

"Well, thank you." He slid his phone toward me. "And if you think I have nothing but dick pics on my phone, feel free to scroll through everything. I'm pretty sure you found the one hidden gem in the lot."

I hit the cock lottery, apparently.

I slid his phone back toward him. "Lucky me. Anyway, do you think it's possible to never mention this again?"

"But you're so cute when you're embarrassed. Seeing as though I'm *not* very cute, however, when I'm embarrassed...we can agree to forget this ever happened."

The fact that he actually seemed uncomfortable about this took me by surprise.

"Thanks."

"No problem." Channing surprised me with his next question as he changed the subject. "So, what do you think I should do about Emily?"

We're on this subject again? I would probably rather talk about the dick pic than her.

"You're asking *me*?"

"Why not? I trust your opinion probably more than anyone's."

He'd totally stumped me. I wanted to tell him that she didn't deserve him, that she'd had her chance. But then I had to wonder if that answer was influenced by my selfish need to not have to witness him with her over the next several weeks. People make mistakes. They misjudge. Everyone deserves a second chance. Right? Still, the right answer was unclear to me.

"I'm not sure what to tell you. I think you should honestly do what's in your heart. I do believe everyone deserves at least one second chance, though."

He kept staring into my eyes then said, "Like the one you plan to give Rory."

"Rory isn't asking for one."

"Yet."

"I don't know what I would do if he did, to be honest. I mean, how can you ever trust someone who left you once?"

He crossed his arms. "I know what my advice to you would be if he ever came back."

"You'd tell me not to take him back."

"You deserve better than someone who's stupid enough to throw you away once."

"Why wouldn't the same apply to you, then?"

"I guess I don't see my situation with Emily in the same way. We'd barely gotten started. I'd also given her no real indication that I was ready for a relationship, even though I might have been leaning in that direction. And looking back, I don't think things had completely ended with her boyfriend. So, all things considered...I do think the situation is a lot different than yours."

"Makes sense. You didn't have a long history like I did with Rory. He was my first...everything. And I thought he'd be my last. It's hard to break away from the future I'd envisioned. I'm doing everything I can to try. But overall, I feel very lost."

Way to change the subject over to Rory, Amber.

He took a while to respond then leaned in. "You're placing value on the distorted idea that the decision he made somehow reflects on you. It doesn't. You're still you, and you have your whole life ahead of you. Fuck him."

His words were momentarily empowering. He always had a way of making me feel better even if it was only fleeting. I placed my hand on his arm. "Thank you. I needed that."

He was staring at me for a bit before he said, "You said that Rory was your first...everything." Channing squinted his eyes like he was challenging me. "You sure about that?"

My heart began to flutter. Was he getting at what I thought he was getting at?

"Not your first kiss, though," he said.

He was getting at that.

I. Could. Not. Believe. He. Brought. This. Up.

It was never something that Channing and I discussed. It was almost like a dream. In fact, I sometimes doubted whether he even remembered or whether it even really took place. We were in such a fog that night. But it still happened. And it was a moment I could never forget.

I finally replied, "No. *You* were my first kiss."

CHAPTER NINE
CHANNING

Was I a dick for wanting her to acknowledge that I had a leg up on Rory in one thing?

I'd always suspected that I was Amber's first kiss. But I never asked her, because we'd simply never spoken about that moment in time. I could never handle talking about Lainey's death, and the circumstances of that kiss were somehow tied into the tragedy of my sister's passing.

As far as first kisses went, ours was far from typical, far from sexual even. It was eclipsed by our mutual sadness and devastation. But in the midst of one of the darkest days of my life, that kiss was like a lifeline—my oxygen. It had given me a reason to breathe just when I thought my lungs were ready to give out.

"I always figured that was your first kiss," I said. "But I never knew for sure until you just confirmed it."

"I wasn't sure if you remembered, Channing. I often wondered if you truly mentally blocked out that whole day."

"Much of that entire time is a blur, to the honest. But *that* moment...that kiss...is not something I could ever forget."

It was the evening of Lainey's wake. I'd managed to pull myself together somehow, standing in that line and shaking hundreds of hands that were attached to blurry black figures.

As much as I knew I needed to cry, I wouldn't allow myself to. It was hard enough to watch my mother breaking down. I didn't want her to have to see me cry because I knew it would kill her. So, I held it in.

The preacher began to read something, and I knew I couldn't take it. So, I slipped away, disappearing to a gazebo out in the back of the funeral home.

To my surprise, Amber was there. Her hair was covering her face. She was alone and crying and didn't see me at first. She'd been composed all night, too, but seeing that she'd stopped fighting it gave me silent permission to do the same.

Unable to hold my tears in any longer, I let go in that moment. Moisture filled my eyes. I was too numb to even realize that I was crying were it not for the vibration of my ribs shaking in pain. Joining her on the bench, I held Amber in my arms and let those first tears fall into her hair. My crying was so intense that it was silent.

We continued holding each other for an immeasurable amount of time. At one point, she turned her face toward me, and I could taste her breath; it felt like oxygen. Suddenly, tasting more of it became all I wanted in the world. Desperate to feel anything other than my pain, I took what I needed and kissed her.

My eyes were closed, my breath shaking. It was hard and passionate and desperate, so different from *any other kiss I'd ever experienced before or ever would experience again in my life. It was an expression of our pain and yet a reminder that we were alive when we'd otherwise felt dead inside. Each thrust of my tongue and each moan into her mouth numbed that pain. It was intense and beautiful and sacred. It provided a momentary peace that words couldn't.*

Interrupted by the footsteps of Amber's father, I pried myself off of her just in the nick of time, even though it was the last thing I wanted to do. My heart was pounding. My palms were sweating. Amber looked dazed as she got up and left.

And we never spoke of it again.

⌒

"I was very lucky to have found you there that night," I said.

Tears began to glisten in her eyes. "I never told anyone about that kiss, not Rory, not anyone."

"Neither did I. It wasn't the kind of kiss you talked about."

"Clearly, *we* didn't."

"Well, you said Rory was your first everything. I thought I would take the liberty to remind you that technically that one belonged to me."

"It definitely did." She smiled.

Feeling the need to lighten the mood, I said, "I think I'm gonna make some tea. You want some?"

It was late, but I was enjoying hanging out with Amber and wanted to prolong our little night cap.

My reaction to her finding those photos on my phone surprised me. It affected me, and I couldn't figure out exactly why. I'd flaunted my body to women enough times that you'd think it wouldn't have. But this was different. This was Amber. She already had some preconceived notions about me, and while many of them were true at one time, I'd changed quite a bit in the past couple of years.

After steeping two hot teas, I handed her one. "So, I finished *The Law of Attraction*. Are you ready to talk about our books?"

She looked down into the steaming hot water and cringed. "Don't kill me, but I haven't finished *The Alchemist*."

"Slacking on our arrangement?" I teased.

"I know. I'm sorry. I've had a hard time concentrating lately. I've been a bit too preoccupied to read. I know I said I'd have it finished."

Whatever could be preoccupying you, Amber?

"I'm just kidding," I said. "It's a book. It will always be there when you're ready to open it again. But I'm ready to talk about *The Law of Attraction*."

She wiped her mouth and eagerly gave me her full attention. "What did you think of it?"

"Well, the biggest takeaway is that if you want something in life, you can't focus on the problem. You have to focus on the solution, or rather, focus on what you truly want. When we stress, we dwell on the things that bother us, and the more attention we give to those things, the more we attract that negativity into our lives. Whether someone believes in the attraction component or not, at the very least, the book teaches the obvious, which is that dwelling on negative shit gets you nowhere."

"Do you believe that you can actually attract something by focusing on it?"

I rubbed my chin and thought about it for a moment. "No way to know for sure. That's a mystery of life. But now that I'm more consciously aware of that possibility, I'll let you know if I experience it happening to me."

She sighed. "I love the concept of the book, but honestly, I've found it hard to implement. Even trying hard to block something out of your mind is still inadvertently focusing on it. It's scary to me to think that if I'm lamenting over Rory, or telling myself that I'll never find anyone else...that I could be attracting that exact situation."

"Okay, so, just in case that's true...try to think about something you really want and practice focusing on that instead."

She looked at me in silence then asked, "What if what you want is something you can never have?"

"Well, that's what you're telling yourself. That may not be true. Maybe you should try to think more positively."

Was she referring to me, or was that just my ego?

Either way, my advice would have been the same, but now I was left feeling rattled and wondering what was really going on in her pretty, little head.

Today was probably one of the most confusing days of my life. There was no doubt I still had feelings for Emily. It was so good to see her, and I was immediately reminded of all of the reasons I fell for her in the first place. She seemed genuinely sorry about the way things had ended between us and made it clear that she wanted a second chance.

When she'd asked me to go back to her place, I almost budged. But I knew what going there would have meant.

It seemed like forever since I'd been inside of a woman. I hadn't slept with anyone since before moving to Boston. This was the longest I'd gone without sex since I was a teenager, and truthfully I was nearing my breaking point. But I somehow resisted, deciding instead not to take advantage of the offer.

While a part of me suspected that it wasn't exactly the end of the story for Emily and me, I couldn't ignore the fact that Amber had been on my mind the entire day. When she appeared at the Common, something shifted. Things were awkward in a way that was different from just running into your friend.

Emily sensed it, too. She asked me if there was anything going on between Amber and me. I told her the truth: Amber and I were just friends.

So, why did it not seem as simple as that answer?

⌒

Emily and I decided to have dinner in Chinatown.

Looking around at the bamboo-style wooden décor and waterfalls at the restaurant, I dragged my fork over the Singapore noodles.

As I gazed out at a window across the street that was dressed with ducks laying upside down in a row, Emily interrupted my thoughts.

"You seem like something's on your mind."

"Just thinking about work."

"Has it been busy?"

"Yeah. I have limited time here to get what I need to get done, so there's a lot of pressure."

Of course, work wasn't really the subject of my obsessive thoughts tonight. I still didn't know what I was going to do about Saturday. The truth was, I was seriously considering just letting the Gentleman Nine thing blow away. Maybe I'd send Amber a message from the G9 email account cancelling tomorrow night, or maybe I could just not show up at all. I honestly had no idea how to handle it. And now with Emily in the picture, things were even more complicated.

Emily leaned in and threaded her fingers through mine. "Can we go back to my place? I can make you forget all about it for a while."

Sex with Emily had been the best of my life. I felt like I needed to go. I needed to figure out where my feelings for her stood, and one way to do that would be to bury myself inside of her, to see if that amazing sexual chemistry we had before still existed.

It had been too long for me. And focusing my sexual energy on someone other than Amber was probably a good idea at this point in time.

I forced the words out. "Sure. Let's go to your place."

⌒

Once back at Emily's apartment in Waltham, she didn't waste time setting up a romantic atmosphere. The shades were drawn, and the lights were dimmed. She played Coltrane and poured me some of my favorite gin, which she'd bought likely knowing I would end up back here.

"I just want to put something out there..." she said.

I threw back the liquor. "Alright." It burned the back of my throat.

"If we decide to give this another try, I would be open to moving to Chicago. I know in the past, I said I was tied to this area, but I feel like a new start could be really good for me. I know we're not there yet, but I just wanted to make sure you knew that—that I would be willing to move for you."

No, we definitely aren't there yet.

"Noted," I simply said.

At one point, she left me in the living room while she ventured into her room. I looked around aimlessly, my eyes landing on her bookshelves then wandering over to a sculpture of an elephant in the corner.

She returned to the living room before taking my hand to follow her back into the bedroom.

Why am I nervous?

This was by no means my first rodeo—far from it.

What the fuck is wrong with me?

Candles that she'd lit flickered around us. She lifted off her dress to reveal a red, lace bra and matching panties. Red was always her color, accentuating her long, dark hair. My dick twitched as I took in the sight of her body.

She pulled me into her, and we kissed as I tried to calm down, caressing her back. Emily was rubbing her bare skin against me. I knew I could have slipped inside of her in two seconds flat and that she'd be wet and welcoming. But for some reason, instead of relaxing into everything that was happening, my muscles tightened. I realized in that moment that I was resisting. *Why?* Why was I moving away from this when my body was turned on? Something was off.

Threading my finger through the back string of her thong, I pulled on it and closed my eyes, determined to let myself get lost in her tonight. The thong made me think of Amber's lingerie. Images of her underwear laying on the grass of the Boston Common flashed through my head. All of my thoughts then moved to Amber. My heart was now palpitating because suddenly the ass I was gripping was Amber's. At least, in my mind it was. And I was getting harder.

To get lost in Emily was what I wanted, but it wasn't what I *needed*. It started to hit me all at once: Amber was showing up to a hotel to supposedly fuck a stranger tomorrow. *Tomorrow.* But she didn't really want him. She wanted *me*. Why *couldn't* it be me? I was leaving town anyway. Why couldn't I be the one to give her what she needed in the meantime? Either I was losing my mind, or this was making a lot of sense. I couldn't figure out which option was correct.

And now, I was painfully hard thinking about this. Shit. I was in no state to be screwing Emily when all I could think about was sex with Amber.

Prying myself away, I said, "I don't think I can do this tonight."

She looked shocked. "What? Why?"

"I've got some things on my mind that I can't shake. I'm really sorry, but I think I need to go home."

The mood was understandably awkward for the next several minutes as Emily got her clothes back on.

"Will you call me when you're feeling better, then?"

"Of course. I just need a little time to sort some stuff out."

Everything was suddenly very clear to me. Before I could focus on anything with Emily or anyone else, I had to get Amber out of my system.

CHAPTER TEN
AMBER

Annabelle picked up. "Hey. Are you on your way?"

My legs felt wobbly as I walked down Grove Street in my heels. "Yes. Can you remind me what the hell I was thinking? Now that this day is actually here, I'm seriously considering backing out."

"You can't back out. You just paid a ton for a Brazilian wax. You need to show that shit to someone."

"Okay, if it doesn't work out, I'll come over in a trench coat and flash you before I drink the night away." I sighed. "I just need to remember to breathe."

"Where are you now?"

"I'm just walking up to the entrance of The Peabody."

"Make sure you call me the second it's over, okay? Even before that if you need me."

I blew out a shaky breath. "Okay. Thank you, Annabelle."

"You got it, friend. Take care of yourself."

With its dark wood décor and elaborate crown moldings, the historic Peabody Hotel was a place of rich architectural beauty. A beautiful Asian woman was playing the harp in a corner. G9's choosing this place meant he had good taste.

My palms were sweaty as I entered the dark lounge, which was located diagonally across from the opulent front desk area. Red tablecloths were draped over the tables, and a massive chandelier shimmered from above.

At the very least, if he never showed, I could just have a drink and leave.

Remember, you don't have to do anything you're not totally comfortable with.

Looking around anxiously, I searched for a man in a black polo shirt.

My heart was pounding, and goosebumps peppered my skin. The room felt freezing cold.

Then, the feel of three fingers tapping on my shoulder caused me to jump before turning around.

That was the moment my heart nearly stopped. His familiar scent wafted in the air, as arousing as ever despite my nerves.

"Channing!"

Channing?

What was he doing here?

This was bad. I couldn't let him find out about this. Gentleman Nine would be here any minute.

"You look beautiful, Amber." He didn't seem as surprised to see me as I was to see him.

Gentleman Nine and Channing could *not* meet!

On the verge of a panic attack, I stuttered, "Um...thank you. What...what are you doing here?"

Fiddling with his watch, Channing looked nervous—very unlike the cool and confident man I knew.

"That's a great question." He let out a single laugh as he gazed at the ceiling. "A *great* fucking question."

"Are you meeting Emily?"

"No, no, I'm not."

"What are you doing here, then?"

"Can we sit down somewhere, please?"

What was I supposed to say?

No, Channing, actually, I'm meeting a male prostitute for sex, so there's no time to sit and chat.

"Um...sure."

"I'm just gonna go get you a glass of wine," he said before he swiftly made his way over to the bar.

I grabbed a seat. Stretching my neck, I kept looking around the room in search of black polo man. There was no sign of anyone who met that description. At this point, I was relieved he wasn't here because I couldn't imagine having to introduce him to Channing. That would have been totally awkward.

Channing returned to the table and handed me a large glass of white wine. "Here you go."

"Thanks."

I was still frantically searching the room when he interrupted me. "Amber, look at me." His voice sounded even deeper than usual.

The look in his eyes told me something wasn't right.

"What's going on? Did something happen?" Paranoia started to set in that maybe he'd heard me talking to Annabelle. *Oh, no!* "Did you follow me here?"

"No. I came to meet you. I know why you're here, and I have to explain."

My heart felt like it dropped to my stomach.

He knows why I'm here?

I swallowed. "Excuse me?"

His face was beet red. I'd never seen Channing's face turn that color in all the years I'd known him. I'd *never* seen him like this.

"I know you're here to see Gentleman Nine."

My stomach was in knots. Hearing that name come out of his mouth freaked me out.

How could this be?

"What...how did you know about that?"

"I need you to understand that I thought I was doing what was best for you."

The room felt like it was swaying. "What was best for me? I'm so confused right now."

"I know you are."

He paused and just looked at me for what felt like a full minute.

"It's me, Amber. *I'm* Gentleman Nine."

What he said registered the wrong way at first. "You're a prostitute?"

"Fuck, no. That didn't come out right. Let me explain."

My ears were pounding. "You'd *better* explain."

Channing downed his drink until it was gone. It was some kind of golden brown-colored liquor.

He took a deep breath in and began to explain. "I came home from my Chicago trip while you were in the shower. I went to use your laptop that was sitting on the coffee table, so I could check Facebook. You left your message to him open, and I read it, even though that was clearly wrong of me. Anyway, I freaked out, Amber. I felt like you were making a mistake and that it was my duty to protect you. So, I sent another message pretending to be you and cancelled your original request."

He what?

"What? You had no right to do that!"

"I know that now. Believe me, I know I crossed a line."

It was finally totally sinking in. "You canceled the request. Then, wait...who was I talking to?"

"That was me."

Oh, my God.

"You pretended to be him?"

"Yes. I created an account so you would think you got a response."

"Why would you do that?"

"It was a stalling mechanism, but it opened up a huge can of worms that I never anticipated. I swear to God...I never meant to hurt you. Please believe that. I only wanted to keep you safe. I just got myself in way too deep, and it spiraled out of control."

"You wanted to keep me safe by lying to me, putting me in a position where I was comfortable telling you certain things I *never* would have admitted to you otherwise?" The realization of exactly what this meant came in waves. I covered my mouth in shock. "Oh, my God—some of the things I said about you to...him...to you! I am so mortified. Channing...seriously?"

Channing looked pained. "I never expected you to say those things about me, to talk about your attraction to me. It really caught me off guard...but not in a bad way, Amber. Fuck...in a good way."

"I can't believe this," I whispered under my breath. I took a long sip of my wine then slammed the glass down on the table a little too hard. Thankfully, it didn't shatter.

"Please, hear me out." Channing placed his hand on my forearm. Despite my anger, my body still reacted to his touch. "I regret how I handled it," he said. "It was an erratic decision based on fear. I really thought I was protecting you and just couldn't handle the thought of you giving yourself to someone who didn't give two shits about you besides collecting your money. But I know now that I had no right to make that decision for you. Once I took that first step, though, I couldn't go back. It was like a domino effect. Fuck, Amber, I'm so sorry."

Taking a few deep breaths, I tried my best to put this in perspective. Channing wouldn't do anything to intentionally hurt me. He just made a really poor judgment call. And he didn't have to fess up at all. He chose to come clean.

"I suppose you could've just never admitted it. That would've been a lot easier. I respect the fact that you told me, even if I still don't really understand how you could do this."

"I never seriously considered not telling you. It crossed my mind, but in the end, I just couldn't do it. My goal in emailing you like that was to buy more time in the hopes that maybe you'd change your mind and not want to go through with it."

"Why did you need to come here tonight to tell me the truth? Why couldn't you have done it at home? Why put me through this?"

"I felt like I needed to face you here, for some reason. I came to a realization last night when I was with Emily. And this time and place seemed appropriate to admit everything to you."

"Why?"

He fell silent then said, "There's more I need to say to you."

"What more could there possibly be?"

He suddenly got up. "Let me get you another drink. You're gonna need it."

Still unable to believe this was happening, I watched Channing as he fumbled with his wallet over at the bar.

He approached holding another white wine for me and more of the same liquor in a shot glass for him.

My instinct was to thank him for the drink, but I stopped myself because technically, at the very least, he owed me alcohol for putting me in this situation.

"What else do you need to say to me?" I asked.

"I never expected you to say the things you did. You told me—him—that you wanted me. I haven't really been able to get it out of my mind. That's not something that I can just forget."

"Yeah, well...try."

He leaned in, suddenly seeming less unsure of himself and more direct. "I don't want to forget it. What you may not realize is that I want you in the exact same way."

To say I was surprised to hear him say that was an understatement. Especially given the reemergence of gorgeous Emily. I never expected to hear Channing say those words—that he wanted me.

"You want *me*? What about Emily?"

"I was with her last night. We were about to...you know...and I couldn't. I was thinking about you—about this. So, that was my moment of clarity. I stopped it and left her apartment. I stayed up all night thinking."

"About *this*? What is *this* exactly? What are you trying to say?"

"I know you don't want anything serious. Neither do I. But we're both adults who respect each other and are clearly attracted to each other. I only have a limited time left in Boston. Why not let me give you what you need while I'm here."

I swear, this felt like a dream, like it wasn't really happening. There wasn't a hint of amusement in his expression. Channing was seriously propositioning me. As much as I wanted to dismiss it, to tell him he was out of his mind, another part of me became increasingly curious—aroused. But this wasn't as simple as he was making it out to be.

"You're suggesting I try to pretend that you're just no one to me? How exactly could this work, Channing?"

"We would have to set ground rules. Keep our personal relationship separate from our sexual relationship."

"And how do we do that when we live together?"

"We could meet here, say on Saturdays, and we wouldn't discuss it the rest of the week. We wouldn't have to discuss it at all. No one will know about this but us. And I promise never to tell Rory. I assume his ever finding out would be your biggest hesitation."

I just kept shaking my head back and forth in an attempt to process everything. "What do you get out of this?"

"I get to be with the girl I've fantasized about since I was sixteen."

Since he was sixteen?

"I never knew you felt that way."

"I hid it very well. But I've always been attracted to you."

My gut was telling me that I was crazy for considering this, but my body couldn't be calmed. It was completely buzzing at the thought of being with him. Everything was suddenly magnified—his scent, the nearness of his perfect body. I wasn't sure if I had the strength to say no, because there was no bigger turn on than being wanted.

My voice cracked. "I really don't know if this is a good idea."

"You don't have to make a decision now. Take some time to think about it. No hard feelings if you decide against it. We'll forget this night ever happened. I promise if you tell me no, we can pretend this conversation never took place. And as much as I hope you don't, if you decide to contact the real Gentleman Nine, I promise not to judge you or interfere, either."

As mad as I was at him, his showing up here was a reality check. A part of me was actually relieved to be sitting here with Channing now and not some male hooker. The longer we sat in this bar, the crazier it seemed that I had come here tonight to pay for sex. At least with Channing, I felt safe.

The idea of unbridled sex with him was extremely tempting. To know that he wanted me, too, made me feel sexier than I had in a long time.

But I still couldn't believe this. And he certainly wasn't going to get an answer tonight. This would change the entire dynamic of our relationship.

It would change my life.

CHAPTER ELEVEN
CHANNING

Apparently, one sure-fire way to get Amber to avoid you is to suggest a sexual relationship. Noted.

The days that followed our meetup at The Peabody Hotel were tense, although the massive relief I felt as a result of having finally told her the truth about Gentleman Nine was the consolation. That was the first and last time I would ever lie to her.

And she hadn't kicked me out of the house or anything. So, that was a plus. Amber also hadn't given me a solid no, either. She'd left the door open to accepting my offer. The last thing she said to me before we left the hotel was that she'd think about it. My body unfortunately chose to focus on that. Whenever we were in the same room, I could feel myself getting turned on from just thinking about the prospect of getting to have sex with her. The fact that she somehow felt it was wrong, made me want it even more. The more forbidden, the sweeter the fruit.

Wednesday night, I'd just gotten home from work when she called my cell.

"Oh, you're home. Thank God," she said, sounding out of breath.

"What's going on? Is everything okay?"

She was panicked. "I need your help."

A rush of adrenaline hit me. "Tell me what's happening."

"I'm around the corner with Milo. I was out with him. I'd taken him to a restaurant, and he spilled split pea soup all over his shirt. Since we were closer to my place than his, I figured I would take him back here and borrow one of your shirts. But now, he's decided to drop to the ground. He's lying on the sidewalk, and I can't get him up. He's too big for me to lift."

Shit.

Already making my way out the door, I said, "I'll be right there."

"Thank you. We're at the corner of Stockton and East Streets."

Amber looked flustered as I approached them. She was huffing and puffing, blowing air up into her bangs, which she often did when she was stressed. Milo, on the other hand, was just sitting on the sidewalk chilling and playing with his iPad as people passed by obliviously, practically walking right over him.

"Hey," I said.

"Hey." She sighed.

I knelt down. "'Sup, Milo. What's happening? You don't want to come hang with us at our place?"

He immediately gripped my head and pulled me into his nose as he sucked in a long whiff of my hair.

His attention then returned to his iPad. A few seconds later, I noticed he had put on a clip of *Archer*. He must have pulled it up quickly in his YouTube history.

"Does he ever play *Archer* when I'm not around?"

"Never." She grinned.

Putting my hand on his shoulder, I said, "You're one complex dude, you know that?"

Of course, he said nothing in response.

I reached for his hand. "Come on, Milo."

Amber was laughing at my attempt to get him up in that way. "If it was that easy, I wouldn't have had to call you."

I scratched my head. "Alright." Moving behind him, I looped my arms under his and forced him up. Lifting him was a Herculean task. Dude was heavy. And I was a big guy. But he was all dead weight, because he wasn't helping me at all.

Once on his feet, he wrapped his arm around me as we walked. I was certain people thought we were a couple. Amber walked alongside us with a huge smile on her face.

"You enjoying this, Amber?"

"I am." She laughed. "Immensely."

Well, if there was one consolation to this, it was that Amber was now talking to me.

Thank you, buddy, for breaking the ice between Amber and me. I owe you one.

When we arrived home, I took Milo into my room and opened the closet.

"Which shirt do you like?"

He began taking some of my shirts off the hangers and throwing them on the closet floor before finally selecting a polo—the most expensive one.

"That's Armani. You have really good taste. Let's see how it looks on you."

After pulling the soiled shirt over his head, I helped him put on the clean one. It fit him like a glove.

"Nice. How about a little cologne?"

I made the mistake of handing him the bottle. He proceeded to spray a shitload onto the shirt and his hair.

"Okay, that's enough." I coughed.

When we entered the living room, Amber was beaming. "Look at you! Such a handsome guy."

"Thank you," I joked. When she turned to me, I winked and she smiled back.

This was good. She didn't fucking hate me for lying and then propositioning her for sex.

Then, she smelled him. "Oh, boy. Someone got a hold of the cologne. I should've warned you. He doesn't know when to stop with certain things."

"I can kind of relate to that lately," I said, hoping she understood that I was referring to my Gentleman Nine fuck-up.

After we got Milo settled with a TV show, I turned to her. "How about I make dinner? What's his favorite food?"

"Everything." She laughed.

"Alright, then."

"Maybe skip the urge to cook something really weird tonight, though. He likes normal food."

"You got it."

"He actually really loves pasta and red sauce."

"Perfect. That's easy enough. I can definitely whip up a good marinara."

Amber leaned against the counter and watched as I boiled the pasta and cooked up a simple sauce with canned tomatoes, basil, and a mixture of spices she had laying around in the cabinet. Milo stayed in the living room watching television.

When we sat down for dinner, I watched in awe as Milo slurped up a massive plate of spaghetti in record time. He seemed so happy to be eating, taking joy in every bite. It only took him about five mouthfuls to completely demolish it. After he was finished, he abruptly got up.

Amber grinned. "He likes to eat and run."

My eyes followed him as he returned to his spot in front of the television. "Where are his parents? How did he end up in that home?"

She wiped her mouth with a napkin. "It's just his mother. He's too big, and she can't handle him. So, she has him in the group home. It's staffed twenty-four hours, so he always has someone there, and being in that environment helps to teach him independence, because you know, his mom's not gonna be around forever."

Still watching him, I asked, "Do you think he's happy?"

"I do. He gets frustrated sometimes because of his inability to communicate his feelings, but overall he lives a different kind of life than we do. He doesn't have an ego, nor is he concerned with what people think about him, so in many ways, that's a blessing. It's like all he needs are food and his favorite shows or YouTube videos, and he's content with basic pleasures."

"Interesting. If only we could all learn to live that way, put our needs first, and not worry about the rest or what other people think."

Her face turned red. She definitely knew where I was coming from. I wasn't even sure if I meant it to relate to our situation, but somehow it did.

After Amber and I finished our own pasta, we joined Milo on the couch, one of us on each side of him.

He was watching some bizarre animated show with a bunch of singing little girls.

"What is this show?" I asked.

"It's called *Kuu Kuu Harajuku*. It's a kids' show. But he loves it."

"What's the gist?"

"Well, see those girls? They're called Harajuku Girls because they live in Harajuku."

"Fascinating." I looked at him and chuckled. "Why do you think he likes it?"

"I suspect he appreciates the mayhem. These girls are musicians, and something is always getting in the way of their gigs. He sometimes laughs when they get into trouble. I think he likes their voices and the chaos. Either that, or maybe he just likes all the flashing colors."

"It is pretty trippy, reminds me of something I would've watched after smoking a bone down in my basement in high school."

"Yeah. You were a bad influence, Channing."

I flashed a mischievous grin. "Some things never change."

She intentionally made sure her eyes were glued to the cartoon after I'd said that.

I took the time to admire her legs that she'd spread out atop the coffee table. They were so smooth and toned. I didn't even think she had to shave because she had this thin layer of blonde hair covering them. I wanted to rub my hand along her skin to see what that peach fuzz felt like. Visions of those legs wrapped around my back floated through my head. Her perfect little toes were painted blood red. I wasn't normally a foot man, but Amber's toes looked good enough to eat. My mouth watered.

Fuck. If she ended up saying no to me, I might never get her out of my system. My eyes continued to devour Amber's legs.

Suddenly, I felt a whack.

And then he laughed.

Milo had smacked me upside the head.

I had no clue whether he was pissed that I was staring at Amber or what, but he'd definitely knocked me out of my trance.

<hr />

That night, it was well past midnight when I'd decided to use the bathroom before bed. Amber was already asleep— or so I thought. She ended up knocking right into me as she was leaving the bathroom while I was entering.

"Are you okay?" My hands were on her shoulders. It was rare that I ever touched her.

Her breathing quickened. My dick immediately responded based on her reaction to me.

"Yeah, I'm fine." She looked up at me in the darkness. "I've been thinking about what you and I discussed at The Peabody."

My heartbeat sped up a little as I reluctantly slid my hands off of her. "Yeah?"

"I'm still mad at you."

"Amb—"

"Hear me out," she insisted.

"Alright."

"I'm mad...but I'm so glad it was you who showed up and not him. You were right. I would've regretted it. Thank you for intercepting what would have been a bad move on my part. Thank you for looking out for me."

"I'm relieved you feel that way."

"Like you said, there have to be some ground rules if we're gonna do this."

My heart really started to accelerate now. Was she taking me up on my offer? My cock twitched. I had to keep my dick in check, especially since it was a dishonest motherfucker. It had been lying to me this entire time just to get what it wanted, trying to convince me that this situation was going to be simple when I knew damn well it wasn't.

"I agree that we have to have rules," I said. "Tell me yours."

"I need to see proof that you don't have any diseases, something from the doctor."

"That's already been taken care of. That's not a problem at all."

"I don't want you sleeping with anyone else while we're doing this."

"That's a given. What else?"

"You have to wear a condom."

Moving in closer to her, I said, "I'll wear two if you want."

"That's not necessary."

My dick was officially getting hard. "Okay. Tell me more."

"We don't utter a single word of this to anyone. It's not just Rory I'm worried about. But I would never want like... say...your mother to know, either."

That made me laugh. "Why would I tell my mother?"

"I don't know." She smiled. "Just don't."

"Done. No one will know. Come on, give me more rules." I wanted everything out on the table so she didn't have any second thoughts later or want to back out.

"I think that's all I've got, actually. I feel like there should be more, but I can't think of any at the moment."

"How about I help?" I said. "I've got a few."

"Okay..."

"I alluded to this before, but a main rule is that we meet on Saturdays only. And we don't take it home with us. We don't talk about it during the week. I think that's gonna be important. As much as we may be tempted, sex happens only in our hotel room on Saturdays, and any talk of what we're doing stays there as well. That way, this arrangement won't interfere with our day-to-day lives."

She nodded. "That's smart."

"You also agree to trust me and to tell me if I'm doing something that you don't like. We need to communicate with each other, at least during the time that we're there."

"I will."

"I'll make all the arrangements."

"We can alternate the cost of the room by week," she said.

I held up my hand. "No. No way. I've got it."

"I want to pay."

"You can pay me back in other ways." I winked. "Just kidding—maybe."

She rubbed her arms. "This is all so weird, Channing. I feel like the past week has been a dream."

"One more rule. There's no pressure. If you're having any doubts, you can change your mind at any time. No hard feelings."

As much as I meant that, I really hoped she didn't back out, that she wanted this as much as I did.

CHAPTER TWELVE
AMBER

"I still can't get over the fact it was Channing all along."

"You and me both, Annabelle. You and me both."

Balancing the cordless phone on my shoulder, I picked out clothes for Saturday, packing them away in a small travel bag.

The outfit I'd chosen consisted of a little black skirt and a nude-colored shirt with black lace overlay that always made my tits look really good. The fact that it was Rory's favorite shirt was my little secret "fuck you" to my ex.

"I swear," she said. "I could write a book about your life in the past month, and it would sell like hotcakes. And we haven't even gotten to the good part."

Throwing some sleep shorts into the bag, I said, "I don't know if I'm doing the right thing. I always said I didn't want to get involved with Channing, but technically this isn't really getting involved. It's just sex."

"I think the whole thing is sexy as hell. Not only was he trying to protect you, but he decided he wanted to be the man to do the job. My only question is...do you think you'll be able to compartmentalize? I know you care about him. Can you really handle this?"

Deep down, I *was* worried. But I still didn't want to deny myself this opportunity. It had simply been too long since I'd been with a man, and I was too weak to resist.

"He cares about me, too, but this is supposed to be separate from that fact. What happens in the hotel room, stays there. It sounds simple in theory, but I honestly don't know how I'm going to feel once we actually do this. The truth is, for this to work, I need to learn to put aside my feelings and see this for what it is—two friends fulfilling a physical need for each other. He gets some thrill out of playing into this sordid hotel room fantasy. And I get what I've always wanted since he moved here, which is to experience having sex with him. This whole thing—my contacting the escort service—really started because of my attraction to him, which put me into this sexual frenzy in the first place. I just never expected that he felt something, too."

"Just go with the flow. You've had a rough year. You're still young. You don't need to be in another relationship. Let Channing give you exactly what you need before he goes back to Chicago. And don't let your worries ruin a good thing."

⊂——

We planned to meet at The Peabody at 3PM. He'd left me a note on my dresser while I was in the shower.

I'll head over to the hotel first, get us a room, and I'll text you the room number. Wear the pink thong you bought. I've been thinking about you in it ever since I picked it up off the grass on the Common.

The muscles between my legs clenched. I still couldn't wrap my head around the fact that Channing desired me when he could basically have anyone he wanted—including Emily. I still had no clue what was going on with the latter.

The Saturday morning breakfast run-in with him in the kitchen had been different than normal, to say the least. We'd sat in silence, drinking our coffees, but the weight of a thousand unsaid words loomed in the air.

Channing's hair had been wet. His tight, white t-shirt stretched across his muscles. My eyes had been glued to his strong forearms every time he'd lift the coffee mug to his mouth—his sexy mouth. I still couldn't believe that body would be hovering over me later, that he would be inside of me. It truly seemed surreal.

And then I'd caught him staring at me and suspected he must have been thinking the same thing. The lust in his eyes was palpable, and I was sure I must have looked the same to him, because I'd never felt like my desire for him was more obvious than that moment. It was one thing to want someone. It was another to want them, knowing you would actually get to have them.

He left after breakfast, and I didn't see him for the rest of the day.

When 2:45 rolled around, I anxiously checked my phone for a text from him. A few minutes later, it came.

Channing: I'm in Room 248. Take your time. I'll be here waiting whenever you're ready.

Despite the feeling that I was forgetting something, I grabbed my bag and forced myself out the door.

By the time I approached The Peabody, the butterflies in my stomach had turned frantic.

Goosebumps covered my arms as I made my way to the elevator up to the second floor.

The elevator dinged open, and my heart was racing as I walked down the long hallway in a fog. I knew I'd be nervous, but my anxiety was much higher than I'd anticipated the closer I got to the room.

After knocking lightly, I took a deep breath in and waited.

When he opened the door, Channing flashed his beautiful grin and moved aside for me to enter. Immediately, his cologne infiltrated my senses as I felt my body temperature rise.

My legs felt wobbly. I guess you really don't know how you're going to feel about something until it was about to happen. Suddenly, all of the self-doubt started to creep in at this inopportune moment.

What if I suck, and he doesn't want to do it again?

What if he doesn't like my body?

What if I come too fast or not at all because I'm nervous?

I immediately ventured over to the window. While a part of me was tempted to jump, I stared down at the busy Boston traffic below. The faint sounds of life outside of the room were muffled by the beat of my own eardrum.

"You okay?" he asked from behind me.

I turned around and rubbed my clammy palms on my skirt. "Yeah, I think I just need some water."

"How about water then some wine?"

"Even better."

Alcohol sounded great right about now.

He opened a bottle of water then poured it into a glass for me. My armpits were sweating, and that became another worry. Had I worn enough deodorant?

I sipped my water and watched as he opened a bottle of cabernet that I knew was pricey.

"That's an expensive bottle of wine, Lord."

"Well, it's not every day I have Amber Walton in a hotel room with me. It's a special occasion." He smiled, and that calmed me down a bit.

Channing handed me the glass then sat at the edge of the bed across from me, watching intently as I gulped the wine down. His stare made me shiver.

He looked so damn good. Everything was on point. His hair was slightly damp. He must have showered in the room right before I got there. He wore a collared shirt that was open slightly at the top, showcasing a few inches of his tanned chest. His dark jeans fit him perfectly, displaying a prominent bulge. Could he possibly have been hard already?

When my eyes made their way back up to his face, I could see he was still observing me.

"You look really beautiful." His smile was almost enough to melt my nerves—almost.

"Thank you. I tried to pick something sexy for you."

"I've been hard all morning, so you could've walked in wearing a paper bag, and I'd still need an ice pack."

Despite my nerves, the confirmation that Channing was aroused made my body buzz with excitement.

Setting my now-empty wine glass down, I asked, "How exactly does this work? "Do we just start going at it or..."

His mouth curved into a smile. "No."

"No?"

"No."

"Then what do we do?"

"We do what comes natural. You're not ready to have sex right this second. I prefer it if the woman I'm with isn't white knuckling her way through it."

"You can tell I'm nervous?"

"Yes. And to be honest, if you weren't, I'd be a little weirded out. It's normal. I think it's adorable how nervous you are, actually."

"I wanted to tell you how nervous I was over coffee this morning, but I didn't want to break the rules. You know, no talking about this at home."

"Well, guess what?" He leaned in, and the feel of his breath on my skin put my body on alert. "I'm nervous, too, Amber. And you can tell me about what you're feeling now. There are no rules in this room. None at all. Tell me what you're thinking."

"A part of me wants to run out of here. But another part of me thinks you smell really damn good and wants to stay. So, yes, I'm nervous, but I still really do want this."

He placed his hand on my knee, and it sent what felt like shockwaves up my spine. "You know what I think?"

"What?"

"I think we should watch TV."

"Watch TV? Surely, you didn't just pay five hundred dollars for a hotel room so that we could watch television."

"We have all afternoon and night. And if by the end of tonight, all you want to do is sleep next to me with no sex involved, that's okay, too," he said. Channing crawled to the top of the bed and began exaggeratedly fluffing the pillows. He kicked his feet back, put his hands behind his head, and let out a deep breath. "Ahh. This is so relaxing. You should try it."

He closed his eyes. So much for our salacious rendez-vous. I laughed, eventually getting up, crawling over to him, and joining him under the covers. The bed was firm, and the pillows were plush. My body sank into the Tempurpedic mattress.

He handed me the remote. "You get to choose what to watch. They have On Demand."

"You're gonna regret that decision, because I'll just watch reality TV on Bravo."

"I'll survive."

He asked for it. I immediately put on one of the *Real Housewives* episodes. It had been a while since I'd binge watched this show.

Channing and I settled into our respective pillows. He really made an effort to try to understand what he was watching. His questions were making me laugh.

"Do women actually act like this?"

"Not the women I know personally."

"So, let me get this straight. Why do they all hate that one chick?"

"They just do."

"I haven't made out one word in the last five minutes. How can you understand what they're saying if they're all talking over each other?"

That cracked me up. "You don't. You just watch."

By pretending to be into my show, Channing had managed to make me forget all about my nerves from earlier. I'd nearly forgotten why we'd come here were it not for the fact that our bodies were ever so slowly molding closer and closer together in a natural way. The side of my leg was up against his, and the heat of his body was ever-present, but I was no longer nervous or stressed. His large foot gently rubbed against mine as we watched, the soft material of his sock caressing my bare foot. He was slowly easing me into things in his own way. It was working.

After nearly an hour passed, I wanted him to know that I hadn't forgotten why we were here. In a brazen move, I slipped my top over my head, keeping my bra on.

He moved closer and whispered in my ear, "Are we playing strip poker, and I didn't realize it?"

God, what just the feeling of his breath in my ear did to my body.

"I wanted to get more comfortable," I said.

His eyes fell to my breasts that were spilling out of my pink, lace bra. My erect nipples tingled, yearning for his mouth on me.

When his eyes met mine again, I said, "Can I ask you a question?"

"Anything." He then placed his firm hand on my hip, and every inch of my body reacted to just that simple touch.

I looked down and could see that his erection was straining against his jeans. Knowing he was perpetually hard for me was perhaps the biggest turn on.

"That night when you told me about Gentleman Nine, you said you've fantasized about me since you were sixteen. I would've never thought that. I guess...I just don't get it."

His hand was still on my hip. Lightly squeezing my side, he said, "What don't you get?"

"You never said anything or gave me any hints. I mean, I had *no* idea."

"That's because I was good at hiding it."

"I know. But why? Why didn't you say anything to me?"

"Well, for one, you were my sister's best friend. If I'd asked you out and fucked things up, I wouldn't have forgiven myself, whether that happened before or after she..." He hesitated.

I didn't want him to have to finish that sentence. "Yeah, I get it," I said, placing my hand in his hair.

Channing closed his eyes for a moment as I ran my fingers through his thick, silky strands. He was so beautiful. It was odd to call a man beautiful, I suppose. But that was the best word to describe him. He was so beautiful to me, and I couldn't believe I was freely touching him like this.

"So...why is this okay now, Channing? Our arrangement? I'm still that same person. Why is it okay to play around with each other like this now? I'm still me and you're still you."

"Because we have a mutual understanding of what we'd both be getting out of it. So, we can't get hurt. Neither one of us is looking for a relationship, and we're clear on that. When you're a teenager, you're too immature to make that kind of a decision."

"Makes sense, I guess." Since we were being honest, I said, "I've always had a massive crush on you, not just because of your looks but because of your personality, too. That's kind of embarrassing to admit, but given I'm half-naked in bed with you right now, I guess I've made it clear how I feel anyway."

He surprised me when he asked, "Why didn't you say anything to me back then?"

"Would it have mattered? Everything you just said implies you wouldn't have pursued me."

"It might have changed things if I knew how you really felt. I mean, I know why I never said anything to you. Like I said, I had my reasons. But why didn't you ever say anything to *me*? We spent a lot of time together."

"I guess I was just old-fashioned and felt like the girl shouldn't make a move. I even once told Rory I had a crush on you." I laughed a little, recalling the time I admitted my crush on Channing to the guy who would eventually become my boyfriend.

Channing suddenly moved his hand off my hip. "You what?"

"Before he and I got together, I once told Rory that I liked you. It's funny to think about that now, considering how things turned out."

"What exactly did he say to that when you told him?"

I wasn't sure whether to admit it. "He told me to be careful of you, that you'd hurt me."

"Really..." His eyes narrowed "When was that? The conversation?"

He was upset.

I scratched my head in an attempt to remember. "Probably shortly before you left for UF."

Channing suddenly sat up against the headboard. My revelation really seemed to piss him off. I could understand why he'd be mad. But I figured he'd understand why Rory would have warned me against him. Channing never hid his philandering ways back then. Rory was his friend, but at the time, Channing *was* a player. That was undeniable. Rory thought he was just looking out for my best interests.

When he continued not to say anything, I asked, "Are you okay?"

CHAPTER THIRTEEN
CHANNING

"Channing?"

Now was not the time to go ape shit. But suddenly, I was eighteen again. I never intended to admit anything to Amber about Rory's and my pact. But hearing what he'd told her was completely jarring. It felt like steam was coming out of my ears. I was ready to blow.

He knew how I'd felt about her back then.

He knew that despite my actions when it came to other girls, that Amber was different.

And now I'd learned that he *knew* she had feelings for *me* before he pursued her.

She could tell my head wasn't right. "Channing, what's wrong?"

"It doesn't matter now. It's old news."

"What doesn't matter?"

"The fact that your ex is a lying douchebag."

"Because of what he said about you?"

My eyes darted to the side to meet hers. "He knew how I felt about you."

She was blinking repeatedly, looking totally confused. "What do you mean?"

Here goes nothing.

"Rory and I both wanted you, Amber. About a year before I left for college, he came to me and told me he wanted to ask you out. I felt compelled to tell him that I had feelings for you, too. At the time, we decided that for the betterment of our friendship, that neither one of us would pursue you. We made a deal, one he broke as soon as I left for UF."

She covered her mouth. "Oh, my God. I obviously had no idea about this."

"No, of course you didn't. You were never supposed to know, but you bet your ass that if you had come to me and told me that you had feelings for *him*, I would've told him about that. I would've abolished that fucking pact if it meant making you happy. Instead, when you went to him about *me*, he did nothing but warn you against me, so that he could move in on you when I left."

She stared off, looking like she was trying to make sense of my revelation. "So, when you came back from UF, Rory and I were together...you were different toward us. That's because..."

"I was devastated. Yeah. I was crushed to see you two together."

"Oh, my God, Channing. I had no clue. None."

"I know that. Why *would* you?"

"I'd based my opinion of you largely on those years after you came home from UF. You always got around, but you just seemed out of control when you came back. I watched your actions and judged you based on them. I never imagined resentment was at the root of it."

Letting out an angry laugh, I said, "I hooked up with all of your friends to get back at you, even though you didn't even do anything wrong. Real mature, right?"

"I kind of hated you in college," she said.

"The feeling was mutual, Amber. I kind of hated you for a while, too, until I wised up and realized that if you were happy—really happy with him—then that was all that mattered."

"Wow."

I couldn't believe I'd let my emotions get the best of me.

Calm the fuck down, Channing.

I chuckled. "Well, so much for just sex tonight, huh?" I'd virtually ruined our evening by bringing the past into this hotel room and throwing a tantrum. It wasn't until this moment that I realized just how much bitterness I was still harboring even after all these years.

She placed her hand on my cheek, and I closed my eyes to relish her touch.

"I'm glad you told me, Channing. I mean, I know it doesn't change anything between us now. But it was a part of the past that I was apparently blind to."

Placing my hand over hers, I said, "Look, I can't even say I blame Rory for what he did. All is fair in love and war, right? He got the girl in the end. He played the game better than me. And you fell in love with him. He won."

Her stare seared through me before she said, "No. I beg to differ. Because now I'm in bed with *you*. So, I'd say *I* won the game in the end."

My heart nearly leapt from my chest. That was the sweetest fucking thing she could have said to me. It felt like she healed an entire decade of anger and resentment with two sentences. She was right. In the end, despite everything that happened, here we were. And tonight, in this moment, it wasn't about any of that shit that happened in the past. It was about us. I could have kissed her for those words.

In fact, I did.

Wrapping my hands around her face, I pulled her into my lips and expelled a breath of relief as I tasted her. She moaned into my mouth and my dick reacted, now ready to burst. As long as it had been since our one kiss all those years ago, the recognition of her taste was immediate. Except this time, it wasn't going to end in just a kiss.

With each moment that passed as I thrust my tongue in and out of her mouth, I became more lost in her. With each whimper and moan that travelled down my throat, I wanted to dominate her more.

I spoke over her lips, "Are you wearing the thong I asked you to?"

"Yes."

"Show me."

She broke away to pull down her skirt then turned her back to me, displaying her gorgeous, taut ass. I ran my hand along her skin and looped my finger inside the string laying within her ass cheeks. Unable to help myself, I pulled on it pretty hard.

"I only want you to wear these when you're with me. I want to see all the different colors. I love your ass in them."

"Okay."

Her thong was wet from the moment I first touched it. "They're soaked. How long have you been wet like this?"

She turned around to face me and grinned impishly. "Since you moved in."

A wry smile spread over my face. "Well, then, it sounds like I created a problem I need to take care of." I boldly slid her hand down onto my cock and pressed it into me. "Feel this. This is what you do to me, except I finally don't have to hide it anymore."

Amber closed her eyes and began rubbing her palm along my crotch as we faced each other. I reached down and massaged her clit before slipping my fingers inside of her hot pussy.

"Fuck, Amber." I closed my eyes and listened to the sound of her wetness as my fingers moved in and out. "My fingers are covered in your come."

I pulled them out and hovered over her as she writhed under me.

"Watch me," I said, unzipping my pants and taking out my rigid cock.

She watched intently as I used her come that was still on my fingers as lube while stroking myself. Her eyes were transfixed on my hand moving back and forth. I couldn't ever remember being this hard before sex. I loved watching her watching me. Amber bit her bottom lip as she reached down and began playing with her clit.

Oh, fuck yeah.

The only sounds were those of our arousal and skin rubbing together. I couldn't peel my eyes away from her fingers moving over the folds of her beautiful, blush pussy. I could have come all over the bed in five seconds if I let myself. There was no way I was going to waste this opportunity. I needed to pace myself. The only place I wanted to climax was inside of her.

She stopped rubbing herself long enough to undo her bra, letting her beautiful breasts spring free. When she looked up at me, there was a certain innocence in her eyes. I had to remind myself that she'd only been with one man before me.

Holy shit. I need to slow down.

My eyes scrolled down her face, to her neck, and then once again landed on her breasts. I took some time to just stare at her creamy tits and erect nipples while my aroused cock hung in the balance, throbbing and ready to go.

As much as I wanted to rub against her opening, I was covered in precum, so that was too risky. Much to my dismay, I'd left the box of condoms in my backpack, which was all the way on the other side of the room. I reluctantly pried myself away from her warm body and walked over to retrieve one.

Amber sat up and gawked at my naked physique, which I fucking loved. I loved how badly she wanted me. Her eyes were glued to the tattoo at the base of my abs as I ripped the condom wrapper open with my teeth and slipped the rubber over my engorged cock.

I couldn't wait a second longer. I crawled over the bed and lowered my body over her before nudging her legs wide open and sinking inside of her. She let out a sound the moment I entered her, and it set me off like a rocket. But she was way tighter than I'd anticipated. I needed to pace myself, or else I was going to blow it in a matter of seconds.

Her legs stayed opened as wide as she could spread them while her tight pussy enveloped my cock. It felt incredible. She was so wet that I didn't worry about hurting her. Her hips moved under me, encouraging me to go faster as her nails dug into my ass.

I'd wanted to go slow our first time, but I just couldn't. It felt too damn good not to fuck her roughly. And it was what she wanted as evidenced by her body's reaction as I pounded into her.

So, I fucked her hard as if it were my one and only chance. A part of me feared she might regret this tomorrow, so I was taking advantage of this moment.

Amber moved my head down onto her breasts, guiding my mouth to her nipple.

Someone likes her tits sucked.

Well, I just so happened to love sucking them—and biting them. I loved that she was showing me what she craved. I also loved that she was going to have marks all over her body by the time I got through with her.

There wasn't one part of me not connected to her. Our hands were locked. My mouth was filled with her perfect breast. My cock was moving inside of her.

"I can't believe I'm fucking you. You're amazing, Amber. You feel better than anything. Tell me when to come. I'm just waiting to explode inside your beautiful cunt."

My words set her off. I felt her pussy convulsing around me. I could literally feel her orgasm squeezing my cock. It was at that moment that I finally let go, pounding into her while my hot cum filled the condom.

Finally slowing my pace, I reluctantly pulled out, even though I wanted to just stay inside of her. The condom was so full it could barely contain my load.

I got up to discard it and quickly returned to the bed. Placing my lips over hers, we kissed long and hard, and within a few minutes, I could feel my cock beginning to harden again. It wanted more.

Amber sighed. A smile spread across her face. She seemed calm, sated, and a little dumbfounded at what we'd just done.

Our faces were close when she ran her fingers through my hair and said, "Well, I'm officially screwed, because I don't know how anything is ever going to top that."

My breath still ragged, I said, "Oh, believe me, I intend to. I'm nowhere near done with you tonight."

I planted my head between her beautiful tits and listened to the sound of her breathing.

After a while, she asked, "Should we go eat?"

"Oh, you mean there are other things you want to do besides fuck me all night?"

She bit her bottom lip and smiled. "The food will give me energy for round two."

"I guess we can break for food, but let's shower first."

"Together?" She looked a little apprehensive.

"Don't be shy. I'll take good care of you."

Amber lifted herself out of bed. My dick was most certainly ready to play again as I got a load of her stark-naked body.

Following her into the bathroom, I made sure to grab a condom on the way—just in case.

Once in the shower, Amber's back was toward me as the warm water rained down on us. My dick was sandwiched in the crack of her ass as I alternated between washing her back and kissing her skin.

"I need to have you again, but this time I want to watch my dick move in and out of you from behind."

"Fuck me," she breathed as her arms trembled against the tile.

Hearing those words come out of her sweet mouth made me crazy. I reached over to the sink for the condom and couldn't get it on fast enough. Thank God I'd had the good sense to bring one into the bathroom.

I slipped inside of her, placing my hands on each side of her ass to guide her over my cock. Watching my dick move in and out of her body from this angle was just about the hottest thing I'd ever experienced.

"Shit," I groaned. "You feel too damn good." This time, I lost it faster than anticipated. "I'm gonna come."

"Me, too," she panted.

My orgasm came on suddenly as my body crashed into her.

Pumping in and out of her slowly, I gently bit her ear and rasped, "I don't ever want you to forget what this feels like, Amber. I know I won't ever forget this."

"That's what I'm afraid of, that I'll *never* be able to forget," she whispered.

⌒

We made our way to a steakhouse down the street. Despite the dim lighting, Amber's face reflected a visible glow that I couldn't help but take credit for.

She was looking down at the menu, but my eyes were firmly focused on her.

"What are you in the mood for?" I asked.

She shrugged. "I'm not really that hungry. I just feel like I *should* eat."

My phone chimed. I refused to check it.

"You can check your phone. I know you think I'll be insulted, but I won't."

"Nope. No need to. There's nothing more important than just enjoying the moment right now with you. Whatever it is, it can wait."

"You're stronger than I am. I would at least need to see who texted even if I didn't respond."

"I don't care who texted." I leaned in so that only she could hear what I was about to say. "All I care about is getting something to eat so I can go upstairs and eat *you*."

She turned red. My eyes stayed fixed on her neck. I was much too proud of the marks I'd left on it.

"What?" she asked.

"Nothing."

"You're looking at me funny."

"I am? I'm sorry. I don't mean to. I guess I can't help it."

"What are you thinking?" she asked. "Give me the honest answer."

"You really want to know?"

"Yes."

Resting my chin on my hand, I stared at her for a bit before I said, "There are a lot of thoughts running through my head. I'm looking at you and thinking that I can't believe I just fucked you—twice. I'm thinking that it felt better than I ever imagined and that I might be fucked if I think I can keep my hands off you for the rest of the week after today. And I'm already thinking about what I want to do to you when we get back to the hotel—namely discovering what your pussy tastes like. I'm enjoying every second of this day, and I feel like the luckiest man alive. I'm also wondering what's going through your head." I reached for her hand. "Your turn."

Amber's face turned an even brighter shade of crimson that trickled down in blotches over her pale neck. "I can't believe how good it felt. In fact, I still feel you in between my legs. I don't want this day to end. That's pretty much the extent of it. I won't allow my mind to go anywhere else because I don't want things to get complicated."

"Good. Just stay with me in the moment. This is what it's all about."

The waiter served us our steaks, and about halfway through dinner, I had to use the bathroom badly. I hadn't pissed since before we'd had sex.

"I'll be right back, okay?"

When I returned from the bathroom, I noticed that Amber's mood seemed a little off compared to before I left.

"What's up?"

"Your phone went off again. I peeked at it. I'm sorry."

"It's alright..."

"It was Emily. Are you mad?"

Shit. Talk about a mood killer.

"Am I mad that you looked at my phone? No, and after the shit I pulled on you with Gentleman Nine, it wouldn't be very fair of me to be mad, would it?"

"Anyway, she wants to know if you're around tonight."

"Well, I'm not, am I? I'm very busy, in fact."

Her lips curved into a slight smile, but I could tell Amber was still preoccupied with thoughts of Emily. I couldn't blame her. I hadn't exactly made it clear what I was doing about that whole situation. I'd sort of temporarily abandoned it. There was certainly not enough mental energy in me to explore that issue tonight. All I really wanted to do was to go back to the room with Amber and forget about anything else.

My dick could not be tamed. I looked down again at the marks I'd left on her neck and chest and suddenly felt the urge to leave and make a few more.

Enclosing her legs with mine under the table, I said, "You feel like taking the food back to the hotel? I'm suddenly starving for something other than steak."

CHAPTER FOURTEEN
AMBER

Channing said he would be working late Monday night, so it was the perfect opportunity to have Annabelle over for some girl time.

It didn't feel right divulging to her everything that Channing and I had done. Even though I shared things with my best friend pretty openly, he and I had agreed not to talk about our business with other people. While Annabelle knew the general gist of what was happening between Channing and me, I chose not to discuss any explicit details with her, and she respected my decision, for the most part. That didn't mean she didn't try to get info.

She poured some wine for each of us. "You sure you don't want to talk about Saturday?"

"I'm sure."

"Okay. But you're good? Everything went okay?" She walked over to me, handing me a glass.

"Yes. Everything was amazing. Too amazing. The only downside of the night was when his phone went off during dinner. He'd gone to the bathroom. I couldn't help flipping it over and taking a peek. It was Emily texting him.

Jealousy crept in. And feeling that way made me think that I've really been kidding myself that we can just stay friends."

"Okay, but you said you both agreed not to sleep with other people while this was going on, right? So, what are you worried about?"

"That doesn't mean he can't have feelings for someone else or even see her. It just means no sex. Anyway, I'm mad at myself for getting so worked up over it. That sort of defeats the purpose of the casual sex arrangement, doesn't it?"

"Well, that's the risk you take when you agree to something like this. I mean, he's your friend. You care about him. When you add physical intimacy into the mix, those feelings are going to get all jumbled. You're only human."

Swirling my wine around in the glass, I stared mindlessly at it. "I don't want to feel this way. I want to be able to enjoy the pleasure that being with him brings without letting in any of the complicated thoughts, but it's hard."

Annabelle took a sip of her wine and placed it down. "You'll figure it out. I don't envy you, though, and I do worry you're going to end up getting hurt. But I'm not going to tell you to stop, because I don't think I would be able to if I were you, either. You need this. I can only imagine that the sex is mind-blowing."

God, yes, it was. I hadn't been able to think of anything else.

"I'm pretty much going with it for the experience, knowing that I'll probably get hurt and taking the risk anyway."

"So much of what we do in life is like that."

The front door opened, startling us. Channing was home from work. He wasn't supposed to be back until much later. My heart started to pitter-patter. I wasn't ready for this.

Annabelle was beaming at the sight of him. It was the first opportunity she'd had to meet him in person.

"Hey," he said as he entered the living room. His eyes fell to the wine bottle and plate of cheese curls lying out on the coffee table.

"Channing, this is—"

"Annabelle." He nodded, offering her his hand and a wide smile. "I know who you are. Really nice to meet you."

"I guess my reputation precedes me?" Annabelle grinned. I could tell she was really impressed that he knew her name.

"Well, Amber's mentioned you several times. I know you're a good friend."

"It's amazing meeting you, as well. I've heard so much about you."

"I'm certain you have," Channing said as he took a seat on the couch. "Mind if I join in?"

I hesitated. "Um...sure."

He poured himself a glass of wine before lying his head back. "Fuck. Today was a long day. I'm so glad to be home."

"I thought you were supposed to be working late."

"My meeting was cancelled. I was psyched about that. I've wanted nothing all day but to get home, eat a nice meal, and chillax."

Kitty ran into the room and jumped onto Channing's lap. He gently rubbed her head as he sipped his cabernet.

Chills ran through me as I thought about those hands on me—in me—a couple of days ago. It was impossible to be around Channing anymore without having the phantom feelings of him touching me, of him inside of me. I felt him all over my body even when he wasn't around, but the feelings were even stronger when he was present. True to his word, ever since Saturday, he hadn't so much as brushed up against me. Being without his touch after an entire day of drowning in him was harder than I'd ever anticipated.

Annabelle couldn't take her eyes off him. She had the goofiest grin on her face. I wished I could've smacked it away.

He shocked the life out of me when he turned to her. "So, I'm assuming Amber told you we're fucking?"

The wine practically sprayed out of my nose. I grabbed a napkin.

Did he just say what I thought he said?

The room went silent. Annabelle looked like a deer in headlights. Then the goofy grin on her face returned in full force. The guilt was written all over her. She was making it very clear without saying anything that, of course, I'd told her.

She looked over at me. "Umm..."

He addressed her, "I mean, we can sit here and pretend like you don't know, but we all know that's not the case." He glanced over at me and said, "Look, I know Amber tells you everything. She's mentioned that to me before. So, I'm not stupid. When I first walked in, the two of you looked like scared mice. I'm certain you were talking about me, and that's perfectly fine. Amber needs a good girlfriend to confide in. I'm happy she has that in you."

Annabelle seemed to be blushing now. "Well, thank you. That's very nice of you to say."

"You're welcome." He kicked his feet up. "Amber tells me you have two kids?"

She looked over at me, seeming really impressed that Channing remembered that. "Yes. Jenna and Alex, eleven and seven."

"They must keep you busy."

"They do. But I love it. Between work and them, I don't have much time to unwind. Needless to say, I live vicariously through Amber's single life quite a bit. Tonight is a rare night out. My husband is manning the house."

He looked between us. "Have you ladies eaten?"

"No, actually. We were going to order takeout," I said.

"I was gonna cook something up for myself. How about I make it for all of us?"

Annabelle looked like he'd just offered her a new car. "That would be gr—"

"That's okay," I interrupted. "We can just do our own thing."

The two of them sitting down together made me nervous for some reason, and I was doing my best to avoid that scenario.

Channing looked a little disappointed. "I get it. I didn't mean to interrupt ladies' night."

"Nonsense," Annabelle said. "We would love to have dinner with you, Channing, and thank you for the offer. It's not every day I have a handsome man cooking dinner for me."

"Well, I don't know about handsome, but I can definitely cook my ass off."

She mouthed over to me, "Freaking adorable."

He is.

And there was no way I was getting out of this dinner now.

Channing ended up cooking us a meal of tapas that included smoked salmon, deep fried bacon-wrapped dates with goat cheese, and Sriracha meatballs.

After we ate, we lingered around the table.

"So, Amber tells me, you two have quite the history," Annabelle said.

"Yeah, Walnut and I go way back." He looked over at me and smiled. Chills ran through me because his every expression, every smile now had an underlying "fuck me" look to it.

"Tell me about young Amber."

Channing's smile widened as he thought about the answer. "Young Amber was awesome. She was like one of the boys, always down for anything, not preoccupied with girly shit, not obsessed with how she looked or anything like that. She was the voice of reason, but she could always somehow be swayed to the dark side. Not much has changed, really. Well, except she's a little more girly now." He winked at me. "But that's perfectly fine with me."

Annabelle's eyeballs were moving and back and forth as she observed us. She seemed to be getting off on his flirting with me.

I turned the topic of conversation back to our childhood. "We never did anything that bad in those days. We might have broken into a couple of abandoned houses, stuff like that. In the couple of years that we were inseparable, you can bet if I did do something bad, that Channing was probably behind it."

"That's true." He grinned. "Anyway, it was just my mother, sister, and me growing up. Amber was always at the house. She was like another family member."

Annabelle played with the last of her food and asked, "You didn't have a father around?"

Channing's expression darkened. "My father left us when we were small. He moved to Nevada and remarried. I'm not in touch with him."

"I'm sorry to hear that."

The only time I'd ever seen Channing's dad was at Lainey's funeral. He showed up with his new wife and didn't really talk to anyone. I knew right away who he was, because he looked just like an older version of his son. The situation with their father walking out on them always made me so sad for Channing and Lainey. But it made me downright angry to see him at her service when he hadn't been there for her otherwise.

"It's okay," Channing said. "I never knew what it was like to have him around after like the age of six, so there was never a huge feeling of loss. Emptiness, maybe, but I've gotten by just fine without him."

I wasn't sure that I believed he really felt that way.

I chimed in, feeling sad that he had to think about his father and wanting to change the subject. "I'm an only child, as you know. I had two happily married parents, the perfect upbringing. But I was bored a lot. I much preferred the chaos of Lainey and Channing's house."

"Anarchy." Channing chuckled. "And all the candy you could eat."

"That's true." I laughed.

I prayed that Annabelle didn't bring up Lainey's death. Thankfully, she seemed to remember me telling her that it was difficult for Channing to talk about.

We stayed talking at the table for about an hour. It made me really happy that Annabelle and Channing got along so well. He ended up calling an Uber for her and insisted on paying for it.

After she left, he and I were by ourselves in the kitchen cleaning up. For some reason, I had a hard time looking at him when we were alone. Without the buffer of another person, I was afraid he would be able to sense the want in my eyes, afraid it would make me look weak.

His voice was low—sexy—when he said, "You can look at me, you know."

My back was to him when I said, "I can't ever look at you the same again."

He inched a little closer so that I could feel his breath. "Well, I sure as fuck hope not."

Clearing my throat, I said, "I'm really happy that you and Annabelle got along so well."

"You weren't planning on bringing her around me, were you?"

I shrugged, unable to properly explain why I was hesitant for him to meet her. "Just so you know, I don't talk about the specifics of what we do or anything. Some things are nobody's business. She just knows in general that we agreed to...you know..." I hesitated.

"Fuck like animals on Saturdays..."

I could feel my face heating up. "Yes."

"I'm fine with whatever you tell her. Like I said, it's important to me that you have someone like her you can depend on and confide in. Clearly, I'm not that friend for you, since I can't be trusted not to fuck the friendship part up in the name of physical pleasure."

We were just staring at each other for a bit, and I was secretly wishing he would break the rules. I wasn't going to be the first to do it. My weakness was eye-opening, a clear indication that I was definitely not going to be able to quit him very easily. Not to mention, losing him altogether was becoming a greater fear by the day.

"I hope that no matter what happens that we'll always be friends, Channing."

"Me, too, Amber. I really mean that."

"We're breaking the rules even talking about this, huh?"

"I'll let it slide this one time." He winked and leaned in closer, the heat of his body palpable. "For the record, I can't wait until Saturday." He was so close yet so far away. My body was in complete agony.

I went to bed that night fully aroused. It was close to midnight, and I was unable to sleep, so I decided to grab a glass of water.

I could hear that Channing was talking to someone on the phone in his room.

Who was he talking to so late?

His voice was muffled, but I struggled to hear what he was saying.

"I've got just under two months left, then I'm back to Chicago for good. I know it feels like forever that I've been gone. But you won't have to wait much longer. I just need this time. Then, I'm yours, alright?"

Returning to my room, I couldn't help the unsettled feeling in my stomach. But I had to remind myself that this situation was temporary. I knew that. So, nothing he said in that phone conversation should have mattered.

I was really good at kidding myself.

CHAPTER FIFTEEN
CHANNING

It had only been a week, but it felt like years. As I sat alone in our hotel room thumbing through a brochure on local attractions, I couldn't wait for her to get here.

Having to look at her all week and not touch her was absolute hell. It had seriously been the longest week of my life. But I made that rule, and I was determined not to break it.

The knock finally came. When I opened the door, I had to stop myself from immediately mauling her as she entered.

She looked good enough to eat in an off the shoulder, flowery top. My mouth watered with the need to devour her neck. It wasn't until I looked up at her face again that I realized something was off.

"What's wrong, Amber?"

Her eyes were brimming with sadness. "I got my period."

Shit.

My balls were aching. The thought of not being able to satisfy the need that had been building all week was unbearable.

"Come here," I said, taking her into my arms and burying my nose in her hair. I then led her to the bed and pulled her close. "It's okay. Don't stress out." I kissed her on the forehead. "How are you feeling otherwise?"

"I'm good. It was a long week getting here."

"Tell me about it."

I couldn't help leaning in to taste her lips. She opened them eagerly to receive my kiss.

My erection was so hard it was painful. I was sure there were other sexual things we could do if she didn't want to have intercourse, but I wasn't going to pressure her into anything if she wasn't feeling well.

We lay in silence for a while until she surprised me when she asked, "Is everything okay back home in Chicago?"

My chest tightened. "Why do you ask?"

"Just wondering."

That was an odd question that seemed to come out of nowhere. There was a lot going on in Chicago, but it was the last thing I wanted to think about right now.

"Everything is fine."

I only wanted to think about her. About her lips that were swollen from my kiss. About her skin that was blushing from the way I was looking at her. About how badly I wanted to be inside of her. I honestly couldn't deal with anything else.

Unable to resist the need to touch her, I brushed my thumb along her collarbone. "Why do you have to look so beautiful right now?"

She sighed. "I don't feel beautiful."

"What can I do to make you feel better?"

"Just keep lying down with me. Let's talk for a little while."

Kissing her neck, I spoke into her skin, "I can do that."

She looked up at me. "Am I being too needy? I know this is just supposed to be sex."

"I like talking to you. *A lot.* I like doing a lot of things with you, as you know, but just talking is cool, too."

"How was work this week?" she asked.

"I'll be happy to be done with this contract. It's been stressful, but it's been worth it just to spend this time in Boston with you."

"I wish you didn't have to leave."

It pained me to hear her say that. "You think you'll ever move back to Illinois?"

"I don't know. I really love it here. And I couldn't imagine leaving the people I work with right now, especially Milo."

"That's true. That would be tough."

"My parents want me to move back. I miss them, but it's been liberating being away and living on my own. Of course, I'd never intended to be alone. I only came out here in the first place because of Rory's job."

"Whereabouts does he live exactly? I never asked."

"He's about thirty minutes from us in Reading. That's north of the city. When we broke up, he moved closer to his work up there. Before that, we lived together in Boston in a different apartment near Fenway Park. After the breakup, my father came out and bought the condo I live in now as an investment property."

"Your dad *owns* your place?"

"Yes. So, I'm paying the mortgage between my rent and then whatever I get from the Airbnb people."

"Wow. I had no clue."

"Do you think I'm a spoiled brat because Daddy owns it?"

"You work harder than anyone I know, so no, of course I don't. You've never taken advantage of your parents' money."

Amber never flaunted her wealth growing up. She started working the first chance she got and never spent money like crazy.

I'll never forget the first time I went to Amber's house back in Illinois. It was after Lainey died. She was always over at our place, so I'd never had a reason to go to hers. I remember at the time being unable to believe that she actually lived in what seemed like a mansion to me because she'd never given us any indication that she came from money.

"Well, I insisted on paying the entire mortgage. Renting out the room really helps with that. Otherwise, I wouldn't be able to afford it."

"Do you rent to only women?"

"There have been a couple of men."

That hadn't even occurred to me until now. I couldn't stand the idea of her living with strange men. Just the thought made my blood pressure rise. *Fuck*. This was going to worry me after I left.

"How do you vet people?"

"Background checks."

"You still don't really know that they're safe."

"Nothing in life is a hundred percent."

"I'm not gonna lie. That freaks me out a little."

"Then stay. You won't have to worry about it."

The smile she flashed was so freaking adorable.

"I wish I could, Amber. Believe me."

Her eyes seemed to be asking me why I couldn't. I desperately wanted to tell her, but I wasn't ready for the emotional toll that would take on me. Instead of thinking about it, I opted to bury my mouth in her neck.

I spoke into her skin, "I want you so fucking badly."

She let out a shaky breath. "I'd give anything to feel you inside of me right now."

Pulling back in surprise, I said, "You *want* to have sex? Then, what the fuck are we waiting for?"

"I didn't think *you'd*...want to. Because I have my period."

"Are you kidding me? I feel like I'm gonna burst, Amber. I was only holding back because I thought *you* didn't want to."

"No. I'm even more aroused on my period. I just thought it would gross you out."

"No fucking way could you ever gross me out." I sighed into her mouth as I kissed her. My dick moved to full mast, so excited to finally get some relief. "God, we really need to communicate better." I got up. "Let me grab a towel to put under you."

She was crazy if she thought there were any circumstances under which I wouldn't want her. Maybe if it were someone else, I would have had to think twice about this scenario. But with Amber, I just didn't care; I wanted her any way I could have her.

I'd never put on a condom so fast in my life. My knees barely hit the mattress before she pulled me down on top of her body.

My cock was throbbing as I entered her. Amber wrapped her legs around my back. It felt like the deepest I'd ever been inside of her. From that angle, it was really hard not to prematurely blow my load.

"I need to slow down."

She nodded, biting her bottom lip.

As I slowed my pace, we looked each other in the eyes while we fucked. The room was so quiet. There were no sounds other than the movement of our bodies and the occasional noise from the air conditioner. I'd never in my life looked a girl in the eyes during sex. With Amber, I wanted to capture every reaction, every emotion as she took me inside of her body. And then I wanted to burn those reactions into my brain, so I could think about them when we weren't together anymore. But it also hurt, because one of the things reflected in her eyes was trust. And I wasn't sure if I deserved it. I wanted to believe I did.

Fuck. What was happening to me?

As I picked up the pace, my hips moving in a circular motion, she dug harder and harder into my back. Then, she went and said something that nearly undid me.

"I want you to come on me. I want to feel it on my skin."

I nearly lost it, pulling out of her and removing the condom before jerking myself off all over her stomach. As I came, she brought herself to orgasm with her fingers.

After, I lowered my body down and kissed the hell out of her, not caring about the sticky aftermath on my abs.

Gently biting her neck, I said, "Remind me to thank Rory for breaking you in for me."

She smacked my ass. "Oh, you're bad."

After I cleaned up, we lay in the bed staring at each other. Sometimes what was unsaid could be so much louder than actual words. I knew we were both coming to the realization that we were kidding ourselves with this arrangement. But I wasn't willing to stop it. I *couldn't*.

She suddenly grabbed my face and kissed me long and hard, breaking only to say, "You're addictive."

"You're beautiful," I whispered into her mouth.

"You know..." she said. "I wasn't sure if I believed you really felt I was beautiful at first. But now, the way you look at me and how your body reacts to me, I know you truly feel that way, which just surprises me, given how much...experience...you have."

I struggled to find the right words to explain just how attracted to her I was. "There's no one like you. There's no one who smells like you, tastes like you. There's no one with the same wide eyes, the same perky nose, the same slight freckles, the same plump lips, the same curve of your ass, the same short but beautiful legs, the same toes I want to nibble on. I don't care how many women I've been with. There's only one *you*, and I can't get enough."

My words put a huge smile on her face. "Do you still see me the same as when I was sixteen? I know you said that before. Have things changed now that you've...gotten to know me better?"

"You mean now that I've owned every inch of your body?" I nuzzled her neck. "Everything's all jumbled now. I still see the old you. But I also see a grown, independent woman I'm really proud of. Every day I see more and more of her."

"Figuratively and literally." She giggled.

"Thank God for that."

Amber's smile faded as she seemed to be pondering something. "What if I see you in the future and can't get past this?"

"What do you mean?"

"I can't imagine ever being around you and not feeling what I'm feeling right now. There's gonna come a day when maybe you're married or I'm married. I don't know. No matter where we are in our lives, I can't imagine ever being in the same room with you and not remembering how this feels, not wanting this. My body will remember, even if I try to tell it not to. I can't fathom ever not wanting you like this."

Hearing her say that tore me up inside, because it was a harsh reminder of the reality of this situation that I'd gotten us into. Could I handle seeing Amber with another man? At this very moment, I knew in my heart the answer was no.

I tried to make light of her comment. "Well, then we'd just have to sneak away and become reacquainted."

She was searching my eyes. "Are you serious?"

"I'm just kidding—maybe." Moving a piece of her hair behind her ear, I said, "Anyway, you're thinking too much. You don't need to worry about that right now."

"I know. I can't help it. I'm sorry."

As much as I'd told her not to worry about it, I felt what she said in my bones. She was articulating exactly what I was feeling. I was just afraid to accept it.

In my heart, I knew our story wasn't going to have a simple ending.

CHAPTER SIXTEEN
AMBER

"This is a surprise. You don't normally call me at this time. Is everything okay?" he asked.

I was out with Milo when I decided to call Channing at work one afternoon.

"Do you think you could sneak out early to hang out with Milo and me? The weather is unseasonably warm, and I was thinking of taking him to walk around the city a bit. I could use the extra hand."

Of course, that was just an excuse. I'd missed Channing a lot this week and really just wanted to hang out with him. Milo really seemed to like him, so it was a win-win situation.

"What time were you thinking?" he asked.

"What time do you normally get off?"

"Get off? He snickered. "Saturdays."

"Funny guy." I rolled my eyes. "Can you leave work by five?"

"Yeah, that's not too early. I can swing it."

"Great. You can meet us at the New England Aquarium. I was going to take him there for about an hour before we meet you. You'll just take the train to Aquarium Station instead of your usual stop."

"Sounds good. I'll see you soon."

Standing in front of the massive ocean tank, I looked over at Milo. He was leaning his hands against the glass as his eyes followed the path of the fish floating by. A bluish green hue was glowing over his skin.

Distant applause coming from a dolphin show in another part of the building could be heard while swarms of children on a field trip lined the area behind us.

My phone buzzed.

Channing: Decided to skip out earlier. I'm at the aquarium. Where are you guys?

Amber: Not far from the entrance over by the giant fish tank.

A large swordfish swam past in the giant tank.

I pointed, "Milo, look at the sword on that one."

"I've heard that before," Channing joked as he snuck up behind me. Chills ran down my spine as the heat of his body resonated at my back.

"Hey." I smiled.

He rustled Milo's hair. "Hey, man." Milo proceeded to sniff attack Channing's head, grabbing it with both hands.

Channing laughed. "Oh, yeah. Get a good whiff. That's good."

Milo then wrapped his arm around Channing and returned his attention to the fish. They stayed like that watching the fish pass by. It was so stinking adorable.

I looked over at Channing and saw that instead of looking at the fish, he had been looking at me. His eyes were glowing in the fluorescent light. They were almost an exact match to the adjacent aquamarine water.

He smiled, and I smiled back. It was one of several moments of silent mutual admiration like that we'd shared this week.

Then, he did something that he'd never done before: he broke the rules. Channing reached for my hand. With my fingers interlocked with his, the warmest feeling came over me. After everything we'd done, you'd think that simple gesture wouldn't have affected me like it did. But there was something very intimate about it. And it shifted things for me. It shifted my expectations, and that was probably dangerous.

We'd had three hotel rendezvous thus far. The last time was the most intense. I'd let him do things to my body that Rory hadn't even tried. With each meeting, I was growing more and more attached, not only in body but in mind. The hopeful thoughts in my head needed to go take a hike.

Why couldn't he stay?

Why couldn't we be more than fuck buddies?

Milo suddenly jerked his body back before running down the concourse. He'd apparently had enough of the giant fish tank. Channing and I both started running.

Once we caught up to him, the three of us exited the building. The aquarium was located down by the Seaport, so it was extremely chilly near the ocean. The faint smell of fish lingered in the air. I hadn't dressed appropriately, so Channing bought me a pink hoodie that said *Boston* on it in navy lettering from one of the nearby vendors.

"Where do you want to go now?" Channing asked, his chestnut hair blowing in the wind.

"We should get dinner."

"There's this Italian place I heard about in the North End," he said.

"Italian place in the North End? You don't say." Seeing as though the North End was the Italian section of Boston, I was totally joking.

"Yes, wiseass." Channing was looking at me like he wanted to smack me hard on the ass. "It's called Fantano's. You heard of it?"

"No, but Milo loves Italian, and I'm down to try anything."

He lowered his voice. "I know you are. I figured that out last weekend."

I must have been blushing like an idiot as we began our evening stroll. It was a beautiful night, and since we weren't all that far from the North End, we decided to walk all the way to the restaurant.

On the way, lights flashed from a field in the distance and that was when I saw it: a massive Ferris wheel. Then, other rides came into my line of sight. There was a carnival in town.

A carnival.

Oh, no.

Since when were there carnivals in the middle of the city and in the colder months?

Milo started walking faster, pulling me in the direction of the action. Once he had his mind set on something, it was hard to convince him otherwise.

Channing trailed behind us as we made our way toward the carnival lights, but I was totally freaking out.

When we got to the entrance, I immediately noticed how pale Channing looked.

This was not good.

"Go home, Channing. I'll stay here with him."

He shook his head. "I can't leave you alone with him here. It's too chaotic."

"I'll be okay."

"No, I can't leave. It's too much for you. I'll be alright."

But it was clear he wasn't. It was written all over his face.

My heart was breaking.

We let Milo lead the way. He mostly just wanted to wander through the crowd.

The sound of screaming children, faint music, and the occasional ringing of bells from the game booths all blended together as I tried to keep my focus on where Milo was leading me.

He pointed to the Ferris wheel, so I paid for a small strip of tickets and stood in line with him while Channing waited for us.

The five-minute ride was excruciating because all I wanted was to be on the ground with Channing.

After we exited the Ferris wheel, I said, "Milo, let's go get something to eat, okay? We're all done with the carnival. All done."

By some miracle, he decided to listen to me. He let me lead him out of the fairgrounds to the exit.

Channing wouldn't look at me as we walked down the street. I knew it was because he didn't want me to see the sadness in his eyes.

When we got to the first intersection, he turned to me. "Will you be okay with him at dinner? I think I'm gonna head home after all, okay?"

I didn't have to ask him why. "Absolutely."

⌒

Illinois Sentinel
September 2, 2006

Investigators looking into a deadly accident at the Briar Park Fair last week say corrosion was the likely cause of damage to metal on the ride that broke, killing two and injuring several others. The Devil's Whip thrill ride had been approved for use just hours before the deadly accident.

Fourteen-year old Lainey Lord and fifteen-year-old Brandy Minor were killed when the car they were riding in detached and hit another car before plummeting to the ground. Five others on board were injured.

All rides at the fair were closed following the accident.

The ride's manufacturer, Oregon-based Kelton, Inc., has ordered all owners of similar rides to cease operations until the investigation into the Illinois accident is complete.

I couldn't get back to him fast enough.

Letting Channing go home alone after the carnival hadn't felt right, but I had to get Milo something to eat before getting him back. I ended up dropping him off earlier than usual.

Channing was sitting alone in the living room when I got home. The TV wasn't even on. He was just sitting in the quiet with a drink in hand. His head was resting back on the couch.

Letting my bag fall lazily to the floor, I made my way over to him. Ignoring our self-imposed rules, I placed my head on his shoulder. I could feel his pulse racing through his neck.

We sat in silence until he finally spoke. "Somehow I'd managed to avoid carnivals all these years. I've driven by a few but never went in. I thought that maybe because so much time had passed that I would be alright, but I really wasn't."

"You've buried so much of it inside of you for so long. It's hard to think about even without the trigger of being in that environment."

The night of Lainey's accident, Channing had driven her and her friend, Brandy, to the fairgrounds. I had been invited to go along but declined because it was my dad's birthday, and we'd planned to take him out to dinner that night. I always felt guilty about that, because maybe if I were there, the course of the evening would have changed somehow. Maybe she wouldn't have been on that ride at the time.

Channing stayed at the fairgrounds and was there when the accident took place. I never knew the extent of what he'd seen because he would never talk about it. But I always suspected he saw it happen.

Right now, he looked so pained. I wondered if he'd ever talked about that night in any detail with anyone or if he'd simply kept it inside all of these years. The few times I'd tried to get him to open up to me about it, he never would.

He finally spoke. "I was terrified every second you were on that Ferris wheel tonight. Crazy, huh?"

"No, it's not." I put my arm around him, not giving a fuck about the rules at that moment. "I know you've never wanted to talk about it. But maybe you should."

His eyes shut tightly as he rested his head on my chest. "I can't."

A tear fell down my cheek. "Okay," I whispered.

He looked up at me. "Was Milo okay the rest of the time you were out?"

"Yeah. It was uneventful. Have you even eaten?"

Shaking his head, he said. "I'm not hungry. I think I'm gonna just head to bed." It wasn't like Channing to not have an appetite.

"Are you sure?"

"Yeah." He leaned in, gently kissing me on the forehead before retreating to his room.

⌒

I couldn't sleep that night, haunted by thoughts of Lainey and of Channing's post-traumatic stress.

Around 2AM, the creak of my door startled me. Channing appeared in my doorway like a shirtless shadow.

Without seeking permission, he slipped into my bed and cradled my body in his.

Closing my eyes, I relished the feel of his warm skin against mine.

His voice came as a surprise. "I saw the whole thing happen, Amber. Everything."

My heart clenched. I turned around to face him in the darkness and placed my hand on his cheek.

He went on, "I'm not sure why I'd been looking up at the time. I wasn't even supposed to be there. I was supposed to just drop them off at the fairgrounds and leave. But then I ran into some people from school and ended up staying. I saw Lainey and Brandy get on the ride. For some reason, I just kept my eyes on it when it started moving."

He paused and let out a long breath.

Running my fingers through his hair, I whispered, "It's okay." I could feel a teardrop fall from his eye onto my hand.

"When the car went airborne...at first, I didn't know whether it was theirs. Everything happened so fast. The world just felt like it stopped. To be honest, I don't remember a lot very clearly after that. I somehow made my way over to the ride, but people were pushing me back. I kept saying, 'My sister's on that ride. My sister.'" His voice trembled. "My sister."

My tears were blinding me.

"Eventually, they started letting people off, and every time someone other than her would come out, my heart would stop. By the time I figured out that it was her car that fell from the sky, they'd cordoned off the area. They wouldn't let me through. I was kicking and screaming, punching at people. I don't remember much after that. Everything is a blur." His breathing became more rapid as he recalled the rest. "Someone called my mother. Mom showed up. Then, someone drove us both to the morgue to identify Lainey. My mother was the one who had to do it. I didn't go in. It was just...a nightmare." It was barely audible when he said, "My sweet sister. She *was* my family. Everything."

My heart was breaking. "I know. I felt that way about her, too. She was my very best friend. As an only child, I didn't have a sister. She was the closest thing I had to one."

"I can't even explain what having you around back then meant to me, Amber. It was such a dark and surreal time, but you being there made it tolerable somehow. It felt less empty. Besides my mother, you were the one person who could relate to how I was feeling. And the thing is, I didn't even have to explain myself to you, because you just *knew*. We both knew what we'd lost."

"That's true." I sniffled.

Channing held me tightly. "I need to tell you something."

My stomach dropped. "Something is going on back home, isn't it?"

His body stiffened. "Yes. But what made you ask that?"

"I heard you on the phone one night. You were talking to someone, and it sounded serious. You were assuring the person that you'd be back soon. I didn't pry, but I've really wanted to."

He nodded in understanding. "That was my mother's boyfriend. He's been working overtime while I'm here."

"Why?"

"Mom was diagnosed with dementia about six months ago."

My heart sank. "Oh, my God."

"Yeah...and it's bad. The diagnosis has been a long time coming. We would notice she would forget little things here and there. She'd call me and forget that we'd just spoken, stuff like that. But it's gotten progressively worse, and the truth is, I feel like my life is about to get a whole lot more complicated soon. I also don't think her boyfriend, Fred, is going to be around much longer. It sounds really awful, but I wanted to get away for a bit while I could, while he's still there to look after her. This opportunity came up and I took it."

"So, wait a minute. You requested the contract job?"

"I had my choice of a few different off-site projects. I didn't have to take them. Honestly, I picked Boston because you're here."

"Wow. I had no clue."

"I wasn't planning on admitting that to you, that I specifically chose Boston. But the truth is, absolutely nothing has played out here the way I planned. And it's kind of scaring the shit out of me." Channing nestled his head into the crook of my neck.

We didn't have sex that night; we just held each other.

My eyes slowly closed as I fell asleep to the sound of his breathing with a plethora of thoughts swirling around in my head.

CHAPTER SEVENTEEN
CHANNING

It was Friday night, marking the end of one of the most mentally grueling weeks I'd ever experienced.

Even though I should have felt better after admitting the situation with my mother to Amber, it was now at the forefront of my mind again and stressing me out.

Before the other night, I'd done a good job of living in denial about the whole thing. Fred would give me daily updates, but for some reason, now I was thinking about my mother constantly.

All I wanted was to come home tonight and spend the evening with Amber. That was the other problem. Now that time was running out, I was starting to doubt whether I was going to be able to handle leaving her.

I'd tried to convince myself that our arrangement was temporary and that once I went back to Chicago, our lives would just go back to the way they were before I came to Boston. But as I walked in from work and found my body aching upon the sight of Amber's smile, I knew better.

"How was your day?" she asked.

"Better now."

In that moment, there were no consequences. All I wanted was to kiss her. I broke my own damn rules when I cupped her face and brought her mouth to mine.

She spoke over my lips, "What about the rules?"

"Fuck them. I made them. I can abolish them." Kissing down her neck, I groaned, "I've thought about you all damn day, Amber. I'm fucking starving."

"Oh, God. Me, too. I couldn't wait for you to come home."

"I want to fuck you hard right now."

Bending her head back to welcome my mouth on her neck, she begged, "Please."

Fuck if I knew how to stop this from happening against my better judgment. Amber was my kryptonite.

She squealed in surprise as I lifted her up and carried her to the bedroom. Can't say I'd ever carried a girl before. It made me feel kind of like a barbarian. She was light as a feather in my arms as I carefully laid her down on the bed.

Ripping open the condom as fast as I could, I felt my body shaking from the urge to be inside of her.

Hovering over her, I took a few moments to stare at her face. The need in her glassy eyes was the best foreplay as far as I was concerned. And then watching her eyes roll back when I finally sank into her body was just about the most amazing fucking thing I'd ever witnessed.

Her tight pussy felt incredible as she took me in. I didn't want to hurt her, but there was no way I could go easy tonight.

As if Amber could sense my apprehension, she whispered, "It's okay. I can take it."

That was all the assurance I needed to move freely at the pace I wanted. She screamed out in pleasure as I rammed into her. She bucked her hips, gripping my ass to push me in even deeper. The headboard was banging against the wall.

"I'll never forget how this feels, Channing."

"You'd better not," I growled.

She was sucking and biting my bottom lip as I continued to pound into her.

This...this was the best sex I'd ever had in my life. It felt different from any other experience: wetter, tighter, more intense.

As I thrust into her while I came, she writhed under me and trembled. The sounds of our mutual pleasure echoed throughout the room.

Collapsing down onto her, I thought about how fast I could make dinner so we could come back for round two. My rules were officially out the window.

When we finally came down from our high, I asked, "Are you okay? I was going a little hard on you."

"That was the most intense orgasm I've ever had," she admitted.

"It's funny you say that...because I was just thinking that it was the single best sex of my life, too."

I carefully pulled out of her. While disposing of the condom, I felt my heart stop. The rubber didn't look right; in fact, my entire dick was sticking out of it—bare. My cum wasn't inside of the condom; it was inside of Amber.

I froze.

This had never happened to me before, and I'd had a lot of opportunities. Never—not once—had a condom broken on me.

Amber noticed that I hadn't moved from my spot by the wastebasket. "Is everything okay?"

Staring blankly at the wastebasket, I answered, "No."

"Channing..."

Just say it.

"The condom broke."

"What?"

"There's no rubber around my dick. It broke. I'm sorry."

She hopped up out of bed as fast as a bolt of lightning and ran to the bathroom before closing the door.

I spoke through the barrier, "I'm assuming you're not on the pill."

"No...I got off of it some time ago because I had a really bad reaction to it."

"Shit. Okay."

Think.

Think.

Think.

Pray.

Think.

No wonder it had felt so good; I was fucking her raw and didn't even know it. Not knowing what to do, I stayed by the bathroom door until she opened it.

Wrapping my hands around her face, I asked, "Are you alright?"

"I hope so."

"I'm really sorry that happened. This is the first time that's ever happened to me."

Amber just kept nodding. "We'll be okay. The chances are..." She looked up, seeming to be struggling with what to say. There was simply no way to know yet if we were in trouble.

I was doing the math in my head. It had been a couple of weeks since Amber had her period. "Do you know when you're...fertile?"

She grabbed her phone and seemed to be calculating something.

"It says there's a window, and today is smack dab in the middle of the ovulation period."

Fuck.

You've got to be kidding me.

She sighed. "It says I have to wait seven to ten days after ovulation to take an accurate test."

Not knowing what else to say, I pulled her into me. "It'll be okay."

I'd be praying to God that I was right.

CHAPTER EIGHTEEN
AMBER

Annabelle was listening to my pregnancy fear woes as I walked and talked on my way home from work. So preoccupied, I'd nearly slammed into three different people.

"Are you sure you can't just take the test now?" Annabelle asked.

"I'm positive. It's too early, and I don't want to have to go through it twice."

"Okay. It's probably fine. It was just one time. Try not to worry about it unless you have to."

"Easier said than done, but okay."

As I approached my building, I stopped dead in my tracks upon the sight of a woman who was sitting on the steps, looking like she was waiting for someone.

"Annabelle, I'll call you back," I said before hanging up the phone.

This wasn't just any woman. It was Christine Lord, Channing's mother.

What was she doing in Boston, and was she even fit to be here?

My heart was beating like crazy as I just observed her for a while. She was looking around and hadn't noticed me yet.

Where's her boyfriend?

Forcing my feet forward, I finally got her attention. "Christine?"

She stood up suddenly. "Amber?"

Still utterly confused, I embraced her.

"Are you waiting for Channing? He didn't mention you were coming."

"He's going to be so mad that I'm here."

My eyes widened. "He doesn't know you're here?"

"No. He wouldn't let me come if I asked him first."

"What made you come to Boston?"

Her eyes welled up. "Fred left me. He said he couldn't handle things the way they are anymore. I didn't know where else to turn. So, I booked a flight. I didn't want to be alone. At the airport, I just gave the cabbie your street number that Channing had written down before he left and here I am."

Swallowing my worry, I tried to remain cheerful for her sake as I waved my hand toward the door. "Well, let's get you inside. It's cold. Come. Please."

My nerves were rattled. Channing was not going to be happy about this.

I made Christine some hot tea, and we sat for a while, catching up. She asked me not to call Channing at work. She didn't want him to feel like he had to come home. I was happy and relieved to see that from what I was observing, she didn't seem like she was losing her mind. That gave me hope that maybe things weren't as bad as I'd imagined them to be.

I filled her in on my teaching assistant job, on working with Milo, and she was asking me how my parents were. Things seemed pretty normal. It was actually really good to see her; she reminded me of my childhood.

Later, Christine followed me into the kitchen, looked me in the eyes and asked, "What is it that you do?"

"Huh?"

"For work?"

I froze. An hour ago, we'd spent several minutes talking about my job. It was then that I saw firsthand what Channing had been referring to.

My heart broke as I began to explain to her what I did for a living as if it were the first time. She enthusiastically listened as I told her the same story all over again.

As we remained in the kitchen, I heard the front door open and braced myself for Channing's reaction to seeing his mother standing there. I could hear him talking to Kitty.

When he walked in, his eyes practically bugged out of his head. "Mom? What are you doing here?"

"Surprise?" She smiled awkwardly.

"Yes, it is, and not a good one. You shouldn't be here. Where's Fred?"

"Fred broke up with me."

Channing's ears were turning red. "He what?" A vein popped out in his neck.

"He left me. He said he couldn't handle things at home anymore. He sent your Aunt Laura over to stay with me for a few days. She left to go food shopping, and I snuck away, headed to the airport." She shrugged. "And here I am."

He looked irate. "How could Fred have not told me he walked out on you? I would've come home right away."

"He said he was going to call you."

"Well, he sure as fuck didn't." Channing rushed away.

I began to follow him. "Where are you going?"

"I'm calling Fred to rip him a new asshole." He looked back at me. "Just go stay with my mother, please? Make sure she doesn't come in while I'm talking to him."

"Sure."

Ten minutes later, he returned to the kitchen. His ears were still red, and he did not look happy.

"What did he say?" I asked.

"Apparently, he sent me this long, rambling email that never got to me because he misspelled my fucking email address. He just forwarded it to me. I don't even care what he has to say. The end result is the same."

Channing walked over to Christine and pulled her into a hug, which warmed my heart and made me incredibly sad at the same time.

"Are you okay, Mom? I'm sorry I didn't ask that first."

"Not really. But I'm better now that I'm here."

He looked her up and down. "You look like you could use a bath."

"I could." She laughed.

"Let me go draw you one."

Channing got Christine set up in the bathroom. I gave him one of my Lush bath bombs for her. Once she was soaking in the tub with a magazine, he came back out to the living room.

Running his hand through his hair, he looked at me and said, "This is bad, Amber. This is really bad."

"You didn't see this coming so soon? Him leaving her?"

"I saw it coming. I was just hopeful that he'd stick around a little longer. And my aunt isn't going to be able to stay there beyond tomorrow. I just got off the phone with her. She just told me she has to have surgery in two days. She lives two hours away. I have to figure something out."

"Can she stay alone during the day?"

"She has been. Fred worked, so yeah. But he was always home by four, and sometimes he worked from home. The neighbor would look in on her from time to time, too." He grabbed my hand and our fingers intertwined. His voice was shaky. "I really don't want to leave, but I'm afraid I'm gonna have to."

Panic set in. I wasn't ready for him to go. And in my mind, there really wasn't a reason that he had to. The wheels in my head were turning.

I didn't even have to think twice when I asked, "Why can't she stay here with us? Your contract isn't for much longer."

"I can't burden you like that, Amber."

"The only burden would be on you. She'd get your bedroom. There would be no burden on me."

He shook his head. "It would be too much."

"On whom? Not on me." I squeezed his hand. "Besides, I really don't want you to leave."

His voice was hoarse. "I don't want to leave, either."

"It's settled, then. Stay. I get home early enough to keep an eye on her in the later afternoon. I can change my hours with Milo to have them start later for a while. Then, there'll be no gap between the time each of us gets home."

Hope filled his eyes. "Are you sure about this?"

"It's just a matter of weeks. Of course, I am."

Channing pulled me into the hardest kiss. It felt like my lips were going to fall off.

"You're amazing. I can't thank you enough for this."

"It will be okay. You'll figure out a situation that works long term, too. Somehow, it will all work out."

We sat quietly for a bit as I lay my head on his chest, feeling like I'd averted one small battle only to have to face another when his contract inevitably ended. This was definitely bittersweet.

He gently caressed my hair. "How are you feeling?"

"I'm fine."

He looked hesitant to ask, "Are you still concerned about...you know..."

The past few hours were actually the first time I hadn't dwelled on my pregnancy fears.

"I'm trying not to think about it until I can take the test."

"Good thinking. I'm so sorry that happened."

"It's okay. It's not your fault. It will be fine. I know it."

"Yeah." He smiled, although he looked nervous.

Christine emerged from the bathroom dressed in my robe. It was the first time I realized she didn't have a bag with her. She hadn't brought any clothing.

"Mom, what do you think about staying here a few weeks until my contract is up? I really can't leave my job yet. I'd like to stay and finish up my responsibilities. You can stay in my room."

"Where will you sleep?"

"The couch. It's fine."

She turned to me. "Are you sure, Amber?"

"I would love to have you. Honestly, I get lonely without people around."

"Me, too. It's why I had to come here," she said.

"I totally get it, Christine."

After Channing whipped up dinner for the three of us, his mother said, "You know, Channing's father used to love to cook bizarre foods. He used to do it to entertain the kids when they were younger. 'Guess what Daddy's making.' It was sort of a game. Of course, there wasn't much time with him before he left us. But I think that's where Channing gets it from."

He didn't respond, but I could tell by the look on his face that he was surprised and upset by the discovery of that correlation. That definitely broke my heart. Whether he realized it or not, in some odd way, maybe he was trying to connect with his father or the memory of him through food. The more time I spent with Channing, the more complex I realized he was.

Christine suddenly stood up from the table. "Channing, can you show me to my room?"

"Yeah, Mom. Of course."

I cleaned up the kitchen while Channing got his mother situated in his bedroom.

The feel of his arms around my waist from behind prompted me to stop drying a dish. He kissed my neck. When I flipped around to face him, the worry in his eyes was palpable.

"She kept asking me questions about what happened with Fred, like she wasn't sure. She's confused. And I'm scared shitless."

I wasn't sure whether to admit my own experience with her but ultimately decided to tell him.

"Earlier, she asked me what I did for a living after we'd been talking about it for a while prior to that. So, I really got to see firsthand what you were talking about."

"Yeah. That's exactly the kind of thing that happens. All of the time." He closed his eyes momentarily and buried his hands in his hair. "The worst is when she realizes how confused she is, and she just looks at me and tells me she's scared. There's honestly nothing worse than that. Nothing, Amber. I almost wish she didn't realize it."

"I wish I could do something to help."

"You already are...just by being here for me."

Really wanting to sleep with him tonight, I said, "I feel kind of weird making you sleep on the couch."

"It's fine."

"Would you want to sleep with me in my bed?"

A smile slowly spread across his face. He arched his brow. "Do you even have to ask?"

"Well, I wasn't sure if we were still playing by the rules."

"My mother is living with us, and there's a small chance you could be pregnant with my child. I'd say the rules went out the window a long time ago."

Maybe that should have made me want to cry, but I couldn't help but laugh.

He followed close behind me as we made our way to my bedroom.

In bed later that night, he spoke against my back. "Can I tell you a secret?"

"Yeah?"

Channing pulled me closer. "The thought that you could be pregnant with my baby turns me on."

"Really?"

"Don't get me wrong...I know it would be a nightmare for us right now, but...the idea that I could've knocked you up definitely makes me a little crazy...in a good way."

"What would we do, though, honestly...if I was?"

"We'd figure it out."

"You wouldn't be upset?"

"Upset is not the right word. Scared, yeah. But upset? No. Maybe because it's you." He paused then squeezed me from behind. "You make me happy, Amber."

His words left me speechless. The idea that he would actually accept the possibility of my being pregnant with his child was not something that I'd considered.

Turning around and touching my forehead to his, I said, "You make me happy, too."

I truly was—for the first time in a long time.

CHAPTER NINETEEN
RORY

B oris stocked his shelves ever so slowly while I sat with my feet kicked up on a chair. His hand trembled as he placed a can of Campbell's Cream of Mushroom soup inside the grainy wooden cabinet of his dated kitchen. With a porcelain sink, Formica countertops, and linoleum floors, Boris's kitchen had a 1950's vibe going on. I felt like I was in a time warp.

I'd go food shopping for my elderly neighbor once a week after work. He'd pay me back by pouring me the best glass of Cognac. And I'd get fucked-up. Best part of the week if you asked me.

"One of these nights, Rory, you're gonna get drunk as a skunk and finally tell me what happened."

I let out a single laugh. "I know not what you speak of, Boris."

"Did she die?"

"Who?" I pretended to not know whom he was referring to.

"The pretty girl in the photo on your phone. The one with the smile that lights up her whole face. The one I've never seen around here because she's either dead or long gone."

I never had the heart to change the screensaver of Amber on my phone. It was my favorite picture of her. She'd been sitting in a pile of dried leaves and laughing. It literally made my heart hurt to look at it, but at the same time I just couldn't get rid of it.

Although I'd never pointed out the photo to Boris specifically, he'd apparently noticed it.

I'd danced around opening up to the old man for a long time now. But tonight was different. Tonight was Amber's and my anniversary. Well, what *would have been* our anniversary—the first one since the break-up. We always used to make a big deal about our anniversaries. This one was supposed to be epic, because I'd planned to propose to her tonight.

I just didn't feel like I could hold it in anymore. I needed to tell someone what had happened. Boris was safe. Who the fuck was he gonna tell my story to? The mailman? Boris didn't leave the freaking house.

Fuck it.

"Her name is Amber." I could hardly believe those words had exited my mouth. Just saying her name was painful.

"Amber! Amber. I like it." He lifted his glass. "Like the color of this here magic juice."

"Damn straight. Amber...just like the Cognac."

He sat down. "Tell me about her."

Where to begin.

Where to begin.

"Well, I'm pretty sure I've loved her for as long as I've known her. But we were together for over nine years."

"Nine years. Wow."

"Yeah. And she loved me with every ounce of her soul."

"Why did she leave?"

"She didn't."

"She died?"

"No. I broke up with her...broke her heart...shattered it."

"You...broke up with her? Why would you do that?"

"Because I love her more than anything in the world."

"I may need more alcohol because this isn't making any sense, son."

"Trust me, we definitely need more alcohol if I'm gonna tell you the rest of this."

Boris poured me more Cognac. "Okay, so tell me why a guy who's hopelessly in love with a girl breaks her heart. How does that happen?"

Drinking down the entire glass of liquor, I smacked it down on the table.

Closing my eyes tightly, I spit it out. "I was driving home from work one night, and a truck hit me head on. I'm really lucky to be alive."

"You get amnesia or something?"

"No. But to be honest, that would have been easier." My heart clenched. "A lot easier."

"What happened?"

"In the weeks after the accident, I learned that..." I hadn't realized how hard it was going to be to get this part out. Only my brother knew, and that was only because he'd threatened to kick my ass for hurting Amber. She'd become like a sister to him. I had to tell him so that he could understand my decision. He hadn't even been speaking to me for a while before he found out the truth.

Boris encouraged me to continue on. "What is it, son?"

"My injuries were such that..." I hesitated. "Basically, I can't have children."

He stared off into space to process what I'd just told him. Then, he said, "What do you mean...like you have no balls?"

I broke out into laughter. "No, I have everything. And it's all working just fine otherwise. But there was damage, and that means I don't make sperm anymore."

"You know that for sure?"

"I had my semen tested."

"You never told her?"

"No. Amber wants kids someday—more than anything. But regardless, I knew she'd never leave me if she knew. So, I had to make a really tough decision. I thought it would be best for her if I broke up with her. It was the hardest thing I've ever had to do."

Boris shook his head in disbelief. "You made a decision for her, that you assumed was the right one."

"That's right. I didn't want her to resent me later in life if she couldn't have a child of her own."

"So, you pretended to what...not love her anymore?"

This was always the part that got me the most emotional. I could almost stand the thought of being without Amber as long as she knew I loved her. But, of course, I made her think I'd fallen out of love with her, because that was the only way she'd let me leave.

"I thought that time would somehow make it—not even easier—but tolerable. But it hasn't. It took a while to get her to stop calling me. Do you know how hard it is to push someone away who you love more than life? I've created this façade to make her think I've moved on. And I think it's finally worked. She stopped trying to change my mind."

"And now you regret it?"

"I love her more than ever." I didn't wait for Boris to pour me more liquor this time. Grabbing the bottle, I helped myself and said, "Today would have been our anniversary, and it was also the day I was planning to ask her to marry me. I can't help but think of her. I suspect she could have met someone by now. But I just don't know because I can't bear to try to find out. She unfriended me on Facebook, too, which was for the best."

"What's Facebook?"

Stopping mid-sip, I said, "You're kidding, right?"

"No."

I couldn't help but laugh. "Yeah, I definitely don't have to worry about you spilling my business."

"Let me ask you something. If you found out today that Amber only had days to live, would you go to her?"

"Of course, I would."

"Days are all we have, Rory. That's all life is...a bunch of days threaded together. All we can be guaranteed is today. No one knows what's going to happen beyond today. We should never make decisions based on an assumed future, but rather on how we feel at this very moment. That's the first thing. The second is, how the hell can you be so sure that she'd rather have a baby over you? Did you even give her a choice? You were the love of her life for nine years. You didn't give her a say in the matter." He leaned in. "Let me tell you something you may not know."

"Alright..."

"My Ellie was barren. Stephanie is adopted. We were in our forties when we got her after years of trying."

"No shit? I had no idea. She even looks like you."

Boris had been married for fifty-seven years when his wife Ellie passed away. Since they had a daughter, I never imagined that Ellie couldn't have kids.

He continued, "I knew about Ellie before I married her. Of course, I wanted to have our own kids, but if it were a matter of losing her or having a biological child, there was no contest. If she'd done to me what you did to Amber, in my mind, that would have been a tragedy. I have no regrets. I have a beautiful daughter."

Maybe it was the alcohol, but suddenly I was doubting everything. Had I made a colossal mistake?

That night, I tossed and turned, obsessing over Boris's advice. My life felt like it hadn't progressed in the months since Amber and I had been apart. I wasn't as strong as I thought I'd be.

Opening the top drawer to my bureau, I took out the one-and-a-half carat Tiffany diamond ring I'd purchased a month before the accident. I'd planned to propose to Amber tonight at the restaurant at the top of the Prudential building. It was going to be perfect. Our lives were going to be perfect. Then the accident happened, and that perfect dream was shattered.

When you love someone, you feel it in your soul, even when they're not physically with you. Maybe it was also possible to feel the moment that you were losing them. If that were true, it was happening to me right now. I felt something strange inside of me tonight, a feeling of loss that I hadn't really felt up until now. I mean, of course, I'd left her, but I hadn't felt like I'd *lost* her until now. It was a feeling of looming finality that I needed to intercept now or never.

It was too late to call her. Amber typically didn't stay up past eleven. It was well past midnight. Still, I didn't feel like this could wait until tomorrow. I had to get my thoughts out now. So, I decided to text her.

What felt like a million words were at the tip of my tongue, but my finger wouldn't move. It just hovered over the keypad.

Ultimately, what I needed to say couldn't fully be communicated in a text.

I typed out a simple message.

Rory: I really need to see you.

CHAPTER TWENTY
CHANNING

Amber's and my mother's laughter could be heard from down the hall. I was catching up on some work in the bedroom but would stop from time to time to listen to their sounds.

Overall, Mom was not doing well. She even called Amber "Lainey" the other day. But as much as the dementia was showing its ugly face, my mother seemed happy here. Amber would do her hair, and they'd bake together. In fact, I must have put on at least a pound this week alone from all of the cookies and brownies. Every night, it was something different.

In a short amount of time, it was starting to feel like we were a family. I hadn't felt that in years.

Closing my laptop, I decided to shut down for the evening and join them in the kitchen.

A tray of some kind of delicious, coconut-covered dessert was cooling on the stove.

Rubbing my stomach, I said, "You two and your sweets are gonna be the end of me."

"Your mother was reminding me about the stage you went through where you refused to wear anything but Ed Hardy clothes." Amber cackled.

That was a blast from the past.

"That was hot," I joked, looking over at my mother. "I can't believe you brought that up."

For someone who was losing her memory, she had to go and remember that shit? But that was the thing...being here with Amber seemed to bring old memories out of my mother's mind bank even when she couldn't always remember what happened a half-hour ago.

Amber slipped away to the bathroom.

When she came back out, I could tell that something was up.

She whispered in my ear, "I just peed on the stick. I have to wait five minutes."

I froze. "I didn't know that was going to be tonight."

"Yeah, well, it's time. It should be accurate now. At least, we'll know...you know?"

I knew the time was coming soon but wasn't expecting it tonight. Deciding not to pressure her, I hadn't been asking when she was going to do the test. So, apparently it was suddenly D-day.

My heart started to pound furiously. It felt like the longest five minutes of my life. The sound of Amber and my mother talking became muffled as I thought about the life-changing impact a positive result would have. Visions of an auburn-haired little girl in pigtails flashed through my mind. The more the situation with my mother deteriorated, the more I was realizing the importance of family. Was I ready for a child now? No. But for the first time in my life, I felt absolutely certain that I wanted a family of my own. And each day it was becoming clearer that it was Amber I wanted that future with.

The kitchen timer Amber had set dinged.

Our eyes met. I took a good long look at her, knowing that things might never be the same again.

Amber turned to my mother. "Christine, would you mind cutting the magic bars? I think they're cool enough now."

"Of course."

Amber ventured down the hall, and I followed a few seconds after.

She was leaning against the sink waiting for me. "Well, here goes nothing."

Just as she reached for the stick, I placed my hand on her arm to stop her. "Wait."

"You don't want me to check?"

"I have to tell you something first."

"Can it wait?"

"No."

"Alright."

"If it turns out that this is positive, I just want you to know that I think it would be a gift from God. It's not the right time for us, maybe, but it will be a gift nevertheless. And no matter what happens, we're gonna be okay, alright?"

She blew out a nervous breath. "Okay."

"Check it."

Amber looked down at the stick then immediately up at me. "It's negative."

My true feelings became apparent to me in that very moment. Because instead of breathing out a sigh of relief and rejoicing over the fact that Amber wasn't pregnant, I felt an emptiness in the pit of my stomach. It was the first time I realized that I might have been secretly *hoping* she was pregnant. That was pretty eye-opening.

My dick immediately stirred with a primal need to rectify this situation as I wrapped my arms around her and kissed her head.

"Are you okay?" I asked.

She nodded against my chest. "I am. This is good news."

"Yeah, I suppose it is. It wasn't the right time."

She pulled back and placed her hands over my cheeks. "We would've had a beautiful baby with you as the father, though."

"Only if she looked like you."

Amber brightened. "She?"

"Yeah." I smiled. "I might have imagined a little girl who looked like you once or twice over the past couple of weeks."

"That's sweet." Her eyes widened. "You know what I'm excited about?"

"What?"

"Getting to have a glass of wine tonight. I hadn't been drinking just in case."

I placed a firm kiss on her lips then nudged my head. "Come on. I'll open a new bottle for us."

We returned to the kitchen to find an unsettling discovery. My mother was sitting at the table with the entire tray of magic bars in front of her. She hadn't cut them but rather had eaten three-quarters of the batch. Under any other circumstances, this might have even been funny.

But given her situation, it wasn't. It was sad. This was the kind of unpredictable behavior I'd become accustomed to.

I felt ashamed. "I'm so sorry."

Amber rubbed my shoulder. "It's okay."

"Really fucking need that wine right now," I said, making my way over to the bottle of red on the counter.

After dinner, Mom turned in early—probably crashed because of all the sugar she'd consumed.

Amber and I stayed up late watching movies. I was incredibly horny, but it had been a long and emotional day, and I suspected she might not have been in the mood.

Her phone, which was in the bedroom, chimed. It was unusual that she would get a text so late at night.

She got up to check it and seemed to take a long time before finally returning to her spot next to me on the couch.

"Everything okay?"

A flush crept up her face. "Yeah. Yeah, everything's fine."

She didn't look fine, but I blew it off, chalking it up to a grueling day.

CHAPTER TWENTY-ONE
AMBER

I'd hung onto Rory's text for two days before I finally responded. He wanted to meet me somewhere to talk, but I didn't feel like I could handle it.

After everything...what could he possibly have to say?

I responded that I would think about a time and place, but that was only to delay what turned out to be inevitable. That lesson was learned the hard way as my doorbell rang one early evening after work.

Channing wasn't home yet, and Christine was in her room watching television when I went to the door.

When I opened, Rory was standing there, and he'd brought our golden retriever, Bruiser. Before I acknowledged him, I bent down to let Bruiser lick my face. Tears started to fall from my eyes from the guilt I'd felt over having abandoned my dog. Seeing Bruiser hadn't been an option without having to see Rory, too. So, it had been several months since I'd smelled his fur and experienced his unconditional love.

"Bruisey...I missed you so much. So much."

Bruiser suddenly started to bark like crazy when he caught a glimpse of Kitty, who had planted herself high atop a shelf. Poor little thing was probably scared shitless at the sight of what may have been the first dog she'd ever seen.

I finally looked up at Rory. My heart hurt from just the sight of his face. It had been a really long time since I'd seen him, yet the wounds of his abandonment still felt fresh.

Rory looked good, like he'd been working out every day. Sporting a five o'clock shadow, he appeared more rugged than ever.

"Why are you here?"

"Well, you weren't exactly responding to my request to see you, so..."

"That was intentional."

"I know. I'm not blaming you."

"What is it that you needed to say to me?"

"I have a lot to say. I just don't know where to begin." Moving past me without permission, he wiped his forehead. "Do you mind if I have a glass of water?"

Without waiting for me to answer, Rory made his way over to the kitchen and the water filter on the counter then poured himself a tall glass. As he gulped it down in a matter of seconds, I could definitely see that he was nervous.

Glancing down at his hand, I noticed a small tattoo of a little bean. "Bean" had always been his nickname for me. He started using it one day when we were in college and never stopped. He never had that tattoo when we were together; it must have been new.

"Did you get a bean tattoo?"

His eyes bore into mine. "Yeah."

"Why?"

"Because I wanted to think of you every time I looked down at my hand."

"That doesn't make any sense."

"I know. But it will. That's why I'm here. To better explain."

What's going on?

Bruiser hadn't left my side. I sat down to grab my bearings, and he immediately followed me. Scratching between the dog's ears, I gave Rory my attention, even though I wasn't sure if he deserved it, but not before taking a dig at him.

"How's Jennifer Barney?"

"Jennifer Barney is a co-worker and a friend. There's nothing going on with us."

"You've moved onto someone else, then?"

"I haven't been with anyone, Amber. Not one person since you."

"I don't believe that for a second. Wasn't that the point of breaking up with me?"

"No. It was never the reason."

"I'm confused."

"I know."

The sounds of footsteps approaching gave me pause.

Then came Channing's voice. "Honey, I'm ho—"

Dead silence filled the air as Rory and Channing stared each other in the face. Bruiser barked once as if to interrupt the tension.

Channing was the first to speak. "What the fuck are you doing here?"

Rory gritted his teeth. "Me? Where did you even come from?"

"I live here." Channing's tone reeked of satisfaction.

Rory's eyes darted toward mine. "What?"

Feeling like I needed to flee, I forced out a response instead. "Channing's working in Boston until the end of the month. He's been staying with me."

Rory placed his hand over his chest. He looked truly flabbergasted and extremely upset. The color drained out of his face. He didn't have a right to feel that way, but the physical reaction he was having proved his shock was very real.

"How long have you been here?" Channing asked.

"Ten minutes."

"Why did you come, Rory?"

"That's not any of your business."

"Amber *is* my business now." Channing's fists tightened, and he ground his jaw.

"Is that so?" Rory looked toward me. "Is something going on between you two?"

I honestly didn't know how to answer that. Not only was it none of Rory's business, but I truly didn't know how to characterize what Channing and I even were. We hadn't labeled our relationship. He gave me no guarantees about what was going to happen once he left. I chose to remain silent.

"To use your own words, that's not any of your business," Channing answered.

Just then, Christine entered the kitchen. Her eyes were groggy as if she'd just woken up from a nap. She squinted. "Rory Calhoun?"

"Mrs. Lord? What are you doing here?"

"I live here. At least, until the end of the month. Amber and Channing took me in. I sleep in Channing's room. Channing sleeps with Amber."

Bruiser barked again, and it echoed throughout the kitchen.

Rory's face turned white as he clutched his chest then held onto his stomach as if he was going to throw up. "I think I'm gonna be sick."

All eyes were on him. No one seemed to know what to say. This situation was as awkward as it got.

His lips trembled. "Amber, can we please go somewhere and talk?"

A part of me wanted to tell him to go straight to hell. But another part of me, the part that knew this man inside and out could see that he was truly hurting right now. Whether his feelings were justified or not, I felt like I at least needed to allow him to say what he came to say.

"I'll grab my coat."

Channing followed me as we left Rory standing in the kitchen with Christine and the dog.

"You want me to come with you?" Channing asked.

"No. I'll be fine."

"Where are you gonna go?"

"I don't know. He's acting really odd, and I know he may not deserve my sympathy, but it's not in my nature to hide from confrontation, even if it might upset me. So, I'm going to hear him out."

Channing looked disappointed, but he respected my wishes. "Text me if you need me."

"I will."

"Did you know he was coming here?"

"No. He surprised me."

"You had no clue?"

"Well...I never mentioned this to you...but he'd texted me asking if he could see me. I never gave him an answer, so he just showed up tonight."

He shook his head. "Unbelievable." As I was about to leave the room, he stopped me. "Wait."

"Yeah?"

He gripped my wrist and pulled me into his arms, planting a firm and possessive kiss on my lips. "I need to tell you something just in case you don't know."

"Alright."

"Whether you realize it or not, he's going to try to convince you to take him back tonight."

"I don't think so. He's just—"

"He is, Amber. There is no doubt. But I can't let you go listen to him without telling you that I'm falling in love with you. This whole thing between us...it was never just sex for me—as much as I might have tried to convince myself otherwise. That delusion ended the moment I was actually inside of you. Every single time we've had sex, I was making love to you." A look of fear spread over his face. "I don't know what shit he's going to be feeding you tonight, but there is no way I could let you go with him without making my feelings crystal clear." Cupping my cheeks, he said, "You don't have to say anything. In fact, I don't want you to. I'm not looking for a response. I just needed to get that out."

The right words escaped me. I wasn't expecting him to pour his soul out like that. "Okay," I simply said.

Channing squeezed me tightly and lingered before letting me go. He walked close behind me as I returned to the kitchen.

Looking over at Rory, I said, "Okay. Let's go."

Rory didn't make eye contact with Channing as he grabbed Bruiser by the leash and headed out of the kitchen toward the door. Channing, on the other hand, didn't take his eyes off of Rory; he was watching his every move.

I looked back once at Channing who was standing with his hands in his pockets. The worry was plastered all over his face. If there was ever any doubt of his feelings toward me, it was diminished in that moment.

My heart was hurting as I followed Rory out of my building and down the sidewalk to where he was parked. It was freezing out, and light snowflakes were starting to fall.

Shivering, I asked, "Where are we going?"

"I don't know."

"You can't just kidnap me. You have to tell me where you're taking me."

"Alright, then…I'm taking you to my house."

"That's too far away."

Rory let me into his car before opening up the back for Bruiser.

He walked around to the driver's side and closed the door before saying, "I know you don't think that I deserve this time with you. But just give me this one thing. I need to talk to you alone. And it's either a hotel or my house. I won't ask anything else of you."

"You're acting strange. I don't understand any of this."

His eyes searched mine. "You will."

The ride to Rory's house in the northern Boston suburb of Reading was quiet. Relishing the warmth of the heated seat beneath me, I spent the latter part of the time in his car trying to clear my mind by meditating on all of the Christmas lights that decorated the houses we passed. The smell of his leather-scented car freshener was familiar and oddly comforting.

We passed through the town center that was aligned with lit wreaths affixed to light poles.

After turning onto a side street, Rory pulled up to a two-story structure. The first thing I noticed was a lone Christmas candle in the window of the lower level.

"Are you on the first floor?"

"No, that's Boris, my neighbor who's in his eighties. I'm upstairs. We have to sneak in quietly so he doesn't see you."

"Why?"

"He'll never leave you alone. He knows who you are."

"How?"

He pulled out his phone to show me his screensaver. It was a picture of me.

Why did he still have that on his phone?

Once inside and upstairs, I took a look around. "This place is nice."

Bruiser retreated to the corner of the room to play with his toy.

Rory's place was cozy. He'd set up a small Christmas tree in the corner of the living room. A pellet stove was going, which made the space warm and toasty.

He walked over to the window and looked out, seeming to grab his bearings. I wandered around and couldn't help noticing a framed photo of us sitting on his end table. This was the second photo of me I'd seen in two minutes.

Why did he still have photos of me?

His old Gibson guitar sat in the corner.

"Have you been playing guitar again?"

"Yeah. I've been trying to teach myself. It's cathartic."

"That's nice."

A long period of silence passed as he continued staring out the window.

He spoke with his back toward me. "How long have you and Channing been…" He wasn't able to finish the sentence.

"Not long."

"Do you care about him?"

There was no sense in lying. "I do. Very much."

"Do you love him?"

Yes.

Do I admit that to him?

Closing my eyes, I spoke the truth. "Yes."

That was the point he finally turned around to look at me, his eyes burning with pain.

Rory slowly approached before lifting his hand to my cheek and gently caressing it. "I'm fucking too late. Is that what you're telling me?"

"What's happening, Rory? Why are you acting like this?"

His voice was hoarse. "I lied to you."

"What?"

"The reason I gave for breaking up with you…it was a lie."

"You didn't really want to see other people?"

"No." He shook his head slowly and whispered, "No way."

Utterly confused, I said, "Okay...what was the real reason?"

"It has to do with the accident."

The accident.

It was one of the worst nights of my life, second only to the night Lainey died. I'll never forget receiving the call that Rory was in the hospital after his truck was hit head on while he was driving home from work. Thankfully, he ended up being okay. But something definitely did change in him after that.

"What about the accident?"

"There's something I never told you."

A feeling of dread hit me. "What?"

He just stared at me for a while before finally spitting it out. "One of the worst injuries I sustained was to my groin area. The doctor had me undergo some tests as a result of the blunt trauma. He said I didn't have to if I didn't want to, but I felt that I needed to know...for your sake."

"What kind of tests?"

"He tested my semen to see if my sperm production was affected. And basically the sample came up empty." Rory looked down at his feet when he whispered, "I can't have children."

No.

Oh, my God.

No.

An indescribable sadness came over me.

"Why didn't you tell me?" My hands naturally fell to his, grasping them tightly.

"I guess...I didn't want you to know, because I knew what you'd say and what you'd do. I knew you'd never leave me because of it. And I didn't want to prevent you from having children of your own. At the time, it felt like the right thing to do. Love makes you do crazy things. I'd convinced myself that I needed to let you go. So, I saw breaking up with you as the only solution."

"What changed? Why tell me now?"

"Because I'm weaker than I thought I was. I thought I could live without you. But I've been so miserable."

Suddenly, everything was finally starting to make sense. "It never felt real. Now, I know why."

He squeezed my hands harder. "How could I leave you? You're perfect for me." His voice cracked. "You're the love of my life, Amber. I love you so much."

I couldn't believe this was happening. It seemed like I could feel my heart breaking, a heart that no longer only belonged to Rory.

Rory suddenly walked away.

"Where are you going?"

"I want to show you something."

He returned holding a Tiffany blue gift bag. His hand was shaking as he took out a small box and opened it, revealing the exact ring I'd always dreamt about—the heart-shaped design from Tiffany's.

"I had planned to propose to you at the Top of the Hub on our anniversary. I'd been holding onto this when the accident happened. I never dreamt that I wouldn't have the chance to give it to you."

My eyes were clouded with tears as I looked down at the ring. I refused to touch it because I didn't feel like it

PENELOPE WARD

was my place to do so anymore. "How did you know about this ring?"

"The file you kept on our old desktop computer with the wedding stuff in it. I noticed you saved a lot of photos of this ring. I went to Tiffany's and bought it." His lips curved into a slight smile. "Anyway, I know it may not matter anymore, but I'm showing you this so you know how serious I was about us. I've had this weird feeling lately that I needed to catch you before I lost you forever. I sensed that something was happening, and now I know exactly what it was." Rory shook his head in disbelief. "I'll tell you one thing...I could never have imagined that you and Channing..." He couldn't get the words out. "I want to fucking throw up."

His devastation penetrated the depths of my soul. This felt like a nightmare.

I struggled to find the words. "I can only imagine how you feel. I honestly don't even know what to say. As hard as it was to accept, I believed that you'd chosen to leave me because you didn't want me. I had to work so hard to try to get over you. Now, I'm finding out that everything was a lie. And on top of that, I'm devastated for you, that you're telling me you can never have children? My God, Rory. You're right. I would have never left you because of that. Not in a million years. I'm so incredibly shocked right now, and I feel sick. You have no idea."

"I think I do know how you feel, because I feel sick, too."

My phone chimed. I knew it was Channing before I even looked down at it.

Channing: Just confirm for me that you're okay.

I quickly typed out a response.

Amber: I'm okay. Talk soon.

I was far from okay. As I looked into the eyes of my first love, the man I thought I was going to marry, the man I thought I was going to have children with, I'd never been more confused in my life.

The truth was, I'd never fully fallen out of love with Rory, even when I thought he'd chosen to leave me. I still wasn't able to shake him. A portion of my heart was still his. But he'd left a void. And Channing had filled it. I'd fallen so hard for him, and despite the truth I now realized about Rory, that couldn't erase what had developed in my heart for Channing.

Now, it felt like my heart had fallen into a state of purgatory. And for the first time in my life, I understood that it was completely possible to be in love with two men at the same time.

CHAPTER TWENTY-TWO
CHANNING

Staring at the clock wasn't helping. That didn't stop me from checking it every two minutes in the hopes that it somehow made her walk through the door sooner.

I'd always known this day would come, that he'd return and try to get her back. It was never a matter of *if...* but *when*.

And since when did Rory look like that? When we were friends, he had no facial hair and never worked out. Now, he looked like goddamn Charlie Hunnam.

My mother entered the room. "Channing, tell me what's going on tonight. I'm very confused."

"You and me both."

The last thing I really wanted to do was talk about this situation with my mom. But I also realized that her mind was deteriorating. How much longer would I have her around to vent to? I would regret not talking to her more while I could. That understanding made me feel obligated to open up to her now, even if it was a little uncomfortable for me.

"I know you sleep with her, but do you love Amber?"

I'd told Amber earlier tonight that I was falling in love with her. The truth was, I knew in my heart that there was no falling happening; I'd already fallen—and I couldn't fucking get up. She was the only woman I'd ever truly fallen in love with.

"I really do love her, yes, Mom."

My mother looked so happy to hear me say that. "Oh, Channing...I wasn't sure if I'd ever see the day."

"Neither was I."

"You never brought girls home to meet me. I just always assumed that would be the way it was, that you'd never settle down with anyone."

"Yeah, well, it still may not happen for me—at least not with Amber."

"Why do you say that?"

"She and Rory were together for nine years. He has a very big leg up on me. She was devastated when he broke up with her. Amber was really in love with him."

Was...or is?

"You've cared about her for a long time—since you were a teenager."

That comment caught me off guard.

How would she have known that?

"How do you know that?"

"A mother can tell. She was a good friend to your sister, and to you, for many years. I watched you interact with her back then. You were always attentive to everything she would say. Your smile would linger for longer than normal when she was around. Little things like that. There was definitely a connection. I could tell there was something there. She's not just some girl. You two have a history, as well. Don't discount that."

It surprised me that she'd picked up on that back then.

My negative mind was kicking into full gear. "Okay... but Rory and Amber have a deeper history and years of memories. We've only been romantically involved for a couple of months."

"I understand what you're doing. You're trying to prepare yourself just in case so that you don't get hurt. You've suffered a lot of loss in your life. Between your father leaving us and Lainey...we're used to being left behind, aren't we? That doesn't mean it will always be that way."

This moment with my mother was a gift. The day would come when I would lose her, too. It was coming faster than I could handle. But she was here now. And even though there were many moments of confusion, I had to appreciate that there were still moments like this, ones of complete clarity. This one came when I really needed it.

She continued, "Don't be so quick to assume that she'll pick quantity over quality. I see the way she looks at you. And I'm not talking about the lustful way most women look at you—even some of my old bag friends who should be ashamed, quite honestly. With Amber, it's different. Her face just lights up when you walk in the room. She admires you. She sees beyond the surface. There is no greater joy for a mother than to know that there's a woman out there who looks at her son like that, who appreciates him inside and out."

"I see that, too. I love the way she looks at me."

"And if this doesn't work out...if she chooses him over you, don't take that to mean that you don't deserve love. The right person will be out there for you. But I do hope Amber's the one, because she's wonderful. I've always felt that way about her. She's the perfect complementary calm to my fiery boy."

It felt great to open up, like a weight had been lifted off of my chest. It made me realize I hadn't spoken about Amber to anyone. I always kept my private life private, especially with co-workers. But sometimes, you just need to talk it out.

"I never told you this, Mom, but I met a girl last year. Her name is Emily. She was honestly the first girl I was ready to hang things up for. Anyway, to make a long story short, she ended up going back with her ex-boyfriend. I was pretty hurt. She's since broken up with him and tried to reconnect with me again. She lives here in Massachusetts."

"Oh, wow."

"Yeah...anyway, I really had it bad for her at one time. But when I met up with her again here...it just didn't feel the same. That was kind of what helped me realize I'd fallen hard for Amber. I just hope that little mini-heartbreak with Emily wasn't just practice for the big one."

I was looking at my mother, waiting for more wise words of advice. Instead, she closed her eyes.

A full minute passed before she opened them. Then, she stared at me blankly. "What were we talking about?"

I could feel my eyes getting watery. She was gone again. "Nothing, Mom." I kissed her on the forehead. "Thank you for listening."

After my mother went to bed, I sat alone in the dark waiting for Amber to return.

She smelled like his damn cologne, and it was irking the hell out of me. She assured me nothing happened between them aside from hugging. Thank fuck.

It was the middle of the night, and it felt like I was in the midst of some kind of bizarre dream where everything I knew to be true was no longer. Amber was distraught as she recalled everything that Rory had admitted to her tonight. She said they stayed at his apartment talking for hours before he finally drove her home. They'd been gone way longer than I ever anticipated.

Amber paced across the bedroom. I couldn't believe what I was hearing. It sort of felt like he'd come back from the dead. I mean, I always knew he'd come back for her. I just never imagined this scenario. There was no plan for how to handle this situation.

I had no words.

The one major thing I'd always had in my corner was the fact that Rory could be deemed untrustworthy for abandoning her to see other people. Turns out, he was a martyr instead.

Fanfuckingtastic.

I understood her reaction, why finding out the real reason behind Rory's abandonment would make her emotional. Even I felt devastated for him. But I wasn't stupid. I knew Amber still had lingering feelings for Rory even before any of this happened. As much as that annoyed me, I always admired how deeply she loved with her whole heart and how loyal of a person she was. My hope was that I'd have more time to make her forget about him completely.

I knew she had strong feelings for me, too. Did she love me? I had no idea. It felt like she might. Things were complicated even before this happened. But now? Now, it was downright messed-up. I had to protect myself.

There was no way I was going to wait for her to tell me she needed time to figure things out. I couldn't even bear to hear those words. I was going to *give* her time before she could say what I knew was coming. As painful as it was, I couldn't allow myself to fall more deeply in love with Amber if there was a chance she was going to go back to him. I also understood what this must have been doing to her psyche.

My mind was racing. The only decision that made sense was to take my mother and leave, give Amber the time and space to sort her head out over this.

"You can't absorb all of this in one night," I said. "You need time to figure it out with a clear head. And I don't think I should be here while you do."

"What are you saying?"

"My contract is almost up. I'm gonna tell them about my mother and that I have to go back home now. Gonna head back to Chicago in the next couple of days. Christmas is next week, so Mom's gonna want to be home for that anyway."

A look of alarm flashed across Amber's face as she gripped my shirt. A fresh tear fell down her cheek. "I don't want you to leave. You were supposed to be *here* for Christmas."

Even though it made me feel good that she wished I could have stayed for the holidays, I no longer knew whether the tears in her eyes were for me or for Rory. I hated having to share anything with him, even her god-damn tears.

My anger at the universe knew no end. I needed to let some of what was inside out.

Placing my hands on hers, I pressed them into my chest and looked deeply into her eyes. "Amber, look at me. I need you to really hear this." I moved my hands to wrap them firmly around her face. "I feel like I didn't really get to make my feelings as clear as I wanted to earlier, because I was crunched for time. I misspoke." Sucking in some air, I said, "I'm not *falling* in love with you. I am *in love* with you." When she started to open her mouth to speak, I cut her off, "Please don't ever tell me you love me back unless you're one-hundred percent mine. I don't want to hear those words otherwise. It will only sting." I leaned my forehead on hers. "I think the moment my feelings for you really hit me was when I felt oddly disappointed that you weren't pregnant. I realized that there was never any fear of being trapped with you because I was exactly where I wanted to be. This has all happened fast with us, yes, but it's very real for me. Every day I've felt closer to you. Even when you'd show me your vulnerabilities, I love those, too. They make you real. I may not have the past nine years to give you, but I can give you many more to come."

I told myself I wasn't going to kiss her but I couldn't help lowering my mouth to hers as she eagerly received my kiss. That made me even more revved up. My words came out faster. "I want to fuck you in our bed every night. I want to read with you, and laugh about stupid shit, make you blush, feed you weird food, and stay up until all hours of the night talking. I want to fall asleep to the sound of your breathing. I want everything we've had over the past few months times infinity. I want it all—the good and the bad. But as much as I want it, I sure as fuck ain't sharing you."

She pounded on my chest in frustration. "Channing...I wish tonight never happened."

I locked her hands to stop her. "I know that, beautiful. I can only imagine how confused you are right now. It pisses me off that he put you in this situation. He should have just been honest from the beginning."

Did I really feel that way? If he'd done that, I never would have had this time with her.

Her lip was quivering. "I'm not ready for you to leave."

"It's not forever. I may be in love with you, but I've been your friend for a lot longer than I've been your lover. I'll always be your friend, even if it pains the shit out of me. And as your *friend*, I know you enough to know that you need this time to figure it all out. If you told me you didn't need it, I'd still make you take it. Don't forget, I had the unfortunate circumstance of being your confidante before I was ever your boyfriend, which means I know exactly how strong your feelings for Rory are. You can't tell me otherwise, and you can't expect me to believe that this news didn't rock your world. I get it. I don't like it...but I get it." I wiped a tear from her cheek. "Only time can show me whether what he's told you tonight changes anything between us. If we're meant to be, we'll survive this. And if you choose to be with him..." I paused to gather my thoughts and curb my emotions. "If you choose to be with him, I won't hate you or hold it against you. I'll understand it was because you were following your heart. I only want you to be with me if it's the only place you want to be."

She shut her eyes momentarily then said, "I know you're making sense, but I just can't imagine you gone in two days. I feel like I need you here to be able to handle this, even though you're part of the dilemma."

"As fucked-up as that sounds, I get it. But I'm giving you space anyway."

With pleading eyes, she said, "There's nothing I can say to make you stay?"

"No. I'm sorry. This is the right thing for now."

Amber just kept nodding. She was finally coming terms in her mind with the fact that I was leaving.

She ran her fingers through my hair. "You referred to yourself as my boyfriend. You'd never used that word before."

"Boyfriend...fuckboy, same thing," I joked, burying my face in her neck. "I'm kidding. I know I never used it. I didn't think I needed to spell it out. I've felt like your boyfriend for a while."

My hands were starting to drift and wander about her body. I was feeling possessive and knew if I slept in the room tonight, that I would want to fuck her. And that would have been a mistake given the turn of events.

"You'd better get some sleep. We'll talk more in the morning." I said, forcing myself to walk away.

She called from behind me, "Where are you going?"

As painful as it was, I said, "It's late. I'm sleeping on the couch."

After a couple of days of tying up loose ends, departure day finally came. The mood around the condo was downright depressing.

Amber focused all of her attention on my mother. She did Mom's hair before we had to head to the airport and helped her pack what few belongings she had. I was pretty sure she was trying to avoid having to say goodbye to me. Of course, I hoped it really wasn't goodbye—at least not permanently anyway—but I had no clue what the next few weeks would bring.

I was putting the last of my things inside a carry-on when Amber walked into my room. "Your mother is lying down. She said to wake her when the Uber gets here."

"Uber's coming in fifteen minutes," I muttered.

Her body was inches from me now, but I wasn't acknowledging her. I wasn't ready.

Amber's voice cracked. "I can't believe this is really happening."

I'd continued to sleep on the couch for the past couple of nights. Amber knew why. I didn't have to spell it out. Sleeping apart from her had been torture. But she didn't try to convince me otherwise. There was nothing more I'd wanted than to spend those nights in her bed. But I just couldn't.

"I need to say something before I leave," I announced.

"Don't make me cry," she said, even though she was already crying.

Sitting on the bed, I prompted her to come to me. Burying my head in her abdomen, I spoke softly, "I don't just love you, Amber. I like you. *Really* like you. You were always my favorite person. But after spending this time with you, seeing how you are with Milo, how much of your life you devote to others, in my book, you're a rockstar. You deserve the world. I just want you to be happy." Looking up at her, I said, "When I first came here...it broke my heart to see how hurt you were. I wanted to help you feel better, like you helped me all those years ago when Lainey died. I wanted to bring you out of your darkness. But in the process, I fucked up and fell in love with you, fell in love with not only the good parts but the dark ones, too—your realness, your vulnerability. And the big irony is that, once again, I needed you just as much as you might have needed me. This time with you has taught me a lot. The way you handle Milo, it's actually really helped me know that even sometimes when someone can't communicate with you that they can have moments of happiness. That gave me hope about my mother's future when very little else does. This trip has been a blessing to me. *You're* a blessing to me. As much as I want you for myself, I want true happiness for you more, whether that's with me or without me. The only thing you need to do for me...is to figure your heart out." I placed my hand over her chest. "I know I'm in there somewhere. But I'm selfish and I want it all."

She sniffled. "You deserve it all."

I stood up from the bed and cupped her cheeks. "I'll miss your face so much."

Amber leaned her head on my chest. "There's just so much I need to say to you that I haven't been able to articulate. I feel like I've been numb, and I owe you so much more than that."

I held her tightly. "You owe me nothing. But if you want to do something for me...just think about me when I'm gone. Spend time with Rory. Do what you need to. But when you're not with him, really *think* about me. Remember everything that I've said and that we've done."

She pulled back to look at me. "I promise, I will."

The sound of a horn outside interrupted our moment.

"Fuck. The car is here. I'm gonna get my mother and the cat situated downstairs. Then, I'll come back up to say goodbye, alright?"

We left the bedroom, and Amber hugged my mother goodbye, promising to see her again soon. I hoped that was really the case. Only God knew how bad my mother would be the next time Amber saw her.

Mom held Kitty in a carrier. The poor cat was meowing like crazy. If you think about it, this must have been scary as all hell for her. Her life literally consisted of breaking out of a truck and then all she knew was me and this place. She probably thought she'd be here forever. And now she didn't know where the hell she was going.

I'm scared of the unknown, too, Kitty.

Grabbing the one black suitcase I'd arrived with along with a small bag of things my mother had accumulated while here, we walked down to the Uber SUV parked in front of Amber's building.

After getting Mom settled in the backseat, I slipped the driver a bonus twenty, letting him know I might be a few minutes and telling him to please be patient.

Amber was waiting by the window when I returned to her bedroom.

She turned around. "This is it?"

I swallowed. "Yeah."

About a week ago, I'd purchased a piece of mistletoe from a shop downtown, planning to take it out on Christmas Eve and play around with it. I pulled it out of my pocket.

Her mouth moved into a slight grin. "What's that?"

"Glittery mistletoe. I was gonna try to be funny on Christmas Eve. I had this idea that I was gonna wrap it around my cock when you came to bed...make you laugh. I bought it before any of this happened."

She wiped the tears from her eyes. "That would have been so funny."

I walked slowly toward her and placed it over her head. "Since we won't be together for Christmas, can I kiss you under this mistletoe?"

"I would love nothing more."

She parted her lips, and I hungrily took them into my mouth. It wasn't my intention to kiss her so forcefully, but the magnitude of this was really hitting me.

What if this was the last time?

Amber was feeling it, too. She gripped my jacket for dear life. The mistletoe slipped out of my hands and onto the ground.

"I have to go," I said huskily over her lips.

"Don't." Her tears were all over my face.

I kissed her harder. And I lost it. Totally fucking lost it. The next thing I knew, she was desperately unbuttoning my jeans. Her ass was on the windowsill, and her legs were wrapped around my back.

It didn't matter that my mother and the cat were downstairs with the Uber driver. All that mattered was getting inside of her again. Secretly, a part of me also needed to know that she wouldn't deny me.

I reached over to the nightstand and fumbled for a condom, ripping it open in record time.

Once the rubber was on, I moaned from deep in the back of my throat as I sank into her. It felt like it had been a hundred years.

My thrusts were fast, hard, and desperate. Her back was banging against the window as I fucked her for dear life, knowing that it very well could have been our last time. Her hands were pulling my hair as I gently bit at her skin.

Groaning into her neck, I said, "I can't fucking quit you, Amber. Don't make me."

"Stay inside of me, Channing. Fuck me harder."

A car horn from outside barely registered through the sounds of our desperation, the slapping of our skin, the clanking of my belt buckle.

Even though I never wanted this to end, I needed release, and I needed to leave.

"I need to go," I whispered in her ear before my body started shaking as I came inside of her, pumping until there was nothing left. She gasped and clenched her muscles around my cock, following suit with her own orgasm.

The coldness I felt as I pulled out of her was excruciating. Our foreheads were still touching as we panted together.

"I really do have to leave now."

I swiftly zipped up my jeans and gave her one last firm kiss on the lips before walking away.

I turned around one last time. "I may not have been your first love, but you're mine."

She silently nodded as more tears fell. I could feel my own eyes getting watery, but there was no way I was going to cry.

At least, not until I got on the plane and out of her sight.

CHAPTER TWENTY-THREE
AMBER

It was the afternoon of Christmas Eve. Annabelle stopped over for some spiked eggnog before she had to retreat home for family time. Her husband apparently wanted her out of the house anyway so that he could wrap her gift.

She bit into a Christmas star cookie that was decorated with green and red sprinkles and said, "Every time I think your life would make a good book, it just gets better and better. Seriously...can anything else crazy happen this year?"

"Please don't ask that. The universe is listening and apparently, she fucking hates me."

"I might have to agree with you." She laughed. When her smile faded, she asked, "Have you spoken to Channing?"

"We're supposed to talk later tonight. He's taking his mother to an early Christmas Eve mass."

"That's nice. He's such a good son."

"He really is."

"And Rory? When will you see him?"

"Rory is with his family in Illinois for Christmas Eve. He's flying back to Boston tomorrow and picking me up. We're heading to his downstairs neighbor's place for Christmas drinks. He wants me to meet him, this old man who lives alone. His name is Boris."

"That's sweet. You're not spending the night there, are you?"

"No, of course not. But you seem very panicked about that."

Annabelle moved to the couch and sat cross-legged. "Well, it's no secret that I'm Team Channing. Even with Rory's situation, which believe me, I am extremely sympathetic toward, I'm totally rooting for Channing here."

"That doesn't surprise me."

She sipped her eggnog and seemed to be observing me. "I have to admit...I'm a little concerned about your well-being."

"You and me both." I sighed and reached for one of the cookies she'd brought.

"What I mean is...you seem very numb, like you haven't really even begun to process everything. You've avoided talking about how you're feeling about either one of them. I know it's complicated, but at some point, you're going to have to face it, talk about it."

I was quite aware of the fact that I was in denial. It was intentional because any time I would think about either one of them I'd burst into tears. Denial was my strategy for getting through the day so that I could function for the kids and for Milo. As soon as I stopped denying what was happening, the pain would creep in.

Like now.

"I let that man go back to Chicago without telling him that I loved him because he told me he didn't want to hear it. There was so much I needed to say to him, and nothing would come out. I've been the same way with Rory. He's been calling me, and I don't know what to say or do. So, I've been bottling everything up. I feel so much for both of them. I *love* both of them. And I'm hurting for both of them for different reasons. The truth is, I've been in denial because this is the most heartache I've ever felt in my life. Apparently, love multiplied is nothing but pain. And I'm scared it's going to kill me." I let out the longest breath and downed some of the eggnog. It felt like I'd just unloaded a heavy weight off my chest.

"Well, congratulations...in talking about bottling it up, you've managed to let some of it out."

"You tricked me." I smiled. Closing my eyes, I decided to divulge a little more. "Channing and I had sex right before he left. Like literally seconds before. We hadn't been sleeping together since the night I went to Rory's, but we both just lost it at the last moment. It was crazy...and passionate. And it broke my heart, because I also knew a part of him felt like that moment might have been it for us."

Annabelle looked like she was going to cry. "That's so sad and romantic at the same time."

"I miss him so much," I whispered.

"With each day, as the shock of all of this wears off, you'll begin to figure it out. You're going to still love both of them. But your love for one of them will shine a little brighter. And you'll just know. Your confused state right now is like a giant cloud of smoke. But it's temporary. When the smoke clears, only one man will be standing there."

I exhaled. "Yeah."

"By the way, do you know how lucky you are to have two good men who love you? Some women wait their whole lives just to be loved one time, by one man."

"Yeah, well, I'd gladly give up this predicament if it meant that someone I love didn't have to get hurt."

⌒

After Annabelle left, it felt strange to be alone on Christmas Eve. This was the first time I'd ever experienced it. I'd always celebrated with either my parents or Rory.

I normally would have been in Chicago, or my folks would have come here, but this was the one year they'd planned a trip to England for the holidays. Of course, I was previously fine with that, thinking that Channing would be here.

Somehow all of the lights in my place were off. So preoccupied, I'd missed sundown altogether, and this was the first instance I became conscious of sitting in the dark.

Walking over to the window, I admired the lights decorating the building across the street. People were rushing down the sidewalk, likely trying to get their last-minute shopping done or in a hurry to make it home to their family parties. My loneliness was starting to feel overwhelming.

When I returned to the couch, I decided to go on Instagram to see if Channing had posted anything. My heart nearly melted upon the sight of a photo of his mother. She had tinsel on her head and was smiling wide. It made me sad that I wasn't there with them. Channing had edited the photo so that everything was in black and white except for the red tinsel. I knew he was really trying to cherish moments like that with Christine. It was simply beautiful.

After staring through Channing's older photos for a while, I decided to go down the line of usual people I stalk on IG. One of them was Channing's ex, Emily. She'd liked one of his posts once, so I kept a note of her profile, which was public. Stalking her was sweet torture.

Tonight, though, I almost wished I hadn't gone to her page. The most recent post was of a huge Christmas tree that seemed to be in the middle of downtown. Except it wasn't downtown Boston. It was downtown Chicago.

The caption read: *Christmas in Chicago.*

Chicago?

She was in Chicago? Her family lived in Massachusetts. Why would she be there if not to visit Channing? My heart was thundering in my chest.

I knew that given the circumstances, it was unfair of me to feel so angry about this, but I couldn't help it. He was very likely feeling vulnerable right now, and she would be there to take advantage, to lick his wounds—among other things.

Sweat was permeating my body. Channing and I were supposed to talk over the phone at eight, but I didn't feel I could wait to call him. I felt like I had to know whether she was there with him.

I picked up the phone, and my finger hovered over his name.

No.

No, Amber.

You have no right to push guilt on him. You'll wait until eight.

The quiet was deafening over the next hour.

When the phone finally rang at eight sharp, I jumped to answer.

"Hello?"

His smooth, deep voice soothed me. "Merry Christmas, beautiful."

I closed my eyes to cherish the sound. "Merry Christmas."

"We just got back from church a little while ago. There was a café still open near there, so I took Mom out for hot chocolate, and now we're back home chilling. I'm making duck with an orange sauce. It's in the oven for an hour."

"Of course. Turkey or chicken would be too boring."

"Damn straight."

After I let out a shaky breath, he could sense something was bothering me.

"What's going on, Amber?"

"Is Emily there with you?" I blurted out, "Is she coming over for dinner?"

After some silence, he responded, "No. But she *is* in Chicago. You knew that?"

"Yes."

"Are you stalking me, Walton?"

Unsure whether to fess up, I admitted, "I...check her Instagram from time to time. She posted that she was in Chicago."

He let out a deep breath into the phone. "I honestly didn't know she was coming here. You remember, she and I have mutual friends. That was how I met her...at their wedding. Shawn and Melanie. They live here. She says they invited her for Christmas."

"So, you've been in touch with her, then. She knew you were back in Chicago?"

"I contacted her before I left Boston. I'd kind of left things a mess with her and felt I should at least have the decency to tell her I was headed home. But she came to see me here yesterday."

"I see." I massaged my temples. "What did she say?"

"You really want to know?"

"Yes." I braced myself.

"She poured her heart out, basically, begged me to give her another chance, tried to fuck me, told me she wouldn't even go back home to Boston if I asked her to stay right then and there."

My blood pressure was rising. That was hard to hear—really hard to hear. I hadn't felt this level of jealousy in my entire life.

When I didn't say anything, he chimed in, "You asked, Amber. I'm just telling you the truth." He sighed. "Nothing happened, okay?"

"What did you tell her?"

"I told her the truth about you and that I was in limbo. I suggested that she move on from the idea of us because I couldn't give her anything right now."

Right now.

My feelings morphed from jealousy to guilt. What if I couldn't leave Rory behind, was stringing Channing along, and ended up keeping Channing from a good, healthy relationship?

"Can I ask you something, Channing?"

"Yes."

"Do you think you would be with her if this whole thing with me wasn't happening?"

He paused then said, "I probably would, but that's irrelevant. With Emily, it was always infatuation. With you, it's different. What we have feels...soul crushing." His tone turned angry. "And by the way, if you think I could be moving on with someone else so quickly right now, clearly you didn't hear one goddamn word I said before I left. And that worries me. It makes me feel like you don't really believe any of it. You have this idea in your head that I'm out with Emily, and meanwhile, I'm home on Christmas Eve, miserable and missing you...just wishing you were here so badly."

I felt like an asshole. "I miss you, too...so much."

Neither of us said anything for about a full minute until he asked, "Have you seen him?"

"No. I'm seeing him tomorrow for Christmas drinks at his neighbor's place. It will be the first time I've seen him since before you left."

Channing's breathing got heavier. "I really thought I could fucking handle this. The truth is, I'm not doing a very good job."

"Who could possibly handle this well?"

He surprised me when he said, "I need to see you."

"How?"

"Skype. Can you do it?"

"Yeah, of course. Let me just log in. My username is Amber Walton Double Zero Eight. I'll add you. Call me when you're ready."

We hung up, and I set up my computer on the coffee table.

A few minutes later, it started ringing. Butterflies swarmed in my belly as I prepared to see him. When he appeared on screen, I was reminded of how beautiful he is. I smiled to see that Channing was actually wearing a Christmas sweater. Even though it had only been a few days, his hair looked longer. He also hadn't shaved.

"Nice sweater."

"Are you being facetious?"

"Only you could look like an absolute god in a Christmas sweater with cats on it."

"My mother bought it. It's an ode to Kitty. I felt like I had to wear it."

"It looks good on you."

"You look beautiful," he said.

"I'm wearing sweats."

"Doesn't matter. You're beautiful, Amber."

Channing was just staring at me, and I felt compelled to say some of the things I'd been saying to him in my head all night long.

"The other night before you left, you really opened your heart to me. I stood there like an idiot, frozen, unable to reciprocate. The truth is, I was a fool for letting you get on that plane without saying something—anything—to let you know how much I..." I hesitated. He told me not to use the word love while we were in this limbo. I needed to honor his wishes. I continued, "How much I care about you. I don't even know where to begin. You blew into my life like a storm. I was so depressed and hopeless. You saved me with your light, with your laughter, with your positive point of view. Before you moved in, I had such preconceived notions about the type of person you'd become over the years. And I was wrong. You shot those down from the very first night when you listened so patiently to me. I'd never smiled so much in my life. I know you say we only had a few months together, but it truly felt like much longer. You saved me from making one of the biggest mistakes of my life leading up to that night at The Peabody, and in turn, you opened a door for us that I never dreamt was possible. I never imagined that you could love me. The idea of that is still so new. But I feel like the luckiest girl in the world that you do."

A long moment of silence passed where I just listened to him breathe. "This is hard," he finally said.

I spoke through my tears, "I know."

"It's Christmas. Don't cry," he said.

There was a knock at the door.

"That's strange. Hang on. Someone's at the door."

"Make sure you look through the peephole."

There was no one there, but there was a box at my feet.

A delivery on Christmas Eve?

I carried it inside and returned to the computer.

"Who was it?"

"No one. There was this box."

"Who's it from?"

"I don't know. It's not labeled."

"Open it." The slight smirk on his face made me think he had something to do with it.

"Channing, what are you up to? What's inside the box?"

His blue eyes sparkled through the screen. "Merry Christmas."

"How did you manage this?"

"I have elves."

"Really..."

As if he hadn't already given me enough with his patience and understanding over the Rory situation, he'd gotten me a present? I felt terrible because I hadn't gotten him anything. I just didn't feel deserving of any of this.

"So...open it. Actually, open everything but the small, flat one."

The box was filled with various individually wrapped gifts. I opened them one by one: Christmas flannel pajamas, a hot cocoa kit, a stuffed white kitten, and a new Kindle. I finally knew what I was doing tonight.

"You shouldn't be alone tonight. I was thinking those things could help."

"I absolutely love them." Cradling the stuffed animal, I said, "Especially my own version of Kitty."

He smiled. "Put the pajamas on. I want to see you in them."

"Okay."

Taking my time, I lifted off my shirt. As I slipped off my bra, Channing's eyes focused on my breasts. Desire pooled between my legs. I would have given anything for him to be here right now, to feel his scruffy beard on my skin.

Once I had the pajamas on, I said, "These are so comfy, thank you."

"Okay, open the last thing."

After removing the wrapping, I began to open the flat, black box. Inside was a thin strand of authentic pearls.

"Oh, my God. A pearl necklace." Then, I started to laugh because I realized why he'd chosen this.

"Not the kind I wish I could give you tonight. But I figured you deserved a real one, unlike the one that dude online and myself would like to give you."

"An actual one!" Running my fingers along the smooth beads before putting it on, I said, "This is so beautiful. I've never actually owned pearls."

"I thought it would look nice around your delicate neck. Anyway, I have one more small thing for you. I'm emailing it to you tomorrow. I'm not finished with it."

Feeling ashamed, I said, "You've gotten me multiple gifts, and I didn't get you anything."

"You can make it up to me another time."

"I need to do something for you tonight. It's Christmas." Something occurred to me. The one thing I could give him right now. "Are you alone?"

"Mom's taking a nap, so yeah."

"Why don't you sit back..."

"What do you have in mind?"

"There's not much I can do from here," I said as I began unbuttoning the flannel pajama top. My nipples stiffened as they hit the air.

The room was completely still as Channing stayed quietly focused on me. He wasn't smiling or laughing. He was transfixed, his eyes growing hazy and filling with need by the second.

His tone was demanding. "Take everything off but the necklace, and take me to your room."

I did as he said, carrying my laptop to my bedroom.

Once situated on my bed and fully naked, I fiddled with the pearls and asked, "Tell me what you want."

"I want to watch you make yourself come."

He'd unzipped his jeans. The tip of his hard cock was sticking out of the top of his boxer briefs.

I positioned the computer in a way that he could see my entire body. Bending my head back, I started to masturbate. There was nothing sexier than the sounds of his moans as he began to jerk himself off while watching me.

Gyrating my hips and curling my toes, I kept circling my swollen clit. I'd never done anything like this before and wondered why it had taken me so long. The need was so much more intense when distance was put between us.

My orgasm rolled through me fast and furiously. Channing groaned out in pleasure. Peeking at the screen through my legs, I could see his fist pumping his engorged cock as cum spurted out. That was an amazingly erotic sight.

When he finally stopped, his head stayed back. His shoulders were rising and falling. He was quiet for a while then wiped his eyes with his sleeve. When his eyes finally met mine again, they were red.

Holy shit.

I took my finger to the screen and traced it along his face. "Are you crying?"

He sniffled and shook his head as if mad at himself. "I just got a little emotional. Can't say that's ever happened to me while jerking off before."

The fact that I couldn't hold him, couldn't comfort him was pure torture.

His voice was hoarse. "I'm trying so fucking hard."

We stared at each other for a while. He'd told me he loved me several times. But I think this was the first moment that it actually had sunk in. This man really loved me. I saw it more clearly than ever. Seeing the tears he was trying to fight, the emotions that a simple sexual act could ignite, I knew. Channing was scared to lose me. He'd been acting calm and controlled and trying to give me space, but he was really hurting.

Any shred of doubt I had about his feelings for me was obliterated in that moment.

⌒

Later that night, I was sitting alone in my new flannel pajamas drinking the cocoa he'd sent me with a big peppermint stick inside the mug when a text came in.

Channing: You sleigh me.

Holding the phone to my chest, I smiled so hard. Sleigh not slay—for Christmas. My fingers hovered over the keys, wanting so badly to type those three words: *I love you*. But I promised him I wouldn't say them unless I was his. That rule extended to text messaging, too. I certainly felt like I belonged to him tonight, but Rory was still in the picture, wasn't he? It wouldn't have been fair to go against Channing's wishes.

How do you tell someone you love them without actually saying it? Ultimately, I couldn't put into words what I felt—especially with that limitation. So, I opted for a simple response and hoped he could read between the lines.

Amber: You sleigh me, too. So much.

CHAPTER TWENTY-FOUR
AMBER

His melodic knock made me jump from my seat. When I opened, my heart sped up a bit. He was dressed to the nines in black trousers and a fitted, sage green sweater with a collared shirt underneath. His sleeves were rolled up, displaying an expensive-looking watch I'd never seen on him.

Rory had come straight from the airport to my house. His blond hair was perfectly gelled, and he'd grown out his beard a little. His blue eyes were glowing. Honestly, he'd never looked better.

He was holding a white poinsettia plant and reached it out to me. "This is for you."

I took it and placed it on a table. "Thank you."

It was weird to not be greeting him with a hug or kiss, but we were both holding back for obvious reasons.

His eyes were piercing. "You look really pretty," he said, slipping his hands slowly into his pockets.

"So do you."

He squinted. "I look pretty? Not exactly what I was going for."

"You know what I mean. Handsome." Shaking my head, I said, "I'm not really thinking straight."

The awareness of Rory's signature Kenneth Cole Reaction cologne immediately brought me a little sense of comfort, reminding me of times when life was far simpler.

"Yeah. You're nervous. It's weird to see you this nervous around me. Try not to be. It's freaking me out a little." He placed his hand on my arm. "It's just me, Amber." His touch definitely didn't go unnoticed.

"I feel like I'm on my first date with you all over again."

"How about we not focus on all of the complicated shit for one day? The last thing I want to do is think about the past week. Just be with me. Let's enjoy Christmas. Plus, Boris has the best booze. It's like a geriatric bar up in there." He flashed a crooked smile that was contagious.

Maybe living in denial was the best way to handle this evening. Rory was not about to acknowledge Channing anyway. Aside from the first night he'd discovered that Channing and I were together, he hadn't so much as mentioned his name. I knew it was too painful for him.

"Well, I can definitely get behind good booze." I smiled. "Good."

We made our way out of the condo. Rory's car was already running when we got outside. His heated seats felt so good against my bottom.

It was completely quiet for the first five minutes of our drive.

Suddenly, Rory pressed some buttons and *The Chipmunk Song* came on. He knew that song always cracked me up. *The Chipmunk Song: Don't Be Late* as performed by Alvin and the Chipmunks was my ultimate favorite Christmas tune.

I didn't know if it was my stress-level as of late or what, but I just lost it and began to laugh so hard that I was practically crying. Those high-pitched voices were just the medicine I needed.

When the song finished, I wiped my eyes and turned to him. "Thank you for that." *Hiccup.*

Oh, no. I'd laughed so hard, I'd given myself the hiccups.

"Hiccups are here! Christmas just got better," Rory teased.

"I'm sorry." I laughed.

"For what?" He glanced over at me while still trying to keep his eyes on the road. "I love your hiccups."

Something about the way he'd said it squeezed at my chest, like he was really trying to tell me he loved *me*, not my hiccups.

"I downloaded the whole Chipmunks album if you want to listen to more," he said. "We could just put it on a constant loop, get drunk, and forget the past year ever happened."

"Wouldn't that be something?"

That was an interesting thought. If I could erase the past year, would I? A part of me wished I could go back to the simplicity of the way things were before the break-up. But another part knew I would never trade the time I had with Channing for anything.

"So, who's gonna be there tonight?" I asked.

"Boris, his daughter, Stephanie, her husband, Mitchell, and their daughter, Sophie."

"Wow, okay. I wasn't sure if it was just gonna be him and us."

"He's normally alone. They live in Connecticut, but they're obviously here for Christmas. They're spending the night at his place."

My breath was visible as we stepped out of Rory's BMW and onto the sidewalk in front of his house. Thankfully, my hiccups had subsided.

I could see Boris and his family through the window. Snowflakes were starting to fall. It was going to be a white Christmas after all.

When the door opened, Boris greeted me with welcoming arms. "There she is...the famous Amber. I've heard a lot about you, darlin.' We only have two rules in this house. You make yourself at home, and you leave your troubles behind."

"Well, this sounds like exactly the kind of place I need tonight."

Rory took my coat, and I followed Boris into the kitchen.

"Rory told me you're a Cosmo girl," he said.

It didn't register at first. "A what?"

"The drink. You like it, right? I had Stephanie pick up the ingredients from the liquor store to make you some."

"Oh! The drink. Yes, it's my favorite. That was really nice of you, Boris."

Rory put his hand on Boris' shoulder. "Thank you."

Stephanie came rushing into the kitchen. She was wiping her hand on her pants so she could extend it to me. "Sorry...peanut butter hands. I'm Stephanie. You must be Amber."

"So nice to meet you."

Stephanie kissed Rory on the cheek. It was clear that they considered him like family.

After she introduced me to her husband and daughter, we sat around the living room enjoying our drinks and the appetizers that were laid out on the table.

The artificial Christmas tree was lit up with piles of presents underneath, and holiday music was playing on low volume.

At one point, Stephanie announced that it was time for the annual people decorating tradition. She divided the room into three teams: Boris and Sophie, herself and Mitchell, and Rory and me. The object of the game was that one person would decorate the other like a Christmas tree. Rory volunteered to be the tree for our team.

Stephanie gave out scissors, construction paper, tinsel, foil, tape, and little jingly balls. Each team had ten minutes to decorate their person.

Stephanie would then post pictures on her Facebook page and let her friends decide the winning team.

Rory was a good sport as I wrapped him up like a present. We would laugh every time pieces of paper or tinsel would fall off of him. Our eyes would lock, and for fleeting moments, I would neglect to remember that he wasn't my boyfriend anymore. With just the right amount of alcohol in me and this fun holiday game, it was becoming easier to forget the heartbreaking situation I'd gotten myself into.

The game finished, and Sophie ended up taking the prize. Afterward, we all sat around the living room again for coffee and dessert. It was really hard not to love these people; they were warm and welcoming.

Rory was being very quiet, overall. He'd steal glances at me as he ate his pie, but we were both pretty much letting everyone else take control of the conversations.

"Let me tell you something about your Rory," Stephanie said as she pointed her cheesecake-laden fork at me. *My Rory.* "He's a saint. He is so gosh darn good to my dad. I don't know what I would do if he wasn't looking after him. I used to worry so much, but with Rory upstairs now, I don't have to."

Rory smiled. "Well, he hasn't kicked me out of the house yet, so..."

She looked at me. "You have an amazing boyfriend there."

The expression on his face dampened. Clearly, Stephanie assumed we were together. I was surprised she didn't know, since Rory mentioned he told Boris everything.

Rory looked unsure of whether to correct her then said, "We're not together anymore, actually."

A look of embarrassment washed over Stephanie's face. "Oh...I'm sorry. I just assumed..." She turned to her father. "Dad, you told me they were together."

"I didn't say that. I said...she was his love."

The room went still for a moment.

She looked over at me and seemed to cringe. "Oh, my God. I'm sorry. I feel stupid now. Well, not that my opinion matters, but you two make such a beautiful couple. Truly. I hope you can work it out. You'd make beautiful babies someday."

Her words were like a knife to the heart. I couldn't believe she'd said that. A pain so enormous filled my chest. Just like that, our joyous, merry evening turned dark.

Rory was just looking down at his shoes. He'd been so cool and calm tonight, so positive, really putting his best foot forward to make me comfortable and to enjoy the evening without bringing up any drama. That couldn't have been easy for him given the circumstances. But that comment was like a huge slap in the face, even though she obviously had no clue what she'd done.

He suddenly got up. "Excuse me." Then, he headed toward the kitchen.

I wasn't sure whether to join him or give him space.

Boris struggled to get up from his seat before walking over to the kitchen.

Left alone with Stephanie and her family, I flashed an awkward smile then dove back into my cake, forcing some of it down.

I could overhear Boris talking to Rory from where I was sitting. Since his hearing was going, he didn't do a very good job of whispering.

"I'm sorry, Rory. I didn't tell Stephanie what was going on because I didn't think it was my place."

"It's okay. Don't worry about it. I'm good. I just needed a breather."

"She's lovely, son. I hope it works out."

Unable to take it anymore, I placed my plate down on the coffee table and headed to the kitchen. Boris made his way back to the living room when he noticed me enter.

Rory poured himself some liquor. He didn't look up when he said, "You didn't have to get up. I'm a big boy."

Placing my hand on his arm, I said, "I know you are. You're the strongest person I know."

He froze for a moment upon my touch. "Are you having an okay time?"

"Yeah...everyone is really nice. I'm pleasantly surprised at how comfortable I am here." As he downed the alcohol, I said, "You sure you're okay?"

He placed the glass on the counter. "I'm good. I already said that. I'm great. Why don't you go back to the living room. I'll be right there, okay?"

I searched his face for the truth. "Alright."

He really wasn't okay, but I had to respect his wishes.

We didn't have a clear plan for the rest of the evening. I assumed I'd be going upstairs with him, and that worried me a little, mainly because I didn't know how to handle myself alone with him anymore.

Rory somehow got finagled into making a gingerbread house with Sophie. I watched as he patiently helped her piece everything together.

I was certain that Rory would make a wonderful father someday, regardless of whether the child was his biologically or not. I'd always known that about him because of how well he always took care of me.

Boris took me aside while Rory was still in deep with the gingerbread house.

"Can I talk to you for a minute, darling?"

Taken aback, I stood up from my seat. "Of course."

Rory's eyes darted over to me when he noticed me walking away with the old man. He looked a little alarmed.

Offering a reassuring smile, I mouthed, "It's fine."

He led me down the hall and into his bedroom, which was more like a shrine to the woman I could only assume was his late wife. There were pictures of her and him everywhere, taking up almost every inch of space on his bureau and walls. The décor in the room was still quite feminine, likely her touches that he never wanted to change.

He picked up one of the framed photos. That's my Ellie. See...in the end, all you have are memories. But you get to choose now who stars in the movie that is your life." He put the photo back. "He really deeply loves you."

I swallowed. "I know."

"He told me the whole story...about this Fanning. He's worried that you've really fallen in love with him and that it's too late."

"Channing," I corrected.

"Yeah. Okay, whatever. Anyway, I know this isn't a simple situation. You might be thinking that I asked you to come in here so that I can convince you to take Rory back, but I'm not gonna do such a thing. I would never tamper with a situation that isn't any of my business. No one can tell someone who to love." He pointed to his chest. "The answer is already in your heart...somewhere in here, and it's not going to come from me or anyone else. Only you know what you really want. What I *can* ask you is to not waste his time or lead him on if you figure it out and have no intention of being with him. He may be putting on a strong front, but he's not that strong. He's not stupid, either. He takes full responsibility for the decision he made when he broke up with you. He doesn't expect sympathy. He just wants your love if it's still there, and he's willing to swallow his pride to get it back. If it's not there anymore, then let him find the person he can make memories with."

The thought of Rory moving on with someone else was still a painful one. Old habits die hard.

"I promise, I don't want to string him along. I'm still trying to figure out what's inside. It feels like a jumbled mess right now, and it's literally making me ill. I feel this constant pain inside of my chest that had never been there before, because I'm in love with both of them."

"You might think so, but you can't really be in love with two people. You *want* to love them both because you care for them both. The stress of not wanting anyone to get hurt is suppressing your ability to decipher your true feelings. Don't force it. Let it come to you."

"Thank you for not judging me, Boris. I know your allegiance is with Rory, and please believe me when I say, I only want the best for him, too."

When we returned to the living room, Rory stood up from the couch. I could tell he was itching to leave.

The gingerbread house he'd made with Sophie looked completely finished, covered in frosting, sprinkles, and gumdrops.

"Are you leaving?" Sophie asked him.

"I think I need to get Miss Amber home."

The little girl pouted. "We haven't even eaten the house yet."

He knelt to meet her at eye level. "All that work, and you want to eat it?"

She looked at him like he was crazy for asking. "That's the fun part!"

Stephanie took the hint that we were ready to go. She stood up and offered me a hug. "Amber, it was so nice meeting you. I just friended you on Facebook. Hope you don't mind."

"Not at all, and so great meeting you, too." I looked down at Sophie and smiled. "And you."

Boris hugged me goodbye. "Goodnight, my lady. It was a pleasure."

"The pleasure was all mine."

Once out in the hallway that connected the two apartments, Rory turned to me. "Will you come upstairs for a little while before I drive you back?"

"Yes, of course."

———

Ecstatic to see me, Bruiser jumped up to lick my face when we entered Rory's apartment. The dog followed me over to the couch and placed his head on my lap.

Rory sat across from us on the chaise lounge. "So, are you gonna tell me what Boris said to you? I hope he didn't embarrass me."

"No, it was fine—nothing like that. He told me he knew what was going on with us. He was just looking out for you—and me. He's a good man, very wise."

We were quiet for a while, but he never took his eyes off me. He looked like he had so much to say, though.

Rory's stare was penetrating. "I can't even think about you with Channing." It surprised me that he mentioned his name.

He went on, "I choose not to, because it's too painful for me. But I'm not gonna stand here and tell you all the reasons why I'm a better fit for you, why you should choose me. That's for you to decide. I'm not bringing him into this because my feelings for you have nothing to do with anyone else." He looked down at the ground and shook his head. "I made a mistake—a big one. Nothing good ever comes out of hiding the truth. I've learned my lesson the hard way."

The dog had fallen asleep on me.

Rory suddenly stood up from his chair. "I put something together for you. I didn't know what else to get you."

He went to his bedroom and returned with a thick book then sat back down, this time next to me. "I printed years' worth of our digital photos. I put them in an album in chronological order."

Looking down at the thick book, I said, "I can't believe you took the time to do that."

"Well, I've been dwelling in the past anyway these last few months. Might as well illustrate it all."

He moved closer to me, and the warmth of his body was unsettling. I slowly opened the album and began looking through the photos, which started from when we had first gotten together. *God, we were so young.* And I was so happy.

Flipping through the pages, I really began to remember all of the reasons I'd fallen in love with him, how happy we were together.

I came across the set of photos that were taken the first night we'd ever made love. We were sitting in front of a fire at the cabin Rory had saved for months to rent.

He and I had waited a while to have sex. I was seventeen and had just graduated high school when I lost my virginity.

We lied to our parents, telling them we were going on a camping trip with friends. In reality, Rory had rented a cabin in the woods for just the two of us. Everyone always complains about their first time, how miserable it was. Not mine. My first time was one of the best nights of my life. We were surrounded by candles and a fireplace. Snow was falling outside. And Rory had taken his time with me. He'd had sex with one other person before we'd gotten together, so I wasn't his first. He knew what he was doing and made love to me so slowly and sensually, making sure to break me in easily. There was a little blood, but there was never any pain. And once we did it a couple of times and it was no longer painful, we couldn't get enough of each other. We stayed holed up, screwing each other's brains out in that cabin for two days straight. It was bliss.

"I'll never forget that night," I whispered.

Rory was lost in thought for a few seconds before he said, "Yeah. It was pretty fucking awesome."

It took the better part of an hour to get through all of the photos he'd printed out. Seeing nine years playing before my eyes like a movie made the ache in my chest even more profound. But he was trying to get me to remember when I'd never actually forgotten.

"I'll always cherish this album. Thank you."

"You're welcome."

Glancing out the window, I noticed that the snow was really starting to come down. Had it been snowing like this the whole time we were here?

Rory turned the news on, and the weather lady was immediately warning against being out on the roads unless it was an emergency. It hit me then that there was no way I was getting home tonight.

He looked at me with a slight smirk. "I swear...I didn't plan this."

"Black ice? That's kind of scary."

His mouth curved into a smile. "Scarier than spending the night here alone with me?"

"Just by a little."

We shared a laugh before he said, "I'll sleep on the couch. But you won't be sleeping alone in my bed. Bruisey's gonna want to sleep next to you, like old times."

"Poor Bruisey. He's gonna be so confused."

"Since we're gonna be here a while, why don't I make us some hot chocolate."

Hot chocolate.

That immediately made me think of Channing.

"Sure."

I slipped out from under the sleeping dog and joined Rory in the kitchen where we sat and sipped the hot cocoa he'd made. Under any other circumstances, being snowed in with this handsome man who'd been my entire life for so long would have been a dream.

He must have been able to sense my inner turmoil when he said, "Don't feel guilty when you look at me. I caused this myself. All of it."

"No, you didn't. You didn't cause the accident. You were in shock, and you did what you thought was right. You thought you were protecting me. This whole situation...it's nobody's fault. I don't blame you for anything anymore now that I understand what really happened."

"My entire reason for coming back was that I could no longer live with you thinking I didn't love you. I just waited too long."

Leaning in and grabbing his hands, I said, "I know you love me. It's one of the few things I'm sure of right now."

My touching him may have been too much because he suddenly ripped himself away from me and walked across the room.

Placing his head in his hands, he said, "When I thought about my future, I always pictured it with you. Now, I see... nothing. I just don't know what it looks like." For the first time, I could see his eyes water. He seemed angry with himself for losing the composure he'd tried so hard for. "So much for a drama-free Christmas," he muttered.

Getting up and pulling him into a hug, I wanted to just take his pain away, reassure him that everything would be okay, that I still loved him. *I did*. But it wasn't that simple. It wasn't just us anymore.

His heart was beating rampantly, and my own was matching his rhythm. He was breathing fast, frantic breaths into my neck. And slowly his lips travelled upward. My body stirred as his mouth landed on mine. I didn't have the heart to pull away, nor did I want to.

The kiss got more intense fast. We'd kissed thousands of times before this, but never had it felt so desperate, so forbidden, so bittersweet.

Somehow, I ended up pinned against the wall. He whispered over my mouth, "I want you, and I can't have you, and that's fucking killing me, because I still feel like you're mine." He leaned his head against mine. The pain in his voice was palpable, and it permeated my entire being. "I miss your laughter, miss the way you used to look at me, miss your love and goddammit...I miss fucking you. I miss fucking you so damn much. I'd just about give my life at this point to be inside of you again." He buried his face in my neck. "I'm so fucking hard right now."

I was beginning to realize how very dangerous this was. His words were making me wet. My body was turned on as he continued to press against me. I was getting carried away. I couldn't remember the last time things felt this intense with Rory.

I'm a terrible person.

I couldn't let this go on a second longer.

Pulling myself away from him, I said, "I'm sorry."

He placed his hand over his face, scrubbing his skin and nodding as if he'd expected me to pull away. "It's okay."

I retreated to his room for the rest of the evening. As expected, Bruiser followed me into the bed.

Drowning in Rory's familiar scent, I cried myself to sleep, my tears seeping through the fabric of his pillow.

⌒

Rory dropped me back off at my place early the next morning.

Once home, when I logged into my messages, I realized an email from Channing had come in overnight.

> **Dear Amber,**
>
> **Attached is something I put together for you today. It's a playlist of songs that remind me of us. Who knew that moving back to Chicago and being away from you would turn me into such a sap? Tell Milo I don't need him to emasculate me anymore; I'm doing a damn good job of that myself. In all seriousness, I hope you like it. At the very least, don't laugh at me.**
>
> **Merry Christmas.**
>
> **Love, Channing**

Plugging my headphones in, I lay back and pressed play on the first song.

It was *Wake Me Up When September Ends* by Green Day. There was no doubt behind the meaning. Lainey had died in September. He'd mentioned once before that this song would always remind him of her. It touched me that he'd chosen to start with that one. As painful as it was, the fact would always remain that Lainey's death was what really brought the two of us together as friends.

The next couple of songs, which included *Best Friend* by Jason Mraz and *You Are The Sunshine of My Life* by Stevie Wonder, I could only assume, represented our friendship as teenagers.

When *What Hurts The Most* by Rascal Flatts came on, it completely changed the tone of the playlist. I knew that reflected the time after he returned home from college— when everything had changed between us.

He'd only included the one melancholy song, which transitioned into another song that made me crack the hell up. It was *Just a Friend* by Biz Markie. That was apparently representative of the beginnings of our time together in Boston and his denial about his feelings for me.

The final song was *Perfect* by Ed Sheeran. The lyrics made me cry because they seemed to represent his ultimately falling in love with me. It truly *was* perfect.

⌒

"I kissed Rory."

The guilt had felt like it was killing me. After hours of listening to Channing's playlist, I finally built up the courage to dial him and vomited out those words the second he picked up.

The silence on the other end of the line was deafening, so I continued, "He was just so hurt and emotional, and I got caught up in the moment and the memories. I felt like I needed to tell you. I don't ever want to keep anything from you."

He finally spoke, "Yeah, well some things I'm not sure I want to know." There was a long pause before he expelled a long breath into the phone. "Did anything else happen?"

"No. It snowed really badly here last night. It was too dangerous for him to drive me home, so I spent the night there. He slept on the couch. I slept in the bedroom with Bruiser. Then, he drove me home this morning. I came home to your playlist. It was so touching. I can't even tell you how mu—"

"Thank you for telling me." Even though he was thanking me, he sounded beyond pissed. "Since we're being honest...I should tell you that I kissed Emily last night."

His admission took a few seconds to compute. I swallowed. "What?"

"Yeah. She came by to say goodbye before heading back to Boston, and we ended up kissing before she left."

My mouth felt parched as I swallowed hard. "Oh..."

It felt like he'd just shredded my heart to pieces even though it was incredibly unfair of me to react that way. My brain felt depleted, unable to form a coherent response.

"Are you still there?" he asked.

"Yes."

"Are you alright?"

"Not really."

"Save your hyperventilation, Amber. It didn't happen. I just made it up, so you would know what this feels like."

The breath I'd been holding finally escaped me. "Oh, my God."

"Feel that relief? Well, I'm feeling the exact opposite right now. A part of me prepared myself for this, but that's not making it any easier."

"Yeah. Well, I completely deserved that."

Sounding understandably pissed, he said, "I need to just...not talk for a little bit, okay? I'm gonna let you go."

He hung up before I could say anything further.

⌒

That night over the phone, Annabelle tried her best to cheer me up after I recalled what happened with Channing.

"Stop beating yourself up over it. No one crucifies *The Bachelorette* for kissing ten different guys in a week or taking three of them to a fantasy suite."

"I'm not the freaking *Bachelorette*. I have no excuse. And Channing didn't sign up for some reality show."

"Anyone in your position would've done the same thing. You're supposed to be figuring things out. This is the rest of your life we're talking about. Kissing Rory was part of the process. This is a man you've made love to countless times. You just kissed him. You didn't let it go any farther. It was a moment, and it passed."

Feeling weakness throughout my entire body, I said, "I don't feel so well, Annabelle. I feel like I can't even stand up."

"It's stress. It will always catch up with you."

"Maybe. It feels like more than that, though. I don't know."

"What does it feel like?"

The answer to that question came easy. "Honestly? It feels like I'm dying from a broken heart."

CHAPTER TWENTY-FIVE
CHANNING

Maybe I was being too harsh on her. After all, she didn't have to admit anything. Amber was being honest, and I'd basically punished her for it.

But I couldn't help my reaction. It downright pissed me off that she'd kissed Rory. It made me jealous as all hell. While I could accept giving her this time to sort things out, I sure as fuck didn't have to be happy about it.

It had been four days since I hung up on her. I was being a dick. And I never called her back. She hadn't called me either, though, so I had to wonder if I was losing this war.

On top of worrying about Amber, I had a lot to handle at home. While Mom was stable, I was spending my days figuring out a daytime situation for her. It no longer seemed feasible to have her all alone while I worked, so I was looking into hiring someone to look after her even if just for parts of the day.

I ended up moving back into the house I grew up in to care for her but kept my apartment for the time being. My life in Chicago looked nothing like it used to and suddenly came with a tremendous amount of responsibility.

But this was my mother—the only family I had left. If it was the last thing I did, I was going to make sure she was safe and well-cared for. No one was going to do that better than I could. No one loved her like I did.

Mom was still sleeping when my cell phone rang on this particular morning. It was Amber's friend, Annabelle. Her number had been programmed into my phone from that one time I asked for her assistance in hand delivering Amber's Christmas box.

But it was odd that she'd be calling me.

I answered, "Annabelle?"

"Channing, hi." Her tone was melancholy.

"What's going on? Is everything okay?"

"Amber doesn't know I'm calling you, but I thought you should know that she was admitted to the hospital a couple of days ago."

"What? What happened?"

"She has pneumonia and severe dehydration. I think she was so stressed out that she stopped taking care of herself...caught something. I'd gone to her condo to check on her after she stopped answering my calls, and she was in bad shape. She told me she felt like she was dying, so I drove her to Mass General. Anyway, she's been here ever since. They're pumping her with antibiotics and steroids, and they're not letting her go until her lungs have cleared. I just thought you should know."

My heartbeat was out of control, and a rush of adrenaline shot through me. I suddenly felt helpless. "Fuck...I obviously had no idea. We...hadn't been speaking."

"I know. She was really messed up over that. She'd kill me if she knew I was calling you right now, but I felt that it was the right thing to do. I figured you'd want to know."

"You said...Mass General?"

"Yes. Room 805 if by some chance you can fly out here."

⌒

I couldn't believe that I had no idea she was so sick. That was proof that I'd let my anger go too far. Were it not for Annabelle calling me, I would've still been in the dark for God knows how long. If something had happened to Amber when we weren't speaking, I'd never forgive myself.

I ended up driving my mother over to her sister's house, which was nearly two hours away from Chicago so that I could head to Boston.

I didn't even know whether Amber was going to want me there; I just knew I *needed* to be there.

The ride from the airport to the hospital was a blur. With only a small backpack, I had no idea how long I'd be staying or what was going to happen.

When the Uber dropped me off in front of Mass General, I rushed to the eighth floor as fast as I could.

It shouldn't have shocked me to see him standing right outside of her hospital room door. But it did. I hadn't expected to have to run into Rory at that moment.

My body went rigid, and my fists instinctively tightened. My guard was fully up when he turned around and noticed me.

"How is she?" I asked.

Rory tossed his empty cup of coffee almost violently into a nearby trashcan.

Nice to see you, too.

"She's sleeping. In fact, she *just* fell asleep. I would wait to go in there. You'll wake her up, and she needs her rest."

"I'm sure if it were up to you, she'd be sleeping all day if it kept me out."

I wasn't about to take his word for it. Peeking through the glass, I could see he wasn't making it up, though. Amber looked like an angel as she lay there with her eyes closed, an IV connected to her arm. She was wearing a light blue hospital gown, and her hair was disheveled

An incredible sadness came over me. It felt like I was breaking inside with each second that I watched her lying there helpless. Look at how much I missed because of my ego. This was a lesson to never, ever part with someone angry—never assume you'll have all the time in the world to work things out. Amber was probably going to be fine, but what if that weren't the case? Pneumonia is no joke.

Rory and I were now both side by side, silently competing for space to look through the narrow window on the door. If testosterone in the air could have cured her illness, Amber's lungs would have cleared in no time

He spoke first. "I've never seen her this sick."

My anger was rising. "We fucking did this to her."

He abruptly faced me. "You're blaming me?"

"I said *we*. Not you. This whole situation. She's been under so much stress that it wore down her immune system."

"I never meant to cause her pain by coming back," he said.

"I know that."

Rory seemed surprised that I'd agreed with him and seemed to calm down a little. "When did you get in?"

"Just now. I came here straight from the airport. Have you been here the whole time with her?"

"She's been here for a couple of days. I've been here the majority of the time."

Still looking through the window at her, I asked, "Is she gonna be alright?"

"Yeah. At this point, they're just monitoring her. This is the first time she's really fallen asleep. She needed it badly."

As much as we were making an attempt to be cordial, you could cut the tension in the air with a knife. It felt like it was only a matter of time before one of us lost it on the other.

"Why did you even come here, Channing?"

And with that, it would seem my losing it would be happening sooner rather than later.

I whipped my head toward him. "Excuse me?"

"She told me you weren't even speaking to her. She didn't even do anything wrong."

I was ready to punch him. "Well, forgive me if I got upset because my girlfriend kissed her ex-boyfriend."

He angrily laughed at me. "*Your* girlfriend? She's not your girlfriend."

"The fuck, she isn't. She became mine long before you came back from the dead and fucked everything up."

"Sorry to ruin your plan of fucking me over the first chance you got. You mean to tell me that Boston job was a coincidence? You heard we broke up and wasted no time pouncing on her."

I bent my head back in laughter. "Are you kidding me? You have some nerve to accuse me of that when *you're* the one who fucking pounced on her the second I went away to college. You knew how I—"

"Excuse me, gentlemen!" A nurse interrupted our sparring. "You're going to need to take this outside. A hospital floor is no place for a fight between two grown men."

Rory and I just death stared at each other for a few seconds. Huffing and puffing, we stalked over to the elevators and down to the lobby.

Exiting the building in silence, I wasn't sure if we were about to roll up our sleeves and go at it outside or what. All I knew was, whatever was about to happen between us had been a long time coming, a decade in the making.

We ended up in a grassy area off to the side of the building that was adjacent to a parking lot. There was no one else in sight, which was probably a good thing.

He held his hands out. "What are we even doing out here? What do you want from me, Channing? It's not enough that you stole the only woman I've ever loved out from under me, fucked her, and manipulated her into falling for you?"

I got in his face. "Is that what you really think? You think what she and I have isn't real? I feel sorry for you if that's the case, because you're gravely misinformed with a false sense of confidence. You weren't there. You have no idea what's developed between us."

"You wouldn't know a mature relationship if it hit you in the face, Lord. Have you ever told her exactly how many women you slept with before her?"

"She knows everything about me. And I'm not the guy you *think* you know. But I don't owe you an explanation of how or why I might have changed. I'm not looking for your opinion."

"I don't believe that you *have* changed. I think Amber was a revenge fuck for you."

Now, he was going below the belt.

"You're really looking to get decked, aren't you?" I unintentionally spit at him when I said, "Don't you ever utter those words again unless you want your face rearranged."

"So, then, tell me why. How was it that you ended up with Amber as soon as we'd broken up? Out of all of the women in the world you could've been with, you ended up with *my* girl?"

"I was there for her because you dicked her over, jackass—or so we thought. No one knew your real reason for leaving her at the time. She was shattered. You'd broken her heart. That was all I knew. Amber and I never stopped being friends even when you guys were together—you know that. Why should it surprise you that I was there for her when you crushed her?"

"'There for her' equals fucking her? Isn't that taking advantage of a vulnerable person?"

"Again, I don't owe you any explanations...but it wasn't my intention to fall in love with her. Believe me, I tried as hard as I could not to."

"Well, you should've fought harder."

I leaned in and took pleasure in saying, "Best thing I ever did was to give up the fight."

He gritted his teeth. "So, that's it? You think you can just appear out of nowhere and steal her from me when she and I have nine years of history together?"

"Out of nowhere? I think there's a little more to the story than that. Do I need to remind you that you stole her from under *me*? You knew she was interested in me before I left for UF. Yeah…she told me. You warned her against me."

"She was innocent. You were not a good fit for her. It was the right thing to do at the time."

"Of course, it was the right thing—for you. It was all part of your plan."

"So, fucking sue me for wanting her so much that I was willing to sacrifice our friendship for it. That was how much she meant to me. I couldn't help that I fell in love with her."

"Well, I can't help that I'm in love with her now. You threw away what you had because of a bad decision you made. You chose not to be up front with her. You ended it and left her completely devastated. I picked up the pieces, and you know what? I don't want to give them back. I love every single broken piece of her. And I can't feel guilty about that, even though I'm really sorry about what happened to you after the accident."

Rory rolled his eyes. "I bet you are."

Shit.

He couldn't have been more wrong. I took a moment to step back and gather my thoughts.

"Is that what you think? What kind of a person do you think I am? You think what happened to you makes me happy?" An unexpected flurry of emotion came over me in that moment when I noticed the true sadness and regret in his eyes. "I'm fucking devastated for you. You were my best friend at one time. I would *never* wish that on you. Never."

We stood in silence just staring at each other, seeming to calm down with each second that passed.

"Yeah, well..." He kicked some dirt. "I still think she'd be better off without me. I just don't know how to *stop* loving her."

"You and me both."

We continued to stand face to face.

"I guess, in a lot of ways, we're right back where we started," he said. "We both want her, and we both can't have her." Rory paused, looking up at the sky and then back at me. "I know you probably think I didn't care about what I did when I broke the pact we made all those years ago, but I felt like a piece of shit for doing that to you. Not that it's any consolation now."

"As much as you did me dirty, I honestly can't say I wouldn't have done the same thing if it were you who went away and if she'd expressed an interest in me. So, I can't hold you to a standard that I couldn't uphold when it comes to myself. I actually forgave you in my head a long time ago."

"So, if you forgive me, why did you look like you wanted to kill me earlier?"

"That was because of your second-guessing my current intentions. Maybe this would be easier for you to accept if you thought all she was to me was a revenge fuck. But I think at this point, we just need to understand that the one thing we do agree on is that we both want what's best for Amber, and we both want her to be happy. None of us chose the situation we're in now. It just happened. And ultimately, it's Amber who decides whom she wants to spend her life with. If she chooses you, I'm not gonna interfere. And I expect the same from you."

I wasn't anticipating what came out of his mouth next.

"I lie awake at night praying she chooses me. And the other half of the time, I'm praying she doesn't...because I'll never be able to give her everything she deserves."

It genuinely did hurt me to think about what happened to Rory. I couldn't imagine having to deal with that on top of everything else. But I knew Amber. And if she believed Rory was the one for her, his not being able to have children wouldn't deter her from wanting to be with him. Amber was naturally loving. I could easily see her adopting and treating that child like it was her own. Just look at the way she was with Milo.

"Don't do that to yourself, man," I simply said.

His hardened expression seemed to soften. "Where do we go from here?"

"We shake hands and agree not to make this more difficult than it already is."

Rory held out his hand to me, and I took it. I didn't know what came over me when I suddenly yanked him toward me into a hug. Then, we patted each other on the back.

"I'm sorry to hear about your mother," he said.

"Thank you."

"She was always so nice to me."

"Yeah. She always liked you." I grinned and joked, "She never was a good judge of character."

He smiled. "Jackass."

As we walked back into the hospital, Rory turned to me and said, "I wasn't thinking I'd be heading back in here unscathed. You disappoint me, Lord. I was expecting at least a bloody lip."

"You hurt Amber again, and I'll be happy to deliver that and more. No matter how this story ends, I will always have Amber's back, which means you'll have to watch yours."

He smacked me hard on the back. "Same goes for you."

The nurse who'd scolded us earlier was watching us like a hawk when we returned to the floor. Assuming our position in front of the narrow window on Amber's door, we could see through the glass that she was no longer sleeping.

"Looks like she's awake," Rory said. "I was gonna go down to the cafeteria and get some coffee. You want anything?"

I knew he was intentionally giving me time alone with her, and I appreciated that.

"Nah. I think I'm just gonna go on in and let her know I'm here."

He nodded once. "Alright."

I watched as he walked toward the elevators. I'd come to Boston hoping to make things right with Amber. I never expected to make peace with Rory.

I guess holiday miracles do happen.

CHAPTER TWENTY-SIX
AMBER

Blinking my eyes open, I had no idea how long I'd been sleeping nor what day it was. The grid-like squares of fluorescent light on the ceiling were giving me a headache as was the smell of the hospital itself, a mix of antiseptic and flesh.

That feeling of dread whenever I thought about my current reality started to seep in as I became more coherent.

The meds they were giving me were working but not fast enough. Grabbing for the remote, I turned on the television and blankly stared at the news program that was on. The bed adjacent to mine was empty, and for that, I was grateful.

There was a slight knock. Assuming it was the nurse coming to take my vitals, I didn't even look in the direction of the door.

When he appeared at my bedside, the recognition of his scent made me realize it wasn't a nurse after all.

As I looked up at Channing, I could hardly believe he was here. As my heart pumped faster, I shut off the television. My eyes closed as his hand slowly reached my cheek. He smelled like the outside mixed with sandalwood, literally a breath of fresh air in this stagnant place.

"How are you feeling?"

"I've been better." I smiled. "But I'm going to be okay."

He exhaled and took my hand. "Thank God. I was worried sick."

A feeling so powerful came over me. I finally understood what people like Boris and Annabelle had been telling me all along—that there would come a time when what I was truly feeling would reveal itself organically. Inexplicably, I would know where my heart was. It was a feeling that couldn't be quantified nor was it premeditated. It just happened upon me naturally and unexpectedly.

This sickness had knocked the wind out of me. But it had also given me more time to reflect on my life. It wasn't until he was right in front of me at this very moment that I became certain of my truest feelings—that I couldn't live without this man. I'd been miserable from the moment he left to go back to Chicago.

"Where's Rory?" I asked.

The expression on his face darkened. He was probably assuming that my question meant I needed Rory more than him. The truth was, I needed to make sure that Rory wasn't going to walk in at this particular moment. I knew Rory had been at the hospital almost the entire time I was here.

"He went down to the cafeteria to grab a coffee."

The sentiment was practically bursting through my chest. "I love you, Channing."

He looked shocked, and then his eyes filled with hope once what I'd just said hit him. "You do?"

He knew that I vowed never to say those words unless I truly meant them.

"I love you. I promised you I wouldn't say it until I was yours. There is no doubt in my mind that I belong with you. I've never been more scared than these past few days when I thought I was losing you for good."

"What about Rory?" The tone of his question and the look in his eyes reflected what seemed almost like concern for Rory. It was an interesting observation.

Of course, the mere mention of Rory's name caused me to start to cry. I would always love him. And a huge part of me felt absolutely terrible right now. But what it came down to was simple.

"My heart beats stronger for you, Channing. I love Rory. I will always love him. And that's something that I hope you can understand. But love isn't always only about the person who makes you feel the safest or even how much you care about someone. Sometimes, it's about the person who ignites your soul, and that may also be the person you fear the most. Sometimes love entails taking the biggest risk. You're the biggest risk, because losing you would be the most earth-shattering thing. My love for you is different. It's something I can't live without. I learned to live without Rory. I can't live without you now that I know what it's like to have you in my life. I never want to know what losing you is like."

He let out the biggest sigh of relief. "God, I was bracing myself to lose *you*. You have no idea."

"I will never make you feel like you have to doubt my intentions again."

Channing's eyes were watery. "I love you so much, Amber. I'm sorry I acted like a dick this week. I was just scared."

"I know you were. So was I." It hit me that he'd come all the way from Chicago and left Christine. "Who's with your mother?"

"I drove her to her sister's house, a couple of hours away from us. She's fine. I told her to expect that I'd be gone a few days. I'll be here with you for New Year's."

"How did you even know I was here at the hospital?"

"Annabelle called me. Don't be mad at her."

Rolling my eyes, I nodded. "I should've known."

He took my hand. "So, what now? Do you think Rory knows where your heart is?"

"I have to tell him. I'm going to need to talk to him today."

He bit his lip, looking pensive. "Okay." It touched me to see how much compassion Channing seemed to have. He wasn't gloating; he seemed seriously concerned for Rory.

Channing lowered his head down on my chest. "I don't ever want to be apart from you again." He continued to lay his head there as I ran my fingers through his hair. It was a perfect moment.

We were in our own world. So much so that when Rory entered the room, I hadn't noticed, until he was standing before us, holding two coffees, and looking like *his* world just ended.

I'd been expecting some sort of confrontation between them, but it never happened. Channing looked somber as he glanced over at Rory. The animosity that previously existed seemed to have disappeared.

Channing squeezed my hand and said, "I need a shower. I'm gonna head to your place. I still have the key. I'll be back soon."

Then, he quietly slipped out of the room, leaving Rory and me alone.

When the door latched closed, Rory put the coffees down and just continued to stand there frozen.

He knew.

"Don't say it. I already know what's going on, and I just can't bear to hear you say the words."

No longer able to contain my tears, I cried, "I'm so sorry, Rory."

Rory stayed at the opposite end of the room. He looked distraught when he said, "This past week—even before you got sick—you'd been completely distant. I knew you were thinking of him. I knew I was losing you for good."

I tried to compose myself to best explain what I was feeling. There was no easy way to do it. I just had to spit it out, even though it hurt me.

"When you told me to explore other people, that's what I did. And I found someone with whom I have a deeper connection, a connection that in retrospect goes way back. The reason why you left isn't important. The fact is, you let me go long enough to realize my feelings for someone else—someone whom I've grown to love. I'll always love you, too. I just can't be with you anymore, as much as that hurts me to finally admit." My voice was shaky. "I hope you can find it in your heart to forgive me."

He was looking down. "I can't look at you right now. It's too painful. But I want you to know that there's nothing to forgive. You didn't do anything wrong. I just hope you made the right decision."

There was a curtain serving as a partition between me and the empty adjacent bed. Rory disappeared behind there for several minutes. I didn't want to imagine he was crying. And I couldn't imagine how he was feeling.

His eyes were red when he reemerged. Rory slowly approached me and took both of my hands in his, kissing them firmly. "Are you gonna be okay if I go home?"

The fact that he even cared hurt my heart. "Of course."

The level of respect I had for how he'd handled himself during this entire ordeal was boundless. My respect for *him* was boundless.

Nothing would ever erase the significance of the time we had together. Everyone who comes into your life serves a purpose to teach you in some way. Rory taught me how to love. And for that, I would be eternally grateful. I would pray every night that he'd find the kind of love he was so deserving of, the kind that would make him realize that what just happened between us happened for a reason.

CHAPTER TWENTY-SEVEN
AMBER

EIGHT MONTHS LATER

Since moving to Chicago, phone calls from Annabelle were always a welcome addition to any afternoon.

"Someone wants to say hello," she said.

His voice was deep as he droned, "Hiiii."

"Hi, Milo! I miss you!"

She came back on the line. "Wasn't that adorable? He's smiling, too."

"You're gonna make me cry."

"I told him we were going to call Amber, and you know what he did? He pulled up an old Daria video on YouTube."

"Shut up! That's so funny. That's the cartoon version of me."

"I know! I remember you told me that."

"Hysterical."

Annabelle proved exactly how much of a true of a friend she was before I left Boston. Shortly after I was discharged from the hospital, it became clear that if Channing and I were going to be together, one of us had to move. Taking Christine out of the only environment she was familiar with was not going to help her ability to sustain her awareness. As heartbreaking as it was to think about leaving Boston behind, the decision was a no-brainer. Channing needed to be in Chicago. He was my home. I needed to move home.

But I refused to go until I could find someone trustworthy to work with Milo at night. It wasn't my responsibility to find a replacement per se. The agency that assigned me to his case technically would find one eventually. But I didn't trust that they would find the *right* person. I wanted someone who would stay for a while and really nurture him, someone who would care for him as well as I did.

During the weeks that I was still in Boston after Channing returned to Chicago, Annabelle could see how hard it was for me living away from him while I tried to get my ducks in order. She insisted that I let her be an interim replacement for Milo and that she would also work to find a permanent person. She pretended like she was welcoming the break from her kids in the evenings, but I knew working those extra hours was a sacrifice she was making for me. Since she had the same level of experience working with special needs individuals that I did, I was comfortable leaving him in her hands. So desperate to be with Channing, I eventually gave in, and thankfully, it seemed to have worked out really well. Eight months later, she was still looking after him, but it seemed to be purely by choice.

"He's really doing okay?"

"He's doing awesome. It's a family affair up in here. He loves hanging out with Jenna and Alex. And they love him. They always ask me if he really has to go back to the group home. It's sweet. The big question is…how are you? I miss my friend."

"I miss you, too...so much." I sighed. "Things here are...busy. Every day with Christine is full of ups and downs, but every day I realize more and more that this is where I belong."

"Oh, I know you're exactly where you're meant to be."

"It's really nice getting to see my parents whenever I want, too. They've been coming over some nights and having dinner with us."

My parents were really shocked at first to find out I was with Channing but finally warmed up to him. They had always been big Rory fans. The idea of me with Channing Lord definitely took a lot of getting used to for them.

"Have I told you how happy I am for you?"

"Once or twice." I laughed.

"I'd better go. I promised Milo I'd take him to get ice cream. The kids are coming, too."

"Have fun. I love you."

"Love you, too.

It became clear pretty quickly after moving to Chicago that the place I was needed most was with Christine. It was hard finding a reliable person to take care of her during the day. So, since I arrived jobless, rather than pay someone, it just made sense that I would be the one to take care of her—at least until it became too difficult.

You couldn't put a price on the peace of mind that granted Channing, knowing I was looking after his mother while he worked. I knew how hard it had been for him as he juggled everything while trying to find the right situation for her. To be able to alleviate the brunt of that stress was a rewarding feeling. Not to mention, I genuinely loved Christine—not just because she was Channing and Lainey's mother, but because she was a kind soul. There were lots of terrifying moments, where she wouldn't acknowledge me or couldn't remember where we were earlier in the day, but there were still so many moments of clarity and humor. As her condition worsened, she seemed to get more and more loving and affectionate—that was typical from what I heard in talking to other caregivers of people with dementia.

The thing about always having Christine around was that Channing and I weren't as free to express ourselves sexually around the house. We'd take advantage of the moments she was in her bedroom to steal kisses or feel up on each other. Sneaking around was kind of fun and made our alone time behind closed doors all the more special. Everything leading up to that was foreplay. Not to mention, we now inhabited Channing's old room, so it always felt a little naughty to be having sex in his old bed.

Even though Channing worked a long day, he always insisted on cooking his mother and me dinner when he got home. He was the better cook—even when he made weird things—so no one complained about that arrangement. Channing claimed that cooking helped him unwind after a long day. He'd pour a glass of wine, play music on his iPod, shake his ass around, and sing while at the stove. Kitty would be weaving in and out of his legs. You could take the cat out of Boston, but nothing had changed when it came to that relationship.

No matter what, each day ended with the three of us sitting down to dinner together. You never knew what you were going to get with Christine. Some nights she was fine, others more confused.

Tonight after we were wrapping up our meal, she threw out a whopper of a question.

"Can you take me to buy a dress, Amber?"

Washing the dishes, I looked over at her. "Sure. What's the occasion?"

"For the wedding."

"What wedding?" Channing asked.

Bracing myself, I hoped to God she didn't momentarily think she was still with Channing's father. How devastating.

"Your wedding."

I momentarily stopped washing the dishes.

Channing placed his hand on her shoulder. "My wedding to Amber?"

"Yes—to that beautiful woman right there. You're getting married, right?"

Channing and I were not engaged. We knew we wanted to spend the rest of our lives with each other, but it was understood that things were a little crazy right now. Although, the truth was, I would have married him in a heartbeat if he asked.

It surprised me when he said without hesitation, "Yes, we are getting married."

My eyes narrowed. "We are?"

"I need a pretty dress, then," Christine insisted.

"We can get you one," he said.

"Tomorrow?"

"Sure. Maybe Amber can take you."

My mouth was ajar. What was he getting at here?

Christine suddenly got up and headed toward her room. "I keep forgetting there's something I have to give you, Channing. It can't wait any longer."

When she returned, she opened a small, red box that had a gorgeous diamond sandwiched inside an antique-looking setting.

"This was your Grandmother Faye's wedding ring. She had given me this diamond for Lainey. But I want you to have it...for Amber."

He took it from her and examined it. "It's beautiful, Mom."

Channing looked like he was deep in thought as he held the ring in his hand.

He put it back in the box, and his eyes flashed up at me. "Can I talk to you for a minute?"

I wiped my hands on a dishtowel. "Sure."

He took me aside in the living room.

"If I asked you to marry me tonight with my mother watching, would you say yes?"

Suddenly, my pulse was racing. "Of course, I would."

"Fuck, I know that this is coming across as really unromantic. But I didn't want to do it in front of her unless you felt you were ready to accept. I'd never want to put you in that position. I know we said we were gonna wait a while. But I want her to see me ask you, to be there—even if she can't remember later. I want her to experience that...if it's okay with you."

Wrapping my hands around his face, I pulled him into a kiss then said, "I would marry you tomorrow."

"You would? Don't you want a big wedding?"

"I want Christine there more. Having a big wedding would require a lot of planning. She might not—"

"I know. That's my fear, that she'll be worse by the time we plan something."

"Of course." I ran my hand along his cheek. "That's a legitimate concern."

"I've known for a really long time that I want to marry you. For me, it doesn't matter if we do it tomorrow or next year. I know you're it for me, Amber."

"Why don't we do something small so that she can be there? And someday if we still want something bigger we can do that, too. Or we can just use the money for a kickass honeymoon."

"You'd really marry me tomorrow?" He smiled. "Okay...maybe not tomorrow...but say...this weekend?"

I didn't have to think twice. "Yes."

He cocked his brow. "Literally? And be careful how you answer."

"Yes...literally."

⌒

We *literally* took our butts down to city hall the next day to apply for a marriage license.

A few days later, that weekend, my father walked me down the aisle in a small ceremony held at The Ambassador Chicago.

We'd called around to a number of places, and it just so happened that the hotel's amazing rooftop wasn't booked on Sunday. With the Chicago skyline and peeks of Lake Michigan as our backdrop, we were able to put together an intimate celebration with just our parents.

By the grace of God, Christine was having a mostly good day, and we got so many photos taken with her.

It meant so much to Channing to have his mother there and somewhat alert. We'd bought her a beautiful champagne-colored dress. I wore a simple A-line, white strapless gown with sequin beading on the bodice.

We chose not to go on a honeymoon yet. Instead, we spent our wedding night like we spent every evening—in our cozy home.

Channing had changed out of his suit and was taking a shower when I decided to venture alone to Lainey's old room. Living in Channing and Lainey's childhood house was a very emotional experience. I'd spend a lot of time in that room, which was now a guest bedroom. There were boxes of her stuff still in the closet. One of my favorite things to do was to spend some quiet time each night reading through her old diaries. I'd debated for a while whether it was even appropriate to read through them. Channing was the one who finally convinced me that Lainey wouldn't care. He pointed out that she'd told me most of her secrets and would want me to find comfort in her words all these years after her death.

The journals mostly contained innocent stuff. She wrote about boys she had a crush on or what she did during a particular day. The normal passage of time meant that I'd become disconnected from Lainey as the years passed, but reading her diaries brought her spirit back to me so clearly. I could feel her presence again. It was like reliving my own childhood in many ways.

On this special night, still in my white wedding dress and lying on the floor, I came across an ironic passage she'd written the year of her death that made me smile from ear to ear.

Today we went to the public pool down on Wellis. It was me, Channing, Amber, and Silas. I'm starting to think that Channing might like Amber. I really hope I'm wrong. Because that would be disgusting beyond belief.

Amber was wearing a bikini with strawberries on it. When she bent down to pick up her towel off the ground, her boobs spilled out a little. Channing kept staring at her. And this went on for the rest of the day. I'd keep catching him gawking.

Anyway: TOTALLY GROSS.

My shoulders shook in laughter as I closed the notebook. That was the perfect way to end this day. It was Lainey's way of congratulating us.

EPILOGUE
CHANNING

My mother's arms were open wide. "Hi! Hi, you beauti-ful, precious thing. What's your name?"

"Lainey."

"Lainey! That's such a beautiful name." She beamed. "And how old are you, Lainey?"

"I'm free."

"Three?"

She held up three fingers. "Free."

"Would you like a piece of candy?"

Lainey nodded enthusiastically.

"Just one," Amber warned.

Mom reached in her drawer for a peppermint starlight mint and handed it to our daughter.

Amber helped remove the wrapper and said, "What do you say, Lainey?"

"Thank you, Gamma."

"You're welcome, sweetheart."

This was probably the twentieth time that my moth-er had met her granddaughter for "the first time." Lainey was a good sport and just went along with it, always wel-

308

coming the grand reception she got. Mom always gave her candy, too, so naturally, Lainey was thrilled with that. We told her that Grandma can't remember things, but I'm not sure she fully understood. Either way, she never seemed to mind being doted on with the same enthusiasm each visit. It was hard to watch, and at the same time, it was beautiful to see my mother's joy repeated over and over.

Mom's condition deteriorated significantly over the years. Her dementia had an atypically fast progression. We tried to keep her at home for as long as possible, but it became too difficult to give her the care she needed, especially after the baby came. We got her into a facility close to home, though, and thankfully, they seemed to be taking really good care of her. Several necklaces adorned her neck. Her hair was done up nice, and her nails were always freshly painted. The women who worked there really made sure she looked and smelled good.

I visited her every single day without fail. Amber and I would only take Lainey to see her occasionally, since that was always an emotionally draining experience.

Our daughter was conceived a year after Amber and I got married. Since we weren't using condoms anymore and Amber could never handle the pill, we just paid close attention to her cycle, leaving things somewhat up to fate. And fate brought us Lainey sooner than we'd anticipated.

My mother caressed her granddaughter's pigtails. "You remind me of someone. You know that?"

Lainey looked just like her namesake—my sister—and even though my mother couldn't figure out the connection, it was comforting to know that on some level, she remembered.

"Mom, we have to go, but I'll be back tomorrow, okay?"

My mother smiled. "Well, aren't you nice."

It definitely hurt when she didn't remember me. Most days she didn't realize why I was coming to visit her aside from me being "some nice guy." That didn't matter; I would still be there for her in the same way that I would if she were a hundred percent aware.

We hugged my mother goodbye before making our way home.

As we drove down the road, Amber turned to me.

"Guess who's getting married?"

"Who?"

"Rory."

"No shit?"

"Yup."

I knew Amber still kept in touch with Rory. He'd moved out to Seattle for work, and about a year ago, he'd told her he met someone, a widow with three kids he'd taken on as his own. He seemed genuinely happy, and that definitely gave Amber some peace.

"Well, good. I'm happy for him," I said.

She smiled. "Me, too."

As we continued to drive, we encountered a traffic jam, and it didn't take long to figure out why. Turned out, the carnival was in town. We had taken a different route home, so we hadn't passed it on the way to see Mom. But it was no surprise. I'd seen the signs posted all over recently.

This wasn't just any carnival. It was *the* carnival, the same yearly fair where the accident happened eleven years ago. I'd passed it before over the past couple of years, but never with Lainey in the car.

She pressed her little finger up against the window. "Mama! I want to go! I want to go!"

My stomach dropped as fear filled Amber's eyes. I knew she wanted to give in to our daughter's request. The only thing holding her back was me, or rather her fear of my freaking out. Amber would never suggest we stop unless I insisted.

It was true that I hadn't been able to stomach the idea of visiting a carnival since my sister's death. Aside from the brief experience in Boston with Milo, I'd managed to avoid them altogether. But I was a father now, and my daughter deserved to visit the carnival if that was what she really wanted. It wasn't fair to allow my fear to affect her life.

My attitude had also changed somewhat over the past few years. Mom's illness had taught me that life was too short to live in fear. Yes, accidents happen, but you couldn't spend your life worrying about the possibility of tragedy. Life was hard enough. I knew it was now or never.

"We can go to the carnival, baby."

Amber looked shocked to hear me say that. "Are you sure?"

"Yes. I need to do this for her."

She placed her hand on mine. "Okay."

One foot in front of the other.

That's what I told myself as we entered the fairgrounds. Yes, I was terrified, but all it took was one look at my little girl's face to calm me down somewhat. She'd never been to anything like this before. Her eyes were flitting all over the place as she took in the sights and sounds.

That was when it hit me. I had two choices. Freak out or calm the fuck down and share some damn cotton candy with my daughter. I chose the latter.

We ended up playing some games, and Amber took Lainey on a few of the kiddie rides—you know, the ones that were safely planted on the ground.

Right when we were about to leave, Lainey pointed to the Ferris wheel. "I wanna go up! Up!"

"Next time, Lainey," she was quick to say.

Was I really going to prevent my daughter from enjoying a ride on the Ferris wheel because of my fear? Yes, I was more comfortable with all of us on the ground, but the guilt of denying her that experience was eating away at me. I knew that would be wrong.

I pushed the words out, "Why don't we all go?"

Amber's eyes widened. "Are you serious?"

"Yes." I swallowed hard. "The three of us."

Amber looked stunned but really proud. "Okay."

If ever I could take a step like this it was going to be today. Both of my girls were my strength. With them by my side and the knowledge that my sister's spirit was with us, I could do anything.

I'm not gonna lie. My heart was definitely pounding as we got situated in the seat and locked in the handle bar. The only real anxiety was on the first go-round. After that, it got progressively easier. Lainey would wave to the people on the ground. With my daughter's laughter in the air, it wasn't so bad.

This Ferris wheel ride was like the story of my life—a little scary with ups and downs but exhilarating and fun at the same time.

Suddenly, Lainey did something she hadn't ever done before. When the Ferris wheel stopped, she was hiccuping from all of the laughing—just like Amber.

Yup. My life had come full circle—with a few hiccups along the way.

ACKNOWLEDGEMENTS

I always say that the acknowledgements are the hardest part of the book to write and that still stands! It's hard to put into words how thankful I am for every single reader who continues to support and promote my books. Your enthusiasm and hunger for my stories is what motivates me every day. And to all of the book bloggers who support me, I simply wouldn't be here without you.

To Vi – I say this every time, and I am saying it again because it holds even truer as time goes on. You're the best friend and partner in crime that I could ask for. I couldn't do any of this without you. Our co-written books are a gift, but the biggest blessing has always been our friendship, which came before the stories and will continue after them. (Who am I kidding? We won't ever stop writing.)

To Julie – Thank you for your friendship and for always inspiring me with your amazing writing, attitude, and strength. This year is going to kick ass!

To Luna –Thank you for your love and support, day in and day out and for always being just a message away. I'm so happy you're back in the US!

To Erika – It will always be an E thing. I am so thankful for your love and friendship and support and to our special hang time in July. Thank you for always brightening my days.

To my Facebook fan group, Penelope's Peeps – I love you all. Your excitement motivates me every day. And to Queen Peep Amy – Thank you for serving as the Peeps admin. and for always being so good to me from the very beginning.

To Mia – Thank you, my friend, for always making me laugh. I know you're going to bring us some phenomenal words this year.

To my publicist, Dani, at InkSlinger P.R. – Thank you for taking some of the weight off my shoulders and for guiding this release. It's a pleasure working with you.

To Elaine of Allusion Book Formatting and Publishing – Thank you for being the best proofreader, formatter, and friend a girl could ask for.

To Letitia of RBA Designs – The best cover designer ever! Thank you for always working with me until the cover is exactly how I want it.

To my agent extraordinaire, Kimberly Brower –Thank you for believing in me long before you were my agent, back when you were a blogger and I was a first-time author.

To my husband – Thank you for always taking on so much more than you should have to so that I am able to write. I love you so much.

To the best parents in the world – I'm so lucky to have you! Thank you for everything you have ever done for me and for always being there.

To my besties: Allison, Angela, Tarah and Sonia – Thank you for putting up with that friend who suddenly became a nutty writer.

Last but not least, to my daughter and son – Mommy loves you. You are my motivation and inspiration!

BOOKS BY PENELOPE WARD

Drunk Dial
Mack Daddy
RoomHate
Stepbrother Dearest
Neighbor Dearest
Jaded and Tyed (A novelette)
Sins of Sevin
Jake Undone (Jake #1)
Jake Understood (Jake #2)
My Skylar
Gemini

BOOKS BY PENELOPE WARD & VI KEELAND

Dear Bridget, I Want You
Mister Moneybags
Playboy Pilot
Stuck-Up Suit
Cocky Bastard

Made in the USA
Lexington, KY
26 February 2018